W9-AKB-732

DID NOT FINISH

A Selection of Recent Titles by Simon Wood

ACCIDENTS WAITING TO HAPPEN
PAYING THE PIPER
TERMINATED
WE ALL FALL DOWN

DID NOT FINISH

Simon Wood

This first world edition published 2011
in Great Britain and the USA by
Crème de la Crime, an imprint of
SEVERN HOUSE PUBLISHERS LTD of
9–15 High Street, Sutton, Surrey, England, SM1 1DF.
Trade paperback edition first published
in Great Britain and the USA 2011.

British Library Cataloguing in Publication Data

Wood, Simon, 1968-
Did not finish. – (An Aidy Westlake mystery)
1. Automobile racing drivers–Crimes against–Fiction.
2. Automobile racing–Corrupt practices–Fiction.
3. Detective and mystery stories.
I. Title II. Series
813.6-dc22

ISBN-13: 978-1-78029-007-2 (cased)
ISBN-13: 978-1-78029-507-7 (trade paper)

Typeset by Palimpsest Book Production Ltd.,
Falkirk, Stirlingshire, Scotland.
Printed and bound in Great Britain by
MPG Books Ltd., Bodmin, Cornwall.

AUTHOR'S NOTE

In the lexicon of motor racing terminology, a Did Not Finish classification is awarded to any driver who does not complete the race and is therefore excluded in the results.

For Dad, Andy and Sam – my faithful pit crew.

First Lap

The security guard blocked my van's path at the competitors' entrance of Stowe Park race circuit. He asked to see my team and vehicle passes as if my Formula Ford racecar on the trailer I was hauling wasn't all the identification I needed. It was a bitter October night, so the poor guy probably needed something to justify spending his Friday night in the middle of the Wiltshire countryside. He handed my paperwork back to me and pulled back the gate.

Dylan took the paperwork from me. He's my best friend and represents one half of my pit crew. My grandfather, Steve, completes the team and constitutes the brains. He worked the pits for Lotus all through its glory days from the mid-sixties until founder Colin Chapman's death in the early eighties. Steve wasn't with us for this one, though. He'd whisked his girlfriend off for a romantic weekend getaway. I swear the man got more action than I did.

Arriving the night before a race meant landing a good spot in the paddock. There are no set places in the paddock so it's a free-for-all. First choice for me is some place flat and close to the assembly area and the scrutineering bay. Formula Fords are single-seater racecars. They look like Formula One or Indy cars, but they are scaled down in size and power. In the evolutionary motor racing scale, they're five divisions down from Formula One. You don't start single-seater racecars unless you have to. That means a lot of pushing the car around. We found a nice spot between two other early arrivals and filled the gap. We quickly wheeled the car off the trailer. I covered it with a tarp in case it rained during the night.

'I need warmth and good company,' Dylan said, so we jogged over to the circuit's clubhouse, The Chequered Flag. It served as a bar during the night and a restaurant on race days.

We stepped inside. The place heaved with half the starting line-ups for tomorrow's races, along with their pit crews, track officials and the circuit's owners, husband and wife team, Myles and Eva Beecham. Bodies four deep crowded the bar and virtually every table was taken. A couple of wall-mounted flat screen TVs close to the bar played the highlights from last year's Formula One championship, but everyone was too engrossed in conversation to care. Tomorrow's race was all that counted.

'Aidy.'

I turned to see Graham Linden waving to me from a table. Graham was a fellow Formula Ford driver and local to the track.

'I'll get the drinks in,' Dylan said. 'Orange juice?'

I nodded, weaved my way through the throng to Graham's table and dropped into a seat next to him. 'I just parked up next to you.'

'Nice.' He slid a set of house keys over to me. 'Those are from Jamie Barrett.'

The keys were to Jamie's house, which he no longer owned. He'd lost the house financing a disastrous year in Formula Renault instead of keeping up with the mortgage. Jamie now lived out of the office of his accident repair business in Bristol. He was cool about the foreclosure, but while the house sat on the market, he let people crash there. It saved me from springing for a bed and breakfast for Dylan and me. It was one of those little benefits that kept my racing habit affordable.

'Have you heard the news?'

I shook my head.

Graham leaned in close. 'Alex is a dead man.'

'What do you mean?'

'Derek's going to kill him to stop him from winning the title.'

Alex Fanning and Derek Deacon were vying for the Clark Paints Formula Ford Championship. It's a twelve race West Country regional championship featuring half the races at Stowe Park circuit with the remainder split between the Anglesey and Pembrey circuits in Wales. Alex held a two point lead over Derek going into tomorrow's final race. As long as he finished ahead of Derek, the title was his. To beat Alex, Derek had to finish two places ahead of him. Barring a catastrophe on Alex's part, it wasn't likely. It looked as if Derek wanted to create the catastrophe.

Graham leaned back in his seat, awaiting my reaction. He looked pleased that he'd cut me in on this latest slice of trackside gossip.

'Where'd you hear that?'

'From Derek. He's telling everyone. Do you think he'll do it?'

I didn't much care. I put my less than enthusiastic response to the paddock gossip down to my racing lot. I currently sat sixth in the championship, which was pretty good going for my first full season, but even if I won tomorrow's race, it wouldn't propel me any further up the standings. Winning wasn't a likely proposition in any case. My engine was done. It had too many miles on it and needed a total rebuild. Unfortunately, I was out of cash, having already burned through my sponsor's money. I would have skipped tomorrow's race if it weren't for my sponsor bringing a client to entertain.

A roar of laughter drew my attention. Derek held sway at the bar surrounded by the usual mix of adoring drivers and officials. He was a local legend. He was a twenty season veteran and had won the southwest title nine times.

He didn't fit the typical race driver mould. In his forties, he was twice the age of most competitors, including me at twenty-one. Physically, he was intimidating. He was a long distance lorry driver and he carried a trucker's build. Whereas the ideal single-seater driver was small and slight, Derek was barrel-chested with arms like legs of beef. He raced like a lorry driver too. Brutality replaced finesse. He tossed his car around, used every inch of the track and wrung every drop of power out of the engine. Catching sight of Derek in your mirrors was like seeing a tidal wave looming.

Was Derek capable of carrying out his threat against Alex? An air of viciousness did radiate from him, and not just on the track. Even though he'd smile and slap you on the back, his penchant for unprovoked violence shone in his eyes.

No one could say it was the drink talking. He was standing at the bar with a Coke in his hand. It wasn't his drink of choice, but it wasn't anyone's the night before a race. A driver couldn't race under the influence and no one wanted to take a chance that anything might trickle over from the night before. The clubhouse was a sea of fruit juices and soft drinks. Even pit crews and friends showed solidarity by staying off the beer. Tomorrow night would be a different story.

'You honestly believe Derek will kill Alex if he doesn't let him win?' I said.

'Don't you?' Graham said. 'Look what he did to Ryan at the beginning of the season.'

Ryan Phillips had contributed to Alex's championship lead in the season's first race. He clipped Derek's car, sending him into a spin. Derek got going again, but managed only a fifth place finish. He made it known that Ryan would pay and Ryan was spotted with a broken nose a week later. He hadn't raced at Stowe since. There were other tales of violence surrounding Derek and car tampering, but all of them were a far cry from killing someone.

Dylan fought his way through the crowded clubhouse with three glasses pressed precariously together. He set the drinks down on our table before sitting down. 'Have you heard this thing Derek's been saying?'

'Graham just told me.'

'If Derek doesn't want word getting around, he's doing a shitty job.' Dylan jerked a thumb towards the bar. 'He's telling everyone about what he's going to do if Alex has the audacity to lead the race. The Beechams are right there. Dumb. Very dumb.'

'Alex is better off skipping tomorrow,' Graham said.

'C'mon, you're not taking this crap seriously, are you? Nothing is going to happen,' I said, annoyed at myself for getting dragged into this soap opera.

'He's serious,' Graham said.

'It's all an act,' I said. 'Derek wants word to get around. This is the perfect place for it. Half the paddock is talking about it now and the other half will be by morning practice. He's playing mind games to screw with Alex's head.'

'Well, we're about to see how serious Derek is,' Dylan said and nodded towards the entrance.

I turned around to see Alex holding the door open for his fiancée, Alison. The usual contingent of Alex's father and Jo-Jo, his mechanic, followed the couple in. A sour-faced, middle-aged man I didn't recognize walked in with them.

Their arrival changed the mood in the clubhouse. An oppressive seriousness replaced the giddy joviality that had been present moments earlier. Suddenly, the rumour wasn't that entertaining. For the first time, the Formula One commentators could be heard on the TVs. The sudden change reminded me of every old western movie where the doomed cattle rancher comes into town to pick up animal feed, unaware that the black hats are saddling up to wipe him and his family out.

Alex seemed oblivious to the mood of the room. I didn't know if he was aware of the rumour flying around. Chances were he knew and was just playing it cool. Alex was aloof at the best of times and had failed to make many friends around the paddock because of it. The same couldn't be said of his dad. He swapped hellos with familiar faces, seemingly unaware of the furtive glances being cast their way.

The tension looked set to continue until Alex broke it. He went up to Derek and put his hand out to him. 'Best of luck tomorrow.'

It was a classy move on Alex's part that made me smile.

'May the best man win,' Derek said shaking Alex's hand.

The move worked. The tension eased and the conversation level rose as Alex and his family sat around a table.

'How'd you think he'll do it?' Graham mused.

'He'll take him out on the track,' Dylan said.

'He might have someone do it for him. He knows people.'

It was the one thing that lent weight to the seriousness of Derek's threat. The rumour was that Derek had connections to organized crime in London despite coming from Bristol. It was a nice bit of spin that helped bolster the don't-fuck-with-Derek myth.

With all talk of Derek and Alex quashed, conversation turned to tomorrow's race and plans for next season. We finished our drinks and it was my turn to get the next round in. I leaned against the bar with a tenner in the air to catch the barman's attention. He looked my way, but continued filling other drink orders.

A path opened and Derek filled a space alongside me. He raised a finger and received an instantaneous response from the barman.

'What can I get you, Derek?'

'Aidy was here first.'

'Two orange juices and a Coke, please,' I said to the barman.

'Tag on to that another two Cokes and a pint.' Derek winked at me. 'Don't panic. It's on me. I'm feeling generous.'

'Coming right up, Derek,' the barman said.

'I hope you don't mind, Aidy. I fancy my chances tomorrow and I want to celebrate with my friends.'

We were friends? We hadn't spoken more than a handful of times all season, but I played along. 'Of course not.'

I felt Derek goading me into saying something to prompt him to reveal his not-very-secret secret, but I didn't give him the satisfaction. I wasn't willing to play stooge, but I did involuntarily. Derek smiled at me and rested an arm across my shoulders. His message was simple: Look at me, Alex. I've got another one on my side.

The barman set the drinks in front of me and I grabbed them. 'Thanks, Derek.'

'Don't thank me. Tomorrow is going to be a great day. Nobody is going to stand in my way of winning my tenth title.'

Lap Two

The following morning, the Clark Paints Formula Ford Championship race had raised its profile in the paddock. Derek's death threat had deposed the Porsche Cup as the feature race on the bill. It was all about Derek and Alex. An uncommon amount of interest went into that morning's qualification session. Drivers and pit crews from all the other races packed the spectator area in front of the start-finish line. The bloodlust was palpable. They wanted to see if Derek would take Alex out during qualifying to make himself a shoo-in for the championship.

I couldn't let their issue distract me. I needed to put up a fast lap during morning practice. I pulled on my race suit and Dylan held out the torque wrench to me.

'You want this or are you going to break with tradition?'

I smiled and took the wrench. I gave the wheels one last torque and went around the car checking that every joint was tight. It wasn't necessary, but it was my habit. I knew every inch of my car and until I was sure every nut and bolt was tight, I couldn't focus on racing. Some might call it superstition. I call it good engineering practice. Well, maybe it is superstition, but it works for me. I completed my pre-race ritual by kissing my mum's St Christopher that I now wore around my neck and prayed for a good day.

I climbed into the car, Dylan helped belt me in and I was good to go.

As I accelerated onto the track, I concentrated on my driving. I worked the brakes hard to get some heat in them before finding myself some space on the track. I used a car three hundred yards ahead as a target to home in on and went for it. I put in a nice set of four laps before I reeled the car in. Dylan held out my time board and I knew I wasn't getting any more out of the car, so I backed off. Late in the practice session, Alex passed me on a flying lap. I gave him room and then tucked in behind him to catch a ride in his slipstream.

No sooner had I slotted in behind him than I veered back out. Alex's tailpipe was shaking violently. It looked as if its support bracket had broken off and only a couple of spring clips and goodwill were keeping it attached. If his tailpipe did break off, I didn't fancy catching it in the face.

The bracket had no doubt suffered a stress fracture, which wasn't an uncommon occurrence. There's little to cushion the punishment inflicted on a racetrack. Take a close look at a racecar and it's held together with duct tape, silicon bath sealant, plastic ties and twist wire.

As I watched Alex's car pull away from me, it occurred to me that the mounting's failure might not be a product of fatigue. Was mechanical failure Derek's way of eliminating Alex from the race? It was more than possible. The honour system operates in the paddock. No one steals anyone's stuff and no one messes with anyone's ride. It didn't mean someone couldn't. If Derek wanted to interfere with Alex's car, it wouldn't be hard.

If Derek had tampered with the car, he hadn't done a good job. All twenty-eight cars returned from practice in one piece. As soon as I parked in my spot in the paddock, I walked over to Alex's area. He, his father and Jo-Jo were clustered around the rear of the car. They all looked up when I walked over.

'Is it the exhaust mounting?' I said. 'I saw it flapping around.'

'Yeah, it looks that way,' Alex said.

'Good, I just wanted to make sure you knew.'

As I turned to leave, Alex stopped me. 'I don't think you know everyone here. This is Aidy Westlake. His dad was Rob Westlake.'

My racing heritage didn't end with my grandfather. I was following in my father's footsteps. He'd made it all the way to Formula One, but never started a race. He slid off the road driving back from Brands Hatch, killing him and my mum. Dad had been gone over a decade and it never got any easier to hear his name mentioned in the past tense.

Alex's dad came forward. 'Eric Fanning. I enjoyed watching your father immensely.'

'So did I.'

'You know my fiancée, Alison, but not her dad, Clive Baker,' Alex said.

He was the sour-faced man I hadn't recognized from the clubhouse the night before.

Alex also introduced me to someone who hadn't been with him last night. He was a tall, athletic man in his late-forties with black hair and a well-groomed beard. He leaned in to shake my hand. 'Vic Hancock of Hancock Salvage.'

Hancock Salvage was the name splashed over the sides of Alex's car in ten inch high letters. Hancock's reputation preceded him. Hancock Salvage was the biggest salvage and car auction business in Britain. He'd sponsored several drivers over the years, but this was the first time I'd seen him at a race.

'I'm glad to see motor racing isn't as cut-throat as the salvage business,' Hancock said with a laugh.

'The racing world is filled with good people,' Mr Fanning said, patting my shoulder.

The irony of the statement wasn't lost on me considering the situation.

We chatted for a few minutes before I left them to the repairs. Everyone thanked me for my considerateness and I headed over to race control for the qualification times.

The head timekeeper emerged and posted the results on the wall before handing out copies to the eager drivers for their own records. I looked to the head of the times first. Derek's mind games had proved ineffectual. Alex had taken pole position from Derek by three tenths, a pretty big margin. I couldn't contain a smile but soon lost it when I saw my qualifying time. I'd qualified fourteenth. I was a second and a half off my times from just two months ago. I really needed to put my engine out of its misery.

Alex winning pole position served to incite the rumour mill. All anyone could say during lunch was if Derek was going to do something, he'd have to do it during the race.

In addition to being the track owner, Myles Beecham was the clerk of the course. He did his best to kill the rumour at the driver briefing. As clerks of the courses went, Beecham was the most pedantic, treating drivers like disobedient children. That was never more obvious than at his driver briefing. He reeled off his usual speech about drivers following track's instructions and using mirrors during the race. Just as I thought he was finishing up, he added a caveat.

'I know racing is a competitive sport by nature and there can be only one winner, but it's not a contact sport. The best driver wins because he outdrives everyone else. Stowe Park has a reputation for fair and fun entertainment. I wouldn't want anything to change that today.'

There it was. Derek was on notice. Myles was watching. As warnings went, it could have come with a keener edge. If Myles's words were an attempt to shame Derek into behaving, he was wasting his time. Derek needed to be struck with something blunter than a verbal warning.

I looked over at Derek. He stood with Jeff Morgan and Matthew Strickland, his usual race day hangers-on. Morgan leaned in and whispered something. Derek shrugged his shoulders as if he didn't understand what Myles was talking about. It was a nice act, but I didn't know who he was trying to fool.

'Thank you,' Myles said. 'Good luck to everyone.'

Walking back to my spot in the paddock, I pushed Alex and Derek from my mind to concentrate on the race. I visualized a lap in my mind, picking out my braking points, turning points and apexes. I studied the starting grid to see who was around me and whether I needed to be careful of them at the start, as well as to concoct a plan of how I'd get the jump on them when the lights turned green.

When the announcement went out over the PA system for the Formula Ford drivers to make their way to assembly area, I needed to pee. After fifteen races, I hoped to be past this point, but nervous tension got me every time. Dylan fired up the engine and broke out his customary bag of sunflower seeds. He ate them all the time; especially when he was nervous and he was nervous anytime I hit the track. I left him to his munching and crossed the paddock to the toilets. I stood over the trough and tried to relax enough to go. I wasn't the only one with this race-related bladder problem. Seven other drivers, including Alex, stood at the urinal with uncooperative prostates. By the time I managed to do what I intended on doing, Alex and I were the only ones left in the toilets. I get quiet before a race, putting all my energy into my thoughts, but I broke my custom.

'Good luck today,' I said. 'I hope you win.'

'Thanks. I won't be back if I don't.'

'Moving up?'

He smiled. 'No, moving out. Win, lose or draw, I'm retiring.

Alison and I got engaged a while ago and the wedding is in the spring. As my wedding gift to her, I'm retiring from racing to concentrate on becoming a chartered accountant. If I'm going to be a husband, then I need to be a grown-up.'

He grinned and it took me a moment to return one. Alex had a promising racing career ahead of him. I couldn't believe he was walking away from it. I knew I couldn't.

'Wow. Congratulations.'

'Thanks. Don't tell Alison, she doesn't know. No one does, and I want to make it a surprise after the race.'

'Your secret is safe with me. Now I really hope you win.'

'So do I.'

I followed Alex out as three other drivers went in.

'What's in your tea leaves, Aidy?'

The opposite of what's in yours, I thought. 'I hope to run in the national series next season and keep moving up through the ranks.'

'And go as far as your dad?'

'If I can.'

'Take this from someone who's a few years older. Don't ever let this come between you and a happy life. This sport crushes more dreams than it creates.'

I was more than aware of this fact. The sport had orphaned me. 'I won't.'

'Then you're smarter than the average driver.'

The call went out again for drivers to make their way to the assembly area. We shook hands and wished each other luck before going our separate ways.

Two hours later, Alex was dead.

Lap Three

I hadn't seen Alex die, just the accident. I'd gotten a good start off the line to take tenth place going into the first major bend at Wilts Corner. Wilts is a second gear right-hand turn and everyone made it through cleanly. Alex and Derek led the field, pulling away from the pack. They were side by side going into

Barrack Hill. It's a fast, right-hand kink that can be taken without lifting off the gas. Just. There's no room for error. Get it wrong and there's a concrete wall to catch you. Everyone was nose to tail going into the bend, making it hard to see anything at the front. I'd just grabbed fourth gear and was looking for my turning-in point when Alex's car popped up on two wheels. The second it crashed back down, it slewed left off the track and into the wall.

Even though my view was obscured, I knew exactly what Derek had done to Alex. Like Formula One and Indy cars, Formula Fords are essentially just a cockpit bolted to an engine with the four wheels and suspension exposed. With these racecars, there's the danger of interlocking wheels with another car. If you've seen the chariot race from Ben Hur then you know what I mean. When it happens, both drivers have to work together to get untangled. It's usually achieved by the drivers matching each other's speed and carefully separating, then going back to racing. It happens by accident, but it also happens by design. Locking wheels is a nasty technique for taking out a car. A driver slips his wheel inside and in front of the car he wants to take out, then slows down. Just taking your foot off the gas for a second will do the damage. The faster car rides over the top of the slower car's wheel, sending it on to two wheels and breaking its suspension when it lands. It's a tricky manoeuvre with the potential for taking out both cars, but usually the faster car comes off worse. To the spectator, it looks like an accident.

Derek had executed the manoeuvre with consummate skill and he exited Barrack Hill with no problem.

The black flags were out on the next bend, stopping the race. Everyone backed off and rolled around the circuit back to the start line. Course officials directed us to our new start positions on the grid before giving pit crews the go ahead to come onto the track.

I couldn't believe Derek had gone through with it. OK, he'd pick up his tenth title, but so what? The Clark Paints Championship wasn't some major title that meant something. It served as a nursery for new drivers cutting their teeth in motor racing on their way up to Formula One and a retirement home for those who were long in the tooth and just wanted to keep racing. In the scheme of things, the title meant very little in the racing community beyond bragging rights. Derek would prove again he was a big fish in a small pond. If he really wanted to show the world what a great driver he was, he should have branched out a long time ago. I felt like pulling out of the race, but remembered my sponsor.

The race restarted after a thirty minute delay. Derek won with relative ease. Thanks to a couple of spins in the pack, I managed to hold on to ninth place.

Afterwards, I returned to the paddock, changed out of my race gear into civvies and collected my race licence from registration. The news floating around the paddock was that Alex was on his way to hospital for a check-up.

As Dylan and I loaded my car onto the trailer, we watched Derek and his crew celebrate his win and his most treasured title. Dylan and I shared a disgusted glance.

Dylan shrugged. 'All's fair in love and war.'

After we were done, I wanted to leave more than ever and draw a line under this season, but I still had work to do. We went to help my sponsor schmooze their prospective client. They left happy and Dylan and I returned to the paddock to make the hundred mile drive home.

The mood in the paddock had changed. Word had filtered down from the marshal's station at Barrack Hill that blood had been seen inside Alex's helmet. The fun and games of gossiping about Derek's death threat turned into guilty silence.

Dylan and I headed home to the excited roar of an ignorant crowd. The race fans had been insulated from Derek's threat against Alex. Their excitement jarred with the muted silence of an embarrassed paddock.

We arrived back at Archway, Steve's classic car restoration garage, where I kept my racecar and found a message on the answering machine from Eva Beecham.

'Aidy, it's Eva. I have bad news. Alex passed away in hospital. I'm letting all the drivers know.'

The news turned my stomach and I dropped into the nearest seat. I was eight again, playing in the garden with my toy racecars, whipping them up and down the concrete path. Gran was leaning out the kitchen doorway asking me what I wanted in my sandwich, but I was lost in my own imagination where my dad and I were leading the race. From within the house, Steve let out a wail, a sound I'd never heard before. He appeared behind Gran and whispered something to her. She collapsed into him and sobbed.

I didn't see what was coming next. What did I understand at

that age? My parents were immortal. I thought they'd always be there.

I left my toys scattered over the concrete path. I didn't run to my grandparents' side. I walked. The sight of my grandparents in so much pain scared me. I stood by them and it took a minute for them to notice I was there. Steve dropped to his knees in front of me. Tears streaked his chalk-white face.

'What's wrong?' I said.

'I've got bad news, little mate,' he said, and my world changed forever.

I sat in the darkness for hours after Dylan had left to go home. I heard the door open and my grandfather make his way through the workshop.

'Aidy, you in here?' my grandfather called from downstairs.

'Up here in the crow's nest, Steve.'

Circumstances had blurred the lines between us. He was my grandfather, surrogate parent and friend. To call him grandfather, grandad or grandpa just didn't work. He was Steve.

He found me in the office overlooking the workshop. Archway Restoration sat underneath Windsor Railway Station. Because Windsor rises to a peak where the Norman castle sits, the station stood on top of a series of archways to ensure the trains didn't have to stop on a slant. The archways had been enclosed decades ago to make business units. The place had plenty of funky appeal with its curved walls and the cobbled street outside. Steve owned the third of the six units sandwiched between a private gym and Mexican restaurant. He let me work on my racecar there and use his van.

Steve flicked on the office lights. I squinted against the sudden glare.

Steve stopped in the doorway. I don't look much like my grandfather. My dad and I both took after my grandmother, who was short, slight and dark. Steve was tall and Nordic looking with strawberry blond hair. He possessed more than a passing resemblance to Steve McQueen which accounted for his success with the ladies.

'I didn't think you'd be back until tomorrow,' I said.

'I came home when I heard about Alex. Dylan told me. I called him when you didn't answer your phone. Don't switch your phone off on race days. You know I don't like it.'

'Didn't Maggie mind you running out on her?'

'She understands. I'll make it up to her.' Steve pulled out a chair and sat. 'What happened?'

I outlined the events of the last twenty-four hours to him from Derek's threat in The Chequered Flag to the details of the crash.

Steve said nothing until I'd talked myself out. 'Alex's death really seems to have affected you.'

It was a challenge I could hardly deny and I picked at a hangnail on my right index finger.

'You didn't know him well, did you?' he said.

'Not really.'

'Then why are you cut up so bad? Is it because of your mum and dad?'

Hanging amongst the motor racing memorabilia on the walls was a picture of my parents. I got up and wandered over to it. It had been taken in the pits at Brands Hatch. Dad held my mum in his arms with his championship-winning Formula Three car behind them. They looked so happy. They died the day after the picture was taken, killed on the drive back. Dad lost control of his car and went off the road a few miles from the track.

I'd lost my parents when they'd been on the verge of a new life where dreams were realized. Alex's death was no different. He'd been on the verge of a new life and it had been snatched away from him.

'This has nothing to do with them.'

'Then why are you so broken up?'

'A man was murdered over a meaningless championship title. And if you want to know the worst part of all this, winning today meant nothing to Alex.'

'What do you mean?'

'Alex and I were chatting just before the start of the race. He told me he was giving up racing to get married. It was going to be a wedding surprise for his fiancée. No one else knew. Not her or his family. He had everything going for him and now he's dead. It's so fucking unfair.'

Another life cut short. Maybe this did have more to do with my parents' deaths than I cared to admit.

Steve studied me with a disapproving look. It was a familiar expression I'd seen throughout my life. He was picking apart something I said to get to the heart of the matter.

'There's more to this than Alex's secret, isn't there?'

I nodded. 'Alex's death could have been prevented if only I'd done something.'

'If only you'd done something?'

'Not just me, but any of us. It only would have taken one of us to report Derek to Myles Beecham or even to tell Alex himself. Instead, we stuck our heads in the sand and pretended nothing had happened. We were cowards and it got Alex killed.'

Steve chewed over what I'd said. 'Sounds like a guilty conscience talking.'

'It is.'

Steve nodded and put his feet up on the desk. 'You're right. You should have done something.' He poked a finger in my direction. 'Your silence helped get Alex killed.'

I knew he was throwing my words back in my face, but it took all my courage to keep looking my grandfather in the eye.

'If that's true, answer me this. Why didn't you step in and put an end to this?'

I dropped onto the sofa behind me and sighed. 'Because it was bullshit. It was nothing more than a scare tactic to intimidate Alex. That's what I thought anyway.'

All the tension went out of Steve's face. 'That's right. And that's why no one got involved. I'll bet you a pound to a penny no one honestly believed Derek was going to kill Alex. Drivers develop grudges, but no driver has gone out of his way to kill a rival to win a race.'

'It doesn't change the outcome.'

'No, you're right.' He smiled at me. 'You're a good lad, Aidy. You're being a little harsh on yourself.'

'Not from where I'm sitting.'

Steve took his feet off the desk and sat forward with his elbows on the desktop. 'OK, it's time for a little different perspective. This could still be an accident.'

'Oh, c'mon.'

'No, hear me out. Let me ask you this. Forget the talk. Do you think Derek really intended to kill Alex?'

'He got his wish, didn't he?'

'Don't be so quick to judge. Look, it's one thing to say you'll kill a person, but it's an entirely different thing to do it. Derek is a bully, I'll grant you that. He uses threats to intimidate and he isn't adverse to banging wheels in order to win. But is he a killer? I'm not so sure.'

I shrugged.

'Have you considered that the situation may have gotten away from him? Maybe he intended to shove Alex off the track to get him out of the race and fate upped the ante.'

Was I letting my emotions and Derek's reputation get in the way of my objectivity? I didn't think so. 'If Alex had gone off at any other corner, maybe, but Derek took him out at Barrack Hill, a flat out corner with no gravel trap or tyre wall for protection. If I wanted to kill another driver, Barrack Hill is where I'd do it.'

'So it's pretty cut and dry as far as you're concerned,' Steve said.

I nodded. 'And the TV will prove it. Redline is showing the race on Tuesday. With everyone watching, Derek won't be able to hide what's he's done.'

Lap Four

I spent Sunday stripping my Formula Ford down to its component parts. I raced a two-year-old Van Diemen. Although the car had gone less than fifteen hundred miles during the season, the punishment racing put on every component was a hundred fold greater than what a street car experiences. After tossing out bent bolts and worn out bearings, I checked the chassis for cracks and found none. I removed the engine for Steve to overhaul. On the whole, things looked good. It would take a lot of work to rebuild everything, but I wasn't looking at much more than a couple of grand to get the car back into race condition.

I worked alone. It helped me decompress. Unscrewing bolts and disconnecting cables made order out of a chaotic weekend. There is no ambiguity in machinery. It does what it's designed to do and nothing more. The distributor feeds electricity to the spark plugs. The fuel pump pumps petrol to the engine. Components don't suddenly decide to kill a person because they don't get what they want.

I had a decision to make: sell or keep the car. There's no love lost on racecars. They're tools, and disposable ones at that. In a few months, when next year's improved cars came out, my trusty steed would be one step closer to obsolescence. Excluding wear and tear, a new car was going to lap half a second faster than my two-year-old Van Diemen. If I wanted to make a bid for the British Formula Ford National Championship next season, then I needed a brand new car. I could only pull it off if I could squeeze some extra money out of my sponsor and save every penny I could between now and next March. I knew Steve would help me out if I got close. He'd done the same with Dad.

I didn't mind using Steve's expertise, but I was reluctant to take his money. I knew the financial burden Dad had put on him. Despite winning a Formula One contract, Dad hadn't lived long enough to be paid and he'd died broke. It almost bankrupted Steve.

I called it a day around nine p.m. I flicked on Steve's computer in the crow's nest and looked up the latest news on Alex's death on the web. The death of a minor racecar driver had failed to make it as a national story. Its newsworthiness certainly hadn't stretched as far as Windsor.

On the BBC Bristol website, I found RACECAR DRIVER'S DEATH INVESTIGATED and clicked the link. The story outlined yesterday's events and mentioned that Alex crashed after contact with Derek's car.

The story featured a quote from Myles. 'Motorsport is a very safe sport and these tragedies happen very infrequently. My thoughts and prayers go out to Alex's friends and family.'

Myles's comment didn't surprise me. It wasn't like he was going to admit he could have prevented the crash if he'd expelled Derek from the race for making a death threat.

I read the rest of the article hoping to see what charges they were bringing against Derek. Instead, the police spokesman talked in terms of an accident investigation. Why weren't they calling it a murder enquiry?

Like most drivers in the lower echelons of motorsport, racing isn't a full time job for me. It's something I have to squeeze in around a day job, so I was back at work on Monday. I'm a design draughtsman for a firm in Slough that manufactures industrial mixers. I don't care much for the job. It isn't a passion like racing is. It's just something I do to pay the bills and give me the money

I need to race. But the job isn't without its perks. After hours, I use their CAD software to design my own replacement parts for my Van Diemen and get the parts fabricated for free by a local fabrication shop in exchange for some ad space on the side of the car.

The management cuts me a lot of slack when it comes to racing by being flexible with my working hours. Now that the season was over, they expected me to make up for their generosity.

On Tuesday, I received an email from Myles Beecham with the news that Alex's funeral was going to be on Friday morning. The email had gone out to all the Formula Ford drivers. I looked for Derek's name amongst the distribution list, but didn't see it. It wasn't much of a surprise. I doubted Derek even had an email address.

I put in a time off request for Friday with my boss. Under the circumstances, he couldn't refuse.

After work, I drove over to Dylan's. On the way over, I stopped in at a florist to order a wreath. The place unsettled me. Flowers marking every kind of celebration surrounded me. When I told the woman I wanted a funeral wreath, she brought out a sample book from under a counter as if death couldn't be looked in the eye. I picked something out and she handed me a card to go with the wreath. I froze with the pen poised over the untouched card. What was the right thing to say? Best wishes? Condolences? All of it seemed so trite.

'Most people write "sorry for your loss."'

I nodded, wrote the words, and signed the card.

I arrived at Dylan's flat in Maidenhead a few minutes before Redline began. Redline is a satellite TV show that rounds up the highlights of the weekly European race scene.

'C'mon in. It's about to start.'

He slipped an arm around my shoulders and ushered me inside. If Steve is my surrogate father, then Dylan is my surrogate brother. He's five years older than me and several sizes bigger thanks to a life spent working as a bricklayer on building sites. Our friendship grew out of Dylan's love of cars. When Dad was still racing, our family rated as minor celebrities. The local papers kept up with Dad's progress and even did a profile on him and Steve. Locals knew where Archway was located and Dylan used to hang around outside to catch a glimpse of one of Dad's cars or one of

Steve's restoration projects. When Dylan was thirteen, Steve caught him sneaking into the workshop. Instead of kicking him out, Steve asked what he wanted. Dylan answered that he wanted to learn about cars. Steve told Dylan that cars couldn't be understood from afar, then tossed him a rag and gave him a job on the spot. I was only eight at the time, but I was already helping out at Archway. At the beginning, we only got to sweep up and put tools away. Despite our age difference, we became tight. Dylan had given me my first misappropriated beer and cigarette and set me up on my first and only blind date. I wasn't thankful for everything.

I followed Dylan into his living room as the show was starting. I dropped into an armchair as the opening credits, a montage of races, filled the screen.

'You want something to drink?'

I shook my head. I just wanted to see what I'd missed on Saturday. I needed to witness Derek's crime spread across the airwaves of Europe. Then, he'd never escape what he'd done.

The show's host talked over snippets of the night's show. 'It's an end of season bonanza this week on Redline. We've got action from the final rounds of the Benelux Formula Ford Championship, British Touring Cars at Silverstone, the French Formula Renault Championship and the Clark Paints Formula Ford Championship at Stowe Park. First up, Formula Three action from *Hockenheim*.'

Hearing Stowe Park mentioned raised gooseflesh. It was going to be hard to watch this. Obviously, Dylan felt the same way since he'd reached for his sunflower seeds.

It was an agonizing forty minutes before Redline got to the Stowe Park race. I went cold when the coverage switched to aerial shots of the circuit. I had an unenviable advantage over all the viewers in their homes. I knew what was about to happen. I wanted to look away when the crash came, but I knew I wouldn't.

Dylan picked up the remote and pressed record on his digital TV recorder. I wondered if Alex's family was doing the same. Then more darkly, I wondered if Derek was recording his handiwork for posterity.

'It's tight at the top going into the twelfth and final round of the Clark Paints Formula Ford Championship. Alex Fanning holds a two point advantage over nine time champion and local fan favourite, Derek Deacon. Here's how they shape up for the start of this hotly contested series. On pole, we've got nine-time champion, Derek

Deacon, giving his championship hopes a much needed boost. Alongside Deacon is Graham Linden in the number two slot.'

'What?' Dylan said and shot me a glance.

The commentator continued to read out the starting line-up as a computer graphic scrolled up the screen showing the drivers' names and race numbers. It became clear what was happening before the commentator said my name.

'They're not showing the race from the beginning,' I said. 'They're showing it from the restart.'

The commentator ran through the complete grid and didn't mention Alex's absence.

'This is bullshit,' Dylan said. 'They have to say something. They can't pretend nothing happened.'

Can't they? I thought. I didn't like where this was going. 'Maybe they're going to say something at the end.'

The race played out from the restart. When it finished, the image cut to Derek shrugging himself from his car and bowing his head to take the winner's wreath and a bottle of champagne from Myles Beecham. Derek didn't show a flicker of remorse for what he'd done. The sight of him basking in his moment of murderous glory made me want to punch a hole through the TV.

I waited for the commentator to mention Alex's death, but nothing was mentioned. As soon as the race ended, the show went to an ad break.

The stink of a cover up radiated from the TV. The sanitized coverage deceived the public, dishonoured Alex, and robbed the police investigation of vital proof.

'What the hell was that?' Dylan said.

'It looks like everyone wants to pretend nothing happened.'

Lap Five

Alex's funeral was held at a stone church on a rainy Friday in Guildford. Dylan came with me. The church's small car park was reserved for the hearse and family, so I parked on the street. The service hadn't started yet so everyone was milling around in groups in front of the church.

The scene sent me back to mum and dad's funeral. I had felt so alone despite my grandparents' presence. It didn't seem possible that I'd never see my parents again. The funeral seemed to take place around me, as if I was invisible. The vicar talked about a future that couldn't be true. I cried more out of confusion than loss.

Graham and about a dozen of the championship drivers stood huddled together in the graveyard, away from the congregation in what appeared to be self-imposed banishment. Derek was the notable absentee, which was understandable under the circumstances. Dylan and I joined them.

Our banishment wasn't entirely self-imposed. I felt a number of the mourners staring at us with disgusted looks. I couldn't blame them. We were an unpleasant reminder of what had killed Alex. If they only knew what we knew about the death threat, they would be chasing us off with pitchforks and torches. At least Derek had the good sense not to show his face.

'Did anyone catch Redline on Tuesday?' John Barshinski asked.

We all nodded.

'Why'd they cut the crash out?' John asked.

'Out of respect?' Graham said.

'Cutting the crash out is one thing. Ignoring what happened is another,' I said.

'I don't think they ignored it,' Graham said.

'Redline excised the crash and all mention of Alex,' Dylan said. 'That's wrong. They didn't have to go into details, but they should have said something about Alex.'

'It could have something to do with the police investigation,' Tony Hansen said. 'The cops have been all over the track.'

Tony and Pete Hansen ran the race school at Stowe Park for anyone who wanted a spin around the track. They operated out of a small office at the circuit.

'Have any of you been interviewed?' I asked. It seemed natural that if they were investigating the crash, they'd interview the drivers.

Everyone shook their head.

'I know they interviewed Derek and Myles,' Tony said.

I hoped the police planned on widening their investigation, but maybe they didn't have to. They might have a strong enough case against Derek already. That could explain Redline's edited coverage of the race. Essentially, it was evidence the police wouldn't want on display before a trial. That might explain why both Pit Lane Magazine and Motorsport News had limited their mention of Alex's death to only a sentence.

'Have the cops mentioned charges?' I asked.

'Why should they?' Tony said.

'Why do you think?' John said. 'Derek's death threat.'

'That was just talk,' Graham said.

'Was it? Alex is dead, isn't he?' I said.

'Jesus, keep it down,' Dylan said. 'We're at a funeral for Christ's sake.'

I took a breath and dropped my voice. 'There's no way this was coincidence. Derek said he'd kill Alex and Alex died.'

'That's a pretty big accusation, Aidy,' Graham said.

'Are you really going to stand there and defend Derek?'

Graham shrugged. 'No, but you can't accuse the guy of being a killer without proof and you don't have it. You were back in the pack and couldn't have seen anything.'

'But you could, Graham,' I said. 'You were behind Derek and Alex. You had the best view.'

Graham glowered. 'They were a hundred yards ahead and I was more interested in the pack behind me than Derek and Alex. I didn't see anything.'

'OK, let's calm down. We're all friends here,' Jerry Watt said. 'Look, it doesn't matter what we think, saw or heard. This is a police matter. We don't know where they are with their investigation. They probably know all this.'

'And if they don't?' I asked. 'Don't we have an obligation to tell the cops what we know?'

'Which is what? Rumour and innuendo? That doesn't help anything.' Tony said.

I wasn't sure what I'd been expecting from everyone, but it wasn't this reticence. I understood it though. No one was under any obligation to come forward. It wasn't their place.

'Can we talk about something else?' Jerry said after a long moment.

'Has anyone seen the car?' John asked.

Pete Hansen nodded. 'It's locked up in the scrutineering bay. It's a mess.'

'Can it be rebuilt?' Jerry asked.

'Bloody hell,' Dylan muttered.

'I'm just asking.'

'Repairable or not, the car shouldn't be raced again,' John said.

Few people would want to drive in a dead man's car, but this had more to do with respect. The car had taken a life and it needed to be retired from the system. Steve had told me about a Formula Three driver killed in the seventies. Every one of the drivers and team owners put money together to buy the car and have it scrapped.

'We should buy the car and have it crushed,' I said.

'That's a good idea,' John said. 'If all the registered drivers chipped in, it wouldn't cost too much. And I really don't want to see that car make an appearance somewhere next season.'

John's willingness ignited unanimous approval. Between us, we formed a plan to get in contact with the other drivers. I would talk to the family about purchasing the car.

The hearse pulled up with two Bentley limousines containing Alex's family. Alex's parents climbed out from the first one. Mr Fanning had to lift his wife from the car. No one should witness this level of human misery. It was private and it should be kept that way. Seeing Alex's mum reminded me of how much I'd lost and I touched my mum's St Christopher.

My parents had died thirteen years ago. I'd been without them for over half my life, but my memories of them remained vivid. I remember squeezing the hell out of Mum's hand as we cheered Dad on at tracks around Britain and Europe. I remember Dad lowering me inside his various cars and telling me that I'd be following in his footsteps. I loved the attention the teams and other drivers gave me. Dad's exploits made me popular at school. They were fun and exciting times.

The years since hadn't been so fun. I grew up without parents. My grandparents were great, but they weren't my mum and dad and when Gran died, Steve was all I had left.

I thought of Alison and Alex's parents going through their version of this; visiting a graveside to reminisce their loss. Nothing could have saved my parents, but I could have saved Alex. If I'd stood up to Derek, I could have prevented this family's pain.

Alex's dad guided his wife up the path into the church. He'd always carried himself with Cary Grant-like composure, but Alex's death seemed to have snuffed out that youthful spark.

Alison and her family got out of the second Bentley. Alison followed behind the Fannings, flanked by her parents. She kept her gaze forward, not taking in her surroundings.

The funeral director called everyone into the church.

Dylan and I filed inside. Ushers directed family and friends to different seating areas. If it wasn't for Derek's selfishness, these same ushers would have been directing people to seating areas for Alex and Alison's wedding.

The racing fraternity and acquaintances were directed to a section at the rear of the church. I had no problems with our second class status.

Myles and Eva Beecham came in and joined us in the pews.

When the congregation was assembled, the vicar asked for everyone to remain standing while the coffin was brought in. The pall-bearers carried Alex in with practised ease and placed his coffin on a stand in front of the altar. Alex's mum broke down. Her tearful sobs bounced off the stone walls.

I thought about the day of the crash. When Derek sent Alex careening off the track, had Alex known he was going to die? I never thought about dying when I had a shunt. Repair costs and the disappointment of not finishing were at the forefront of my mind. Mortality never entered into it. I hope Alex hadn't seen it coming.

'Are you going to continue racing?' Steve had asked me over breakfast this morning.

I'd said, 'Yes,' but it was said without mourners and a body hidden from everyone in a coffin. I asked myself the question again. Did I want to continue? My answer remained the same. I still wanted to race. Racing was a part of me. Alex's death didn't and couldn't change that.

The vicar gave an eloquent service. He'd done his homework on Alex. He tied his tribute, even down to the hymns, to a racing and sporting theme. It could have come off as hackneyed or insensitive under the circumstances, but it was a touching and fitting send off for any driver.

When the service came to an end, Alex's body was carried back outside. The burial itself was to take place at the family plot across town. This part of the service was for invited guests only and the drivers weren't included. The congregation filed back outside as the pall-bearers loaded Alex back into the hearse.

Everyone formed back into their groups. Myles and Eva Beecham herded the racing fraternity to one side.

Mr Fanning emerged from the church and shook hands with the vicar before heading over to us. 'I just wanted to say thank you to all of you for coming here today. It means a lot.'

'We're honoured,' Myles said.

He shook each of our hands and I saw in his eyes that he was barely holding it together. He thanked us again before moving on to other mourners.

Alison went by, cosseted by her parents.

Myles took his wife's hand. 'We're moving on to the burial. I wanted to thank you all for attending too.'

He turned to leave, but I stopped him with a question. 'What's the latest on the investigation?'

'The police made a thorough investigation and have reached their conclusion.'

'Which is?' I asked.

Myles looked confused. 'That it was a terrible accident.'

'An accident?' I said. 'They didn't think Derek's threat was suspicious?'

Myles's expression tightened and he grabbed my arm and dragged me to a far corner of the graveyard. 'What are you inferring?'

'Don't play dumb, Myles. We all heard what Derek said that night.' I lowered my voice. 'Don't pretend you didn't hear him say he'd kill Alex.'

Myles leaned in toward me. 'I heard him. It was talk.'

'It's funny how talk turned into reality.'

'You need to watch your mouth, Westlake.'

'If threatening someone's life and making good on the threat has no consequences, I've got nothing to worry about.'

Myles's cheeks flushed with anger. I knew I was pushing too hard, but I couldn't help myself. I was angry too. I was sick and tired of everyone trying to rewrite events.

'Considering what happened to your parents, I thought you would be more sensitive.'

I wouldn't let Myles distract me with my parents. 'Why did Redline edit the coverage and not even mention Alex's death?'

'Why'd you think?' Myles snapped. 'Some people understand the meaning of respect.'

'Respect for whom – Derek or Alex?'

'You're a piece of work.'

'Have you seen the TV coverage?'

'I've seen the footage. It showed nothing. You should get your facts straight before you start mouthing off.'

Myles knew the dirty tricks of the racing trade. He was either lying or deluding himself. Alex's car hadn't simply spun out. It was launched into the air from locking wheels with Derek's car.

'Yes, Derek said something stupid, but it was just words. Alex died as a result of a terrible accident. You'd do well to remember that. I have to go now. I'm attending the burial on behalf of people like you.' Myles couldn't have injected any more disgust into his words if he tried.

He turned away from me to leave, but I grabbed his wrist. 'Does this mean you'll be installing a tyre wall and gravel traps at all the bends now?'

Stowe Park was one of the only tracks not to have installed gravel traps. In Myles's opinion, dragging stranded cars from gravel traps slowed down the action for the spectators. It was a fair point, but gravel traps saved lives and drivers' money.

My backhanded remark struck a nerve. Myles put his face in mine, but kept his voice down to a growl. 'You little shit.'

Eva grabbed his wrist. She was a small, squat woman but she knew how to handle her husband. 'Leave it. He isn't worth it.'

Myles didn't let go of his anger, but he obeyed his wife and headed toward his car. I'd lost the support of my fellow drivers. They'd already started walking away. If I had any backing for getting to the truth, it was gone now.

Our little row had failed to reach the other mourners, except for Alison. She was looking directly at me as she climbed into the idling Bentley.

Dylan waited until Myles walked away before approaching. He passed Myles and Eva on his way and gave them room as they hurried past.

'That looked like it went well,' he said.

'I'm sorry, but I'm sick and tired of this crap.'

'You're preaching to the choir, mate. You just need to be careful. There are more people than just you involved in all this.'

I nodded and remembered Alison looking my way. 'Did anyone overhear us?'

'No, you got lucky, although any louder and you would have been in trouble.'

'I'm glad to see everyone stuck around to back me up.'

'What do you expect, Aidy? People are scared. They've seen something and they're not sure they can believe it. They don't know what to do. Hell, I don't know what to do.'

'Well, I do.'

I pulled out my mobile phone and dialled Steve's number.

'I'm not sure it's respectful to make a call in a graveyard.'

I knew Dylan was trying to lighten the mood, but it wasn't working.

When Steve answered, I switched the call over to speaker. 'You're on speaker with me and Dylan.'

'What's up?' Steve asked.

'I just found out that the police have completed their investigation. They're calling it an accident. Case closed.'

'And that bothers you?'

'Yes, it bothers me. The TV coverage was cut, Myles is pretending nothing happened at The Chequered Flag and the cops closed the case. Unless someone steps up, Alex's lasting memorial will just be a Did Not Finish classification on the official race record and that isn't right.'

'Why is this so important to you, son? Alex wasn't a friend.'

Steve was testing me. I felt him pushing me from the other end of the phone line. There was no sidestepping the answer he wanted to hear.

'Because I don't want to see someone get away with murder again,' I admitted. 'They did with Gran. The hospital closed ranks to protect the surgeon who killed her.'

'But he never worked again.'

'He should have gone to prison.'

Six years ago, Gran died from blood poisoning after a routine replacement hip operation. It was obvious something was wrong during recovery. The excessive bruising should have told the surgeon something, but he ignored it and first signs of septicaemia. By the time he finally acted, it was too late. The post-mortem revealed a catalogue of mistakes that had occurred during the operation. Instead of this sparking a criminal investigation, acceptable risk got plastered over all the mistakes.

Steve exhaled. 'God, you sound just like her. She was a terror when it came to injustice. She always fought for what was right and she instilled that in you.'

'And is that such a bad thing?'

'No. She'd be very proud of you.'

'I know,' I said.

'So what do you want to do about this situation?'

'Build a case against Derek and take it to the cops.'

'Then let's do it,' Steve said.

Lap Six

The first part of our investigation was to examine the scene of the crime. Saturday morning, I drove out to Stowe Park.

I went down in Steve's pride and joy, a 1972 Ford Capri RS2600. When it came to affordable coupes of yesteryear, the Americans had the Mustang and the British had the Capri. Steve had bought it new and he'd kept it in mint condition. He'd made a number of modifications that ensured it kept up with its more modern counterparts. I got to drive it when he needed the van, which was pretty often.

For my cover, I went armed with a laundry list of replacement parts I needed to rebuild my car. Like most tracks across the country, someone ran a parts and equipment business on the track's premises. The stores all did a roaring trade on race days and survived the rest of the time through mail order. Chicane Motorsports, located in the paddock at Stowe Park, was the most reasonably priced outfit across the country.

I ignored the signs for the paddock entrance and followed the ones for the flea market. On non-race weekends, Myles rented the general parking area out to the market. The track was acres and acres of overhead and the income earned from ten race meetings throughout the year wasn't going to cut it. He needed other sources of revenue and the market was a great moneymaker.

I parked and cut through the market. There was no security on hand to stop me from exploring the track.

It took me fifteen minutes to cover the distance from the start-finish line to the spectator area at Barrack Hill. During a race, I would have covered the same distance in less than thirty seconds. You don't really understand how fast you're travelling until you have to cover the same distance on foot.

I climbed the dirt embankment at Wilts and followed it to where Alex had crashed at Barrack Hill. The concrete wall he hit is built into the embankment. Spectators are allowed to watch from the mound. Last Saturday, anyone there got a close-up view they weren't expecting.

I looked to see if anyone was watching me before bringing out my digital camera and snapping a couple of shots of the track from the embankment. I wanted pictures of the skid marks before the weather and other cars ruined them. I climbed down the embankment and over the gate onto the track.

Alex's tyre marks were impossible to mistake. There was the usual array of skid marks where drivers locked up their brakes before going into the turn. Only one set of skid marks started in the middle of the bend. Alex's skid marks. You don't brake in the middle of a turn. It's suicidal.

These skid marks might not have meant much to most people, but they told me a story. The marks were in two parts. The first set occurred part-way through the bend. It was a heavy, violently drawn S-shape. This came from the initial contact with Derek which kicked Alex's car onto two wheels. The second set of skid marks began just as the first ended. A set of four ugly black lines slewed off the track at an angle and dead ended into the wall. These short skid marks indicated Alex's futile gesture. He would have scrubbed little to no speed off before hitting the wall.

Alex had to have known the impact was going to be serious. Had he had time to pull his knees up and take his hands off the wheel to prevent the shock wave from going through his body? Hopefully, but in a big shunt, panic takes over and you ignore the correct course of action.

I followed Alex's fatal trajectory, snapping close-up shots of the marks until I reached the wall. Cars striking the wall over the years had left their mark in the form of gouges in the concrete. Amongst the collection of gashes, it was easy to recognize the fresh impact left by Alex's car. Red paint and fragments of fibre-glass were embedded in the gash left behind. I took a final shot.

I'd seen enough and returned to my car. No one seemed to have noticed my excursion. I drove out of the flea market over to Chicane

Motorsports. I walked inside the cramped building filled with mannequins dressed in racing overalls and holding steering wheels. Chicane's is big, but the customer area is small. The majority of the space is taken up with floor to ceiling racks filled with car parts.

At the end of one of the aisles, I waved to Chris who was sitting at his desk typing away at his computer. Chris owned Chicane's, but never looked the part. I'd never seen him in a pair of jeans. He always dressed in designer clothes. Considering the oil and grease content of his business, it was a mistake to be that well-attired, but somehow, he never managed to get a drop of oil on him.

'Hi, Aidy, what can we do you for?'

I held up my list.

'I'll get Paul.'

Chris called out for Paul, his only full time employee.

'Coming,' Paul's familiar voice called back. He climbed down from a ladder and came out to the counter.

Paul was the antithesis of Chris. He was always grubby. His hands were black from oil and his complexion was leathery from a lifetime spent in the elements.

'Watcha, Aidy. Is it that time of year already?'

'It is. Time to make up for all the damage I've done this season.'

I pushed a box containing my rear shocks over to Paul. Oil from their leaking seals stained the cardboard. Paul looked them over.

'For rebuilding?'

I nodded.

'I've got everything on your list on the shelf, but the shocks will take me a week to turn around. That OK?'

'No worries. I'll take what you've got and I'll be back for the rest.'

Paul grinned and scurried off to find the bearings, rose joints and everything else on the list.

Chris called out, 'You go to Alex's funeral yesterday?'

I peered down the aisle to see him. 'Yeah.'

Chris shook his head. 'Too bad. I can't remember there being a death here.'

'I can,' Paul chimed in. 'Barry Telfer, August bank holiday, 1972. He rolled a Ford Cortina at Church corner, broke his neck. Nasty.'

Chris rolled his eyes and I smiled. Paul was an encyclopedia of motorsport. He absorbed every race result, fact and rumour. If there was something he didn't know, then it wasn't worth knowing.

'I sent flowers, but I didn't go,' Chris said. 'It didn't seem right.'

'I know what you mean,' I said.

'Did many go?'

'Most of the regulars.'

Chris nodded. 'Did Derek?'

'No.'

Chris shrugged in a 'what are you gonna do' gesture.

'Are you coming to the championship bash?' he asked.

There was an end-of-the-season banquet to celebrate the season and to present awards, including the championship trophy. Under the circumstances, I hadn't intended on raising a glass to honour Derek Deacon, but I changed my mind. I saw some value in attending. The dinner was an excuse for everyone to get dressed up, drink too much and forget how much money they'd spent on a season of racing. It meant people would be more forthcoming than usual.

'Yeah, I'll be there.'

Paul emerged from the shelves with everything I'd requested. He checked it all off against my list and when he was sure all was good, he rang it up on the register.

'I hear Alex's car is here.'

Paul stopped punching numbers into the till and shared a look with Chris.

Chris got up from his seat and came up to the counter. 'Yeah, it's locked up in the scrutineering bay.'

'I know you've got keys to the bay. Do you think I could take a look?'

'Why would you want to do that?' Myles Beecham said from behind me.

Shit. Another minute and I would have pulled it off. Was dumb luck biting me in the arse or had he been watching me walk the track from the control tower? I turned to face him. He looked ready to throttle me. Obviously, he hadn't gotten yesterday out of his system.

'Well?' he demanded.

'Some of the drivers agreed that no one should drive Alex's car again. We're looking to buy it to have it crushed.' While that was true, I wasn't planning to melt the car down until I'd gone over it. Just like the skid marks, the car would help me construct a case against Derek.

My explanation worked. The tension in the room broke and Myles seemed to shrink by a few inches as his suppressed anger bled out of him.

'But why do you want to see the car?' he said.

'So I can make a realistic offer. We want to make a gesture, but none of us are made of money.'

Myles chewed that one over for a moment. I guessed he was deciding whether I was bullshitting him or not.

'Come with me. I'll show you.'

We crossed the paddock to the scrutineering bay in silence. This was no good. If I wanted to get to the bottom of Alex's death, I needed everyone's cooperation. That included Myles. 'Look, I'm sorry about what I said at the funeral. It was uncalled for.'

Myles kept walking without looking at me. 'That's OK. Nerves are a little frayed at the moment. It's a sensitive time for everyone.'

'Sensitive times or not, I was rude.'

'I appreciate you saying that.'

Myles unlocked the double garage doors to the scrutineering bay and swung them open. What remained of Alex's car sat ruined in the middle of the bay. My mouth went dry at the sight.

The car was a mess. The impact had flattened the aluminium nose box, snapping off the brake and clutch master cylinders in the process. A pool of fluid stained the floor. Splintered fibreglass bodywork exposed the chassis underneath. A Formula Ford's chassis is a spiderweb of tubular steel. It's immensely strong, especially in a head-on collision, but Alex's chassis had buckled. Only one tyre remained inflated. The other three were either punctured or hanging from buckled rims. The front wheels only remained attached to the car by the brake cables and the wishbone suspension assembly was nothing more than a knot of folded steel.

Despite the devastation, Alex should have survived. Formula cars are one giant safety cage. The wheel and suspension arrangement is designed to shear off so that it reduces the energy during a crash. The cars fold up like a garden chair, allowing the driver to walk away in one piece.

Crouching down to examine the cockpit, I discovered what had killed Alex. The harness mounts over his shoulders had sheared off during the high speed impact. Unrestrained from the waist up, his momentum hurled him head first into the steering wheel. Even with his crash helmet, he didn't stand a chance. When the car hit the wall, physics took over. The deceleration was massive. His body went from one hundred and thirty to zero in the blink of an eye. The resulting force at which he would have hit his head on the steering wheel would have been staggering. I climbed to my feet, unable to speak.

'How much do you think you'll offer?'

There was thousands in damage here. The car wasn't worth much in this condition. The chassis wasn't salvageable and most of the ancillaries were write-offs. There was very little of value. The whole thing was worth a grand at most, but that wasn't a figure to toss out at a grieving family. Nobody wants to hear their son's life could be reduced to a few hundred pounds.

'How much do you want?' I asked.

'It's not down to me. You'll need to deal with Alex's family.'

That wasn't going to be a fun call.

'You're making a very nice gesture here, but I don't think they'll be interested in receiving offers for it. I talked to Alex's father yesterday about returning the car. He doesn't want it back.'

'I don't want to see any part of this car back on the track next season, Myles.'

'I don't disagree. I think the family will give you the car if you ask. Have you raised any money?'

'I have commitments from several of the drivers.'

'It's a shame for that money to go to waste.'

'We could start a fund and put the money towards upgrading the crash team's equipment or something.'

Myles smiled. 'I like that. It's a fitting memorial.'

And it gave me an excuse to stay close to the activities at Stowe Park.

'Come back to the office,' Myles said, 'and let's make some phone calls.'

Eva Beecham fixed me with a disapproving glare when I followed Myles into the administration building. Myles diffused the situation quickly.

'Aidy is putting a fund together in Alex's name and I think we should help. Pull out the list of registrants for the Clark Paints Championship and we'll make some calls.'

Eva printed off a list of drivers with their contact information. The list consisted of names, addresses, phone numbers and emergency contacts. Alex's was there alongside Derek's and my own. It also listed the name and number for emergency contacts. Next to Alex's home address was his father's name and mobile phone number.

We decided amongst us that it was best the money was sent care of Myles and Eva. Any donation was fine, but we would push for a donation matching a race entry fee, which was two hundred pounds. Getting that from every person seemed steep, but it was possible considering the emotional weight attached to the request. Every driver would like to think others would cough up the price of a race entry if they should die on the track. With two hundred multiplied by just the forty drivers registered to the series, we were looking at an impressive sum.

'I'll call Alex's father to get the go ahead,' Myles said.

'You should call *Pit Lane* magazine, *Motorsport News* and the TV stations about what we're doing,' Eva said. 'They should talk to you two about this.'

I liked the idea of the press attention, specifically from anyone at Redline. I wanted to see the uncut footage from the race.

For the next couple of hours, the three of us called dozens of drivers from across the country. The support was fantastic. About two-thirds agreed to donate the price of a race entry and none but a distinct minority refused to donate anything. It was a fulfilling, yet draining experience. I hung up on my last call and sat back in my seat. Eva was smiling at me.

Myles finished his call. 'Aidy, that was Alex's father. He'd like to meet with you tomorrow to talk about the fund-raising and the car. I said that would be OK. If it's a problem, give him a call back.'

'No, that'll be OK.'

Myles handed me a post-it note with a phone number, an address and two p.m. circled.

'Your father would be very proud of what you're doing.'

'Thanks,' I said and wished someone had done something like this for him. Dad had died without receiving his Formula One signing bonus or taking out a life insurance policy.

The door opened and Derek Deacon walked in. He smiled at us. I felt like we were being sized up by a shark.

Derek's appearance unsettled Myles and Eva. Despite being on their own property, they looked as if they'd been caught stealing. They didn't have anything to feel guilty about. None of us did, but I tensed up along with them.

'Eva, I got a message that you called. I was in the area and thought I'd drop by. What's going on?'

Even though the question was aimed at Eva, Derek's gaze was fixed on me.

I returned his gaze. I'd been glad when Eva had called Derek. He, more than anyone, had reason to give something back after he'd taken so much.

'We're putting together a fund in memory of Alex,' she said.

'That's nice,' Derek said in a sneering tone. 'Whose idea was that?'

'Aidy's,' Myles said.

'That's very good of you.'

I shrugged.

'I'd like to do my bit. How much is everyone putting in?'

'The price of a race entry,' I said.

Derek smirked. 'I like that. I'll tell you what. I'll go one better. I'll donate my prize money for winning the championship.'

The championship winner received a thousand pounds. Derek looked to be trying to buy his innocence.

'Are you sure?' Myles said.

'Deadly,' he said turning his attention to Myles then back to me. 'I don't race for the money.'

'That's very generous,' I said.

Derek shrugged the compliment away. 'I'm a generous kind of guy. See you at the banquet,' he said on his way out.

It was a nice performance. He was responsible for Alex's death and he was acting magnanimous. His philanthropic gesture would get back to the racing community. He was going to come out smelling like a rose.

It was getting dark, so I stood up. 'Look, I'd better go. I need to settle up at Chicane's before they close.'

Myles shook my hand before seeing me out.

By the time I got back to Chicane's, Chris and Paul had boxed up my order. I paid them and carried the purchases out to the Capri. Derek was leaning against the driver's door.

I unlocked the boot and put the box inside. As I came around to the driver's side, Derek made no move to stand aside.

'That's a really decent thing you've masterminded,' he said. 'I didn't realize you were so philanthropic.'

Masterminded was an unusual choice of word. Philanthropy is never masterminded. I didn't point out his poor choice of words.

'It seemed the right thing to do.'

Derek nodded his agreement. 'I saw you and Alex chatting on race day. You looked very chummy. I didn't know you two were so tight.'

'We weren't.'

'So why the big effort?'

'I know what it's like to lose someone close.'

'That's right, your mum and dad. I remember your dad well. I raced against him here in Formula Fords. Did you know that?'

I shook my head.

'Nice guy. Terrible what happened to your parents. It just goes to show you can't avoid accidents. Your parents couldn't and Alex couldn't.' Derek stepped out from in front of my driver's door and opened it for me. As I slid into the seat, he leaned in close and whispered, 'Careful how you go, Aidy. I wouldn't want anything to happen to you too.'

I'd just received my first warning.

Lap Seven

Alex's parents lived on a tree-lined street in an upscale neighbourhood in Guildford. They lived in an elegant Edwardian era detached house with a double garage and U-shaped gravel driveway. I parked Steve's Capri alongside the familiar Range Rover I'd seen Mr Fanning drive to race meetings.

Mr Fanning stood waiting for me on the doorstep. He took my hand and pumped it two-handed. His eyes shone with unspilled tears. 'Thanks for coming.'

'My pleasure,' I said.

He led me into the living room. It was tastefully furnished, if a little dated. Pictures of Alex ranging from when he was a toddler up to very recent covered a table underneath the window. Not one of the photos showed him racing.

Alison sat on the sofa with her arm around Mrs Fanning. She looked up and gave me a half smile, but Mrs Fanning kept her gaze aimed at the carpet. Alison was an unexpected and unwanted surprise. I knew my presence would be upsetting to the Fannings. I didn't need to upset Alex's fiancée too.

'This is Adrian Westlake,' Mr Fanning said.

'Call me Aidy,' I replied.

'He's one of Alex's racing friends.'

Mrs Fanning tore her gaze away from the ground to look at me. She murmured a hello before rising to her feet. 'If you'll excuse me, I have some things to do.'

She kept it together until she reached the stairs, then broke into sobs. Alison went to go to her, but Mr Fanning shook his head as he sat alongside Alison.

'Myles says you're spearheading a collection to buy Alex's car,' Mr Fanning said.

'Yes.'

'Why?' Alison asked.

'To make sure the car isn't raced again. It's a mark of respect.'

'I don't think it's in any condition to be raced,' Mr Fanning said.

'You'd be surprised. The car could be restored.'

'I'm not sure anyone would want to race the car after what happened to Alex,' Alison said.

I didn't want to tell her how many people would. I wouldn't be surprised if the Fannings had received calls from the vulture element already.

'What would you do with the car?' Mr Fanning asked.

There was no way of saying it without it sounding crass or callous. I was glad Mrs Fanning wasn't in the room to hear it. 'I would have it compacted to make sure nobody could use it.'

I said nothing about wanting the car so I could prove that Derek had killed Alex. 'The car has little residual value, but I'm willing to pay a price you're happy with. We're trying to make something good out of something tragic.'

'How much money have you raised so far?' Alison asked.

'Around six thousand. An appeal will go out in *Pit Lane* magazine and *Motorsport News* for others to contribute. I'm hoping we can double that figure.'

'That's more than the car is worth,' Mr Fanning said. 'What would you do with the excess?'

'I spoke to Myles about using the money on safety upgrades at the track. It might just save a life.'

Mr Fanning and Alison exchanged a look. She nodded.

'We talked about what to do with Alex's car before you came over,' Mr Fanning said. 'We decided we don't want any money for it. It belonged to Alex. He bought it. Taking the money would be pointless. You can have the car with our blessing.'

Alison took Mr Fanning's hand and both of them smiled at me. Tears welled up and robbed me of the ability to say thank you. Seeing these people act with such grace after what had been done to them was too much.

I wasn't the only one with tears in my eyes. Alison's eyes glistened.

'There's something we want to do,' Mr Fanning said. 'Motor racing robbed my wife and me of our son. Alison lost her husband-to-be. We should be crusading for the end of motorsport, but I know how important racing was to Alex. He knew the risks and still he raced. I can be upset by what happened, but I can't be bitter.'

He was talking about Alex's death in terms of an accident. Did he still not know of Derek's death threat?

'In that spirit, the last race of the series will be the Alex Fanning memorial race. Myles has given it the OK. There'll be a special prize fund for the winner each year.'

I smiled and said it was a great idea, but I didn't like it. I foresaw Derek winning next year's race. The idea of him winning a race honouring the person he killed was abhorrent.

'Vic Hancock has offered to dispose of the car,' Mr Fanning said. 'He has the facility and he's more than happy to take care of matters for you.'

I couldn't let that happen before I got to see the car. 'No, I'd like to do it. I know several of the other drivers would like to be involved. It would be our way of saying goodbye to Alex.'

Mr Fanning smiled and nodded his agreement. 'You understand more than most about what we're going through. I can't imagine what it must have been like to lose your parents.'

'And I can't imagine what it's like to lose a son.'

'But we all understand an untimely loss.'

There was no dispute there.

Mr Fanning held out an envelope. 'Myles asked for a release giving the car to you.'

I took the envelope. I had my first piece of evidence. 'Thank you. I really appreciate this.'

'No, thank you. You're looking out for my son even after none of us can. I appreciate that.'

I nodded and rose to my feet. 'I should be going. I've intruded enough on your time. Please pass my condolences on to your wife.'

Mr Fanning stood, squeezed out a pained yet grateful smile and shook my hand.

'I should be going too,' Alison said.

'I'll run you over to the railway station,' Mr Fanning said.

'No, that's OK,' she said. 'Do you mind giving me a ride to the station, Aidy?'

The request surprised me. 'Sure. No problem.'

'I'll just say goodbye to Laura before we go.'

'I'll wait for you in the car,' I said.

Mr Fanning insisted on shaking my hand again and telling me what a great guy I was. The atmosphere inside the house was stifling and I had to get out. I wanted Alex's car for all the right reasons, but I was deceiving these people. I thanked him one last time and walked over to the Capri.

The blast of afternoon wind cleared the nausea that had been building. I sucked in the cool air. It cleansed me of my guilt.

I got behind the wheel. The car was cold and uninviting. I gunned the engine and turned on the heater. It was a couple of minutes before the warmth spilled over me. I released a relieved breath.

Alison stepped from the house a few minutes later. She wiped at her eyes with a tissue as she climbed into the car. She kept her gaze dead ahead.

'Which station?'

'London Road.'

I pulled onto the street and accelerated away. Alison looked back over her shoulder at the Fanning's house. When I turned onto the next street, she turned around and sighed.

I felt for Alison. She was trapped in an awkward situation. She was a final connection to the Fanning's son, but the connection that made them family no longer existed. Alex was the glue that had tied them together. Without him, there was no bond.

'Do you think you'll stay in touch with the Fannings?'

'For now, yes. We need each other. Who knows in the future? It depends on how we heal. You know better than all of us. Do you ever get over something like this?'

'No. Not really. Alex will always be a part of you. You'll always be reminded of something he said or did. You'll wish he was around when something great or terrible happens. It won't stop you from living your life, but you'll never let him go.'

We said nothing after that. I drove, threading my way through the streets of Guildford over to the London Road railway station. As I stopped the car, a train slowed as it headed into the station.

'That's my train,' she said.

'OK,' I said. 'Have a safe journey home.'

The station announcer's voice drifted across the air. 'The three-twenty service for Waterloo is now approaching.'

I waited for Alison to move, but she remained seated.

'You're going to miss your train.'

She said nothing.

We watched the people climb aboard the train. It paused for a moment for that one final passenger and when that person didn't arrive, its diesel engine growled and it pulled out of the station.

She waited until the last carriage passed the end of the platform before speaking. 'Why are you going to all this trouble?'

She fixed me with an expression that wasn't hostile, but was certainly demanding.

'I guess I understand loss,' I said, sticking to my cover story.

Her expression tightened, squeezing the softness from her face. 'I get that, but it seems a little excessive.'

'Alex was a friend.'

She nodded, but her tension failed to leave her. 'Funny, I don't remember Alex ever mentioning you. What were you, pen pals?'

There was no point in deceiving her anymore. 'You're right, Alex and I weren't really friends. From what I knew of him, he was a nice guy and for that, I liked him. I talked to him just before the race. It might sound stupid, but we shared a guy moment. He told me about getting married to you and his plans. Two hours later he was dead. One moment Alex had a future, the next he didn't. It affected me. I had to do something.'

I left out the part about Alex retiring from racing as a wedding gift to her. She was putting on a tough act to get me to talk, but her façade was eggshell thin. It would shatter in a second if she knew. I didn't know anyone who could handle the news that a loved one was killed an hour from walking away from the thing that killed them. To tell her would be a cruel punishment.

What I said seemed to work. She sank into her seat and the softness returned to her face. She looked like herself again, except sad. I wished I could put a smile on her face instead of pain.

'So that's why you're doing this.'

'Yes.'

'It has nothing to do with Derek Deacon saying he'd kill Alex? I saw you and Mr Beecham arguing at the church.'

It was stupid on my part to assume she hadn't heard about the death threat. There was no way Alex could shield her from it. 'OK, it does.'

'So you think Derek killed Alex?'

'I don't know for sure.'

'Don't give me that.'

I was trying to be kind. It wasn't working. Alison had probably had enough kindness in recent days. She needed someone to be honest with her.

'Yes, I think he killed Alex. I can't prove it, but I'm trying to. Derek shouldn't be allowed to get away with it.'

We were silent with each other. Only the drone of the engine filled the void.

'I didn't think you knew,' I said.

'I didn't have much choice. Everyone was eager to let me in on the news. Like I wanted to hear my fiancé had been marked for death.'

'Did you say anything to Alex?'

'Yes. He told me not to worry about it.' She shook her head. 'He said none of it mattered and the best man would win.'

Alex couldn't have been more wrong.

'What about his parents?'

'Eric knows. He hasn't told Laura. She's not taking this well.'

'What does Mr Fanning think?'

'He thinks it was an accident. He believes all racecar drivers are honourable and do right by each other.'

'Is that how you feel?'

'No.' Alison shoved the car door open and walked over to the railway station.

Lap Eight

I spent the rest of my Sunday at home with the photos I'd taken at Stowe Park. I printed out all the images I'd shot and spread the sheets out on the dinner table. I arranged them in storyboard fashion, showing the sequence of the crash from beginning to end.

'So that's how it happened,' Steve said over my shoulder.

I'd been too absorbed to hear my grandfather come in. He'd been on a make-up date with Maggie.

'Yeah,' I said.

He nudged me aside to get a better look at the photographs. 'How'd you get on with the Fannings?'

'They gave me the car. I'll pick it up next weekend. I should be able to see where Derek's wheels made contact with Alex.'

Steve nodded. He picked up the picture of the wall showing the imprint of Alex's impact. He examined it for a long moment. He'd witnessed a lot of fatal crashes working the pits. The sixties were a dark time. Safety measures were primitive to say the least, and track deaths were commonplace compared with today. He'd been there when Bruce MacLean died at Goodwood. It had been hard to get him to work the pits with me. The deaths of Mum and Dad were still too raw for him, but he relented. He needed to be there to watch over me like he had with Dad. He returned the picture to where he'd found it.

'So you've got a public death threat, the car and these skid marks,' he said tapping a picture. 'It's a start. What else have you got?'

The pictures looked damning, but only because of what Derek had said. To an outsider, the police, a jury, these were merely skid marks. They didn't show malice. These pictures told a story, but without a narrator, the story was meaningless. 'Nothing.'

He pulled out a seat alongside me and sat. 'We can't do this alone, Aidy. I understand this is important to you, but we don't have all the answers and we have little influence over the outcome.'

I wanted to argue, but I'd never be able to twist Derek's arm into confessing and I didn't have the power to secure the raw video from Redline. I wasn't trying to bring Derek down by myself. I just wanted to produce some evidence that would turn the investigation in the right direction. Looking at the photos now, I saw I had little capability of swaying anyone, even myself. I reached over and picked up the pictures.

Steve put a hand on my shoulder. 'You're doing the right thing, Aidy. People are trying to make this all go away for some reason. That's not right. Someone needs to speak up. It looks like it's going to be you.'

'So what do I do; call Derek out?'

'No. Talk to the cops.'

'They've closed the case.'

'Because they don't know any better most likely. They aren't motorsport people. They need to be educated. Find the cop in charge and tell him what you know. It'll turn things around.'

I nodded. It seemed like a smart plan.

'Just know though, if you talk, it won't win you many friends.'

It wouldn't, but I didn't see what choice I had. Alex's death couldn't go unpunished. Someone had to stand up for him. I just wished it didn't have to be me.

'Yeah, I know, but it has to be done.'

Steve smiled. His pale grey eyes sparkled under the ceiling light. 'Good, lad. Call them tomorrow.'

'I won't have to. I'll be able to do it in person on Tuesday after I finish the press conference.' There'd been a message from Myles on the answering machine telling me to be at Stowe Park Tuesday morning for a press conference about the Alex Fanning appeal. He'd gotten the motorsport press and TV to turn out.

I arrived at the track Tuesday morning. Myles had set the press conference for ten thirty and I arrived just in time. A bunch of cars and a BBC news van were clustered around the race control tower. I parked next to the BBC Bristol news van. It didn't appear there'd be any national coverage for this story and my hope that Redline would attend went unanswered too. As I got out of my car, two other vehicles stood out for me. Mr Fanning's Range Rover and Derek's aged Ford Granada.

Whose idea had it been to include Derek; Myles or Derek

himself? I could see either being responsible for this move. Neither of them wanted me airing dirty laundry. They had nothing to fear. I wasn't going to say anything. Steve was right. I didn't have enough. Yet. I was biding my time.

It was a beautiful day. Bright, clear skies, but bitterly cold. A biting wind sliced across the track. I hurried inside the building and everyone looked my way. Mr Fanning and Alison were among them.

'Now that Aidy's here,' Myles said, 'I think we're ready to start.'

Myles led everyone upstairs into the control tower. Once there, the BBC cameraman ordered us around. He put Myles in the middle with Mr Fanning, Alison and Vic Hancock on Myles's right and Derek and me on his left. We were positioned with our backs to the track in order to have a panoramic view of the circuit in the background.

While the BBC set up, we ran through the interview with *Pit Lane* magazine and *Motorsport News*. These two publications accounted for everything motorsport related in the UK. I didn't recognize Andrew Marsh from *Motorsport News*, but I knew Fergus Kane from *Pit Lane*. He raced VW Beetles and worked in the ad sales department at the magazine. He'd been hustling for a reporter gig and it looked as if he'd gotten his wish. He smiled at me.

Marsh got things rolling. 'You want to tell us what's going on here today?'

'As you all know, we lost a promising competitor in Alex Fanning,' Myles said. 'It's a loss we all share and one we're not willing to forget. That's why I've been collecting donations all weekend from drivers in the Clark Paints Formula Ford Championship in Alex's honour. The money will be going towards safety improvements for our paramedic crews here at the track. The initiative was spearheaded by Aidy Westlake.'

'What made you do this, Aidy?' Fergus asked. 'Does it have anything to do with your father's untimely death?'

The second part of Fergus's question stung for a second. 'I know what effect a racing death has on a family and the racing community. We live in times where safety measures make driver deaths rare, but when they happen, we can't ignore them. Raising funds to improve safety seems like the natural thing to do.'

'How much have you raised so far?' Marsh asked.

'Over seven thousand pounds so far from the drivers in the series,' Myles said, 'but we're looking for others to donate. We're hoping that all drivers across the country will contribute.'

'Is there a preferred donation sum?'

'Two hundred pounds. That's the equivalent of a race fee. But we will accept donations great and small. Derek Deacon, this year's champion, donated his championship purse to the fund.'

'Why the generosity, Derek?' Fergus asked.

This was an answer I wanted to hear. Did it help him ease his conscience? Judging from Derek's smirk, a guilty conscience wasn't something that needed easing.

'I won this championship because Alex died, so it's a hollow victory. I could never enjoy the proceeds.'

Someone had been practising his lies in front of the mirror.

'I wonder if I could step forward a moment,' Vic Hancock said. 'Hancock Salvage sponsored Alex. We miss him dearly. As a mark of our respect,' Hancock said as he removed a check from his suit jacket pocket, 'we'd like to add five thousand pounds to the fund.'

Hancock received a small round of applause as he handed the check to Myles Beecham.

'How can others make a donation?' Fergus asked.

'Through us here at the circuit,' Myles said.

'Are there any events planned in honour of Alex?' Marsh asked.

'Yes,' Myles said. 'From now on, the last round of the Clark Paints Championship will be the Alex Fanning Memorial Trophy. Alex's father will be putting up a trophy and an additional cash prize for the trophy's winner.'

'My son lost his life doing something he loved,' Mr Fanning said, filled with pride. 'While that hurts the ones he left behind,' he said as took Alison's hand, 'I can't turn my back on a community that has gone out of its way to honour him.'

Mr Fanning broke free of his spot in Myles's seamless arrangement to shake my hand along with Myles's and Derek's. It disgusted me to see Derek enjoying the adulation for something he'd caused. I told myself to take it easy. Let him enjoy the applause because it wouldn't last. His crimes would catch up to him sooner than he thought.

'All those who have helped here are truly princes amongst men,' Mr Fanning said, 'and I thank them all for their kindness and camaraderie.'

We ran through it all again for the BBC, then the affair broke up into individual interviews. Each reporter got their sound bite from everyone concerned. The photographers from both magazines corralled us for pictures. What expression was I meant to show? Happiness for the good we were doing? Sadness for the loss of a comrade? I let the photographers guide me. The only shot where I could raise anything like a smile was when Alison brought out a framed photo of Alex. It was a head shot of him in his racing overalls, smiling. It killed the smiles that had been present until then. I looked over at Derek. Even he couldn't grin his way through that one. I almost took pleasure from watching him squirm, but Alison killed it. The photographer lined her up in the front with Mr Fanning at her side. The shot reminded me of a photo taken at my parents' graveside. It's a pretty famous picture of me standing over their coffins holding my dad's crash helmet with Steve standing behind me. This new pose, with a different face, but the same unquenchable sadness, smacked too much of déjà vu.

After my part in the affair ended, I hung around outside. I needed to talk to Fergus. I had a ten minute bone-chilling wait. When he came out, I caught him on his way to his car.

'Fergus, got a sec?'

'Sure,' he said. 'Pretty screwed up about Alex, eh?'

'Yeah, I wanted to talk to you about it.'

Fergus grappled for his recorder.

I placed a hand over his. 'This is off the record, OK?'

He hesitated for a moment, then nodded.

'Did you see the TV coverage of the race?' I asked.

'Yeah. What was that about? They didn't mention Alex at all.'

'I know,' I said. 'I have a favour to ask. Is your dad still friendly with some of the people over at Redline?'

'A few.'

'Do you think he can get a copy of the unedited footage of Alex's crash?'

Fergus pulled back from me. 'Why do you want that?'

'A bunch of us wanted to see the accident to know what happened.'

'Look, don't bullshit me. I've heard the rumours of what went on during that race. Do you know something?'

'I might, if I got to see the footage.'

Fergus frowned.

'If I find out anything because of what I see on that tape, I'll come to you and you only. Sound good?'

I was dangling a carrot in front of him. Obviously, he'd been given his break as a reporter and a big story would cement the position. If he wanted to be a full time reporter, he couldn't turn me down and he didn't.

'OK. I'll get my old man to ask, but I'm going to hold you to your word that you'll give me everything you know.'

When I had all the proof, I wouldn't hesitate telling Fergus everything. I told him we had a deal and we shook on it before he left.

I got as far as my car before I heard my name being called. Vic Hancock emerged from the control tower and jogged over to me.

'Do you have a minute, Aidy?'

'Sure.'

'I just wanted to say you're doing a great thing masterminding this fund-raiser in Alex's honour.'

I tried to shrug the compliment away. The attention was embarrassing me.

'Look, my company still wants to be in racing, so I was wondering if you would like to talk about sponsorship for next season.'

Normally, I'd be biting a potential sponsor's arm off, especially one I didn't have to solicit. Motor racing is a hard game. It's not like any other sport where you can just kick a ball or pick up a bat. It takes resources just to get to the starting line. Hancock was piling the cash up in front of me and I wasn't in a position to turn it down, but the circumstances felt more than a bit ghoulish. Alex hadn't even been dead two weeks and here we were talking about replacing him. Worse still, I saw the business angle here for Hancock. He could earn himself some points with his clientele by parading me around as Alex's replacement. If I said no, he'd find someone else. I would hate it if that someone else was Derek Deacon.

'I'd like that,' I said.

'That's great. Get a proposal and a budget together and give me a call to make an appointment.' He handed me his card. 'I look forward to it.'

I watched him go. The word budget sounded very nice. Racing with a solid budget was the air bag all drivers wanted in their cars.

You could race with freedom and without the fear that an accident would keep you off the track for an indefinite period. Sadly, the circumstances of my good fortune sullied my excitement.

I checked the remaining cars for Derek's Granada. It was still there. I needed to get away before Derek did. I didn't want him seeing where I was heading next. I should have said goodbye to Mr Fanning and Alison, but I didn't want my farewell to trigger an exodus.

I went to the Stowe village police station, but the duty officer directed me to the Chippenham station, since they were handling Alex's case. I followed the officer's directions into Chippenham and entered the station. There was no one in the waiting room. A Plexiglas partition separated me from the duty sergeant.

'I'd like to speak to the officer in charge of the Alex Fanning case.' When the officer didn't react to Alex's name, I added, 'He was the driver killed at Stowe Park race track.'

'You want Detective Len Brennan, but he isn't here right now.'

'When do you expect him back?'

'I can't say.'

'Does he have a mobile number or something I could call?'

The officer dug out a business card and handed it to me through a slot in the Plexiglas. It had all I needed, an office number and an all important mobile number. I thanked the officer and left.

In my car, I dialled Brennan's number on my mobile. The call was going unanswered and I expected it to go to voicemail when the rasping voice of a serious smoker came on the line.

'Brennan.'

'You're in charge of the Alex Fanning case?'

'I was. That case is closed.'

At least Myles hadn't lied to me about the police involvement. 'Would the case be reopened if you received new information?'

'Yes, but let's dispense with the hypothetical and stay with the facts. Let's start with your name.'

I told him my name. I wanted the police to know it. It put me under their umbrella of protection. If Derek went after me, he'd play straight into their hands. It was scary to think in those terms, but my refusal to let Alex's murder go put me in this position.

'OK, Mr Westlake, what is it you know?'

'Derek Deacon threatened to kill Alex Fanning the night before the race. He didn't make a secret of it. He told plenty of people.'

'I see,' Brennan said.

It wasn't quite the reaction I was expecting, but then again, I hadn't been that fired up by Derek's threat when he made it.

'Why did Mr Deacon make this threat?'

'Alex was going to win the championship if Derek didn't stop him. He hadn't been able to beat him straight, so he had to do it crooked.'

Brennan was silent for a moment. 'That's a pretty weak reason to kill a person.'

'Is there ever a good one?'

'Good point. OK, Mr Deacon says he's going to kill Mr Fanning. How could he do it? The statements I have say Mr Fanning's crash was an accident.'

I explained to Brennan how it's possible to interlock wheels to force an opponent out of a race while making most people swear they'd seen a simple accident.

'You were in the race?'

'Yes.'

'So with your trained eye, you witnessed this wheel locking manoeuvre, yes?'

I winced. I'd hoped Brennan wouldn't ask this question. 'No, I didn't have a clear view.'

'But you think you know better than the people who were actually witnesses?'

I saw where Brennan was going, but I'd be damned if I'd let him dismiss me. 'The race was filmed for TV. Have you seen the footage?'

'Yes.'

'The actual crash?'

'Yes.'

That was music to my ears. Brennan had seen the uncut video, which meant he could get his hands on it.

'If we watch it together, I can show you what I mean. It'll make total sense.'

Brennan cut me off. 'I've seen the crash and it was what it was. An accident. Plain and simple.'

'Yes, that's how it looks to the uninformed person. If I were to go over it with you, then you'd be able to see.'

'See what? Your version of events? I might be an uninformed person, but I'm not stupid.'

'I didn't say that you were.'

'Didn't you?'

Shit. This was all going wrong. 'No.'

'Look, let me explain a few things to you, someone who is uninformed about the ways of law enforcement. I investigated Mr Fanning's death. I spoke to witnesses. I viewed the TV footage. And guess what? None of it matches your accusation, not one bit.'

I should have conceded defeat. My attempt to reopen Alex's case had been shot to pieces, but I wanted an answer to one more question.

'Did you speak to Derek about what he said the night before the race?'

Brennan let out a frustrated sigh. 'Yes, I did. He even volunteered the information.'

'And you didn't think that was worth pursuing?'

'Excuse me?'

I'd burnt my bridges with Brennan. Being rude to him now made no difference. 'A person threatens to kill someone and when that someone dies, you don't take it seriously?'

'Let me ask you this. If you heard Mr Deacon make the threat, as did dozens of others, why didn't you come forward until now?'

I didn't say anything. Brennan had me. I couldn't decide if Derek was lucky or a criminal genius. It was all playing into his hands and he didn't need to lift a finger.

'What's that Mr Westlake? I don't think I heard you.'

'I didn't think Derek was serious.'

'Exactly. You can call Mr Deacon a poor sportsman, but you can't call him a killer.'

Brennan was dead wrong. I didn't care what he said. It was all too coincidental that Derek threatened to kill Alex, and then, as if he'd invoked a genie's wish, Alex died.

'Let me make a suggestion to you. I would keep your remarks about Mr Deacon to yourself. You're leaving yourself open to a defamation suit.'

Brennan didn't give me a chance to respond and hung up.

No, I wasn't going to be brushed aside by Brennan. The man was going to listen to me whether he liked it or not. I jumped out of the car and shoved my way back into the police station.

'You again?' the duty officer said.

I bottled my frustration and put on a smile. 'Yes, I spoke to

Detective Brennan. He was very helpful. I did want to meet with him though. I was wondering if you know where I can find him.'

The duty officer frowned. I understood it. My story was full of holes.

'I just need ten minutes of his time and I don't want to do it over the phone. I drove all the way from Windsor to find someone to speak to. I don't want to drive back empty-handed.'

The duty officer looked at his watch. 'If he's not on a call, he'll be having lunch about now. Do you know Langley Hill?'

'Yeah.'

'You'll find him at the Green Man. They do a good pub lunch there.'

'Thanks,' I said and walked to the Capri.

I floored it to Langley Hill. I was under no illusion that the duty officer wouldn't be straight on the phone to Brennan. Brennan would either be conveniently gone or he'd be waiting there to read me the riot act. I hoped for the latter. He could bark at me all he liked, as long as he listened to my side of the story.

I slowed when I reached Langley Hill. It had a quaint thoroughfare and all the buildings were at least a couple of hundred years old. It looked to have been a highway rest stop for anyone on their way back from London. Despite its tourist trap possibilities, it remained a well-kept secret. I'd never seen a tourist within twenty miles of this place, just the locals. I don't know if the locals wanted it that way, but it worked. I spotted the pub on the left and parked across the street.

I jogged across the street, which was free of traffic, and climbed the steps going into the pub. I stopped in the doorway. I realized I hadn't asked the duty officer for the detective's description. I searched the sea of faces for him, but no one's manner screamed cop. My search came to an abrupt end. Derek Deacon sat next to a middle-aged guy in a suit playing with an unlit cigarette in his hand. Derek and his friend were laughing and Derek slapped his companion on the back.

I couldn't walk in there. Derek couldn't see me talking to Brennan. I needed Brennan to come outside. I pulled out my mobile and redialled the detective's number while keeping my gaze on Derek. A sense of dread came over me seconds before Brennan answered the phone. The man sitting next to Derek, sharing a joke and a pint, reached inside his suit coat pocket and brought out his mobile. He eyed the caller ID for a moment before answering. As he spoke, Brennan's voice came over the line in my ear.

'Is that you again, Mr Westlake?'

Lap Nine

'So the cops are in bed with Derek?' Steve said.

'It sure looks that way. Who interviews a suspect in a pub?'

'Good point.'

Steve and I were sitting in the quiet and relative safety of the office at Archway. What I'd stumbled on to made so much sense. It explained why Brennan hadn't interviewed any of us who'd been in The Chequered Flag the night Derek tossed his death threat around, the short reach of the investigation, and why a lid had been placed on the TV coverage.

But none of it explained why Brennan was protecting Derek. Were they friends? That was a pretty big favour to ask a friend, especially a cop friend. Was there something more? Did Derek have his hooks into Brennan? Anything was possible.

'Now Derek knows you're gunning for him.'

'I don't need reminding,' I said. I'd driven back to Windsor with one eye permanently on the rear-view mirror fully expecting to see Derek there. If he was willing to kill to win a championship, he was going to tear me apart for informing on him.

'I might have put Derek on the defensive, but he won't stay that way. If he thinks I'm on to him, then he's going to come after me and chances are I won't see it coming.'

Steve nodded slowly. 'I know. You're going to have to watch your step.'

'Oh, God. How can this be happening?'

'It shouldn't be, but it is. You've got two choices open to you now: walk away or take him down.'

'Some choice.'

'Be thankful you still have choices.'

'Am I even in a position to walk away?'

'I think so. Word can get back to Derek that you're backing off.'

Walk away. The idea of it sounded appealing, but Alex's death had been eating away at me for over a week. The thought of Derek getting away with murder burned a hole right through me. Alex deserved justice and he wasn't getting it. If I didn't finish what I'd started, the injustice would keep eating away at me.

'I can't walk away,' I said.

A thin smile spread across Steve's face. It lasted a moment before it fell away. 'We have to decide what we're going to do to protect you.'

I liked that Steve saw my problems as a joint issue.

'So what do we do now? Talk to police here? The Windsor cops aren't connected to the Wiltshire force. Derek and Brennan won't have any influence over them. The police will want to get involved with a corruption scandal within their ranks, won't they?'

'They might,' Steve said not sounding convinced. 'Let's say we go to the locals. What do we have to give them?'

All I had was hearsay, photos of skid marks and a belief. I already knew what would happen if we contacted the Windsor police. They would go straight to Brennan. He'd tell them how I'd accused Derek of killing Alex with nothing to back it up and what a monumental pain in the arse I'd been. If I told them about Brennan's meeting with Derek, Brennan could easily dismiss it and I had no way of proving it. Even if Brennan did admit to meeting Derek, it still didn't mean anything. Derek wasn't a suspect. My claims were worthless. Telling the police would only make matters worse.

'Nothing. So what do you suggest?'

'Stay off Derek's radar. Concentrate on working the information you have and don't go off half-cocked. Tie up the loose ends and when you have something solid enough then go to the cops. They won't be able to ignore you when you have something no one can refute, even this Brennan guy. In the meantime, give Derek a wide berth.'

'I was going to pick up Alex's car on Saturday. Should I wait?'

'No, go. If we're going to prove anything, we need that car. Just don't go alone.'

Steve was good. He made it all sound simple. 'OK.'

Music from the Jumping Bean Mexican cantina next door bled through the brick wall. The management only turned the music up when they had a crowd. Considering it was only a Tuesday night, it looked as if people were having as rough a week as I was and were starting the weekend early.

Steve looked at the wall where the music threatened to crack the mortar holding the bricks in place. 'Want to go next door to get some dinner? There'll be some ladies there.'

'What will Maggie say?'

'Nothing if she doesn't find out.'

I smiled. 'You're a terrible man. Let's go.'

We went next door. It felt good to be surrounded by people who knew nothing about the racing world. We got a table and ordered food and drinks.

A group of a dozen hotties on a girls' night out had a long table running down the centre of the restaurant to themselves. Every one of them was dressed to kill. Steve tried to distract me from the subject of Derek by pointing out their various attributes, but I wasn't having any of it.

'Do you know Derek?' I asked.

'By reputation. Why?'

'He said he knew Dad and they'd raced against each other.'

Steve pondered, flicking through more than thirty seasons of pit lane memories. He nodded slowly when he struck upon something. A wry smile creased his lips. 'Your dad did what Alex almost accomplished.'

'He beat Derek for the championship?'

'Not quite. The year your dad won the Formula Ford Junior series, the last race of the season was at Stowe. He double-entered, racing in the junior race and the Champion of Stowe Park race. It was a one-circuit series back then. Your dad won both races. Derek crashed in the Stowe race in a frustrated move to overtake your dad. The crash cost him the championship.'

Great. Another reason for Derek to hold a grudge.

For the next few days, I followed Steve's advice and kept a low profile. From then on, after going to the office each day, I either worked on my Van Diemen at Archway or worked on my proposal for Vic Hancock. I mailed it out to him on Thursday and called him to let him know it was coming. We made an appointment to meet the following week. He sounded eager to put money in my hands. I tried to sound enthusiastic.

Thursday was also the day the new issues of *Motorsport News* and *Pit Lane* magazine came out. I turned to the pages with Alex's tribute in them. Alex was being heralded as a lost star. *Motorsport News* even went so far as to suggest his death was the greatest loss in motorsport since my father. Both magazines patted me on the back for my good deed. Naturally, Derek got talked about in glowing terms. Reading it all just made me more determined to bring out the truth.

Keeping to myself seemed to work. Derek made no move on me. I wondered if Brennan had reined him in. A man in his position wouldn't want Derek making life more difficult for him. Of course, Derek could be playing the same waiting game to see what I would do next. That put us in an uneasy stand-off, which sounded good, but wasn't a permanent solution. Eventually, one of us would have to make a move. Hopefully, my inactivity had convinced him to lower his guard. It didn't make me lower mine. I lived in fear that at any moment Derek would appear with a baseball bat trailing from one hand. Time dragged. I thought Saturday would never come.

I picked up Dylan in the morning and we drove down to Stowe Park in Steve's van. I didn't bother with the trailer. With so much of Alex's car in pieces, we would easily be able to fit it inside the vehicle.

Part way through the drive, Bob Dylan's 'Knockin' on Heaven's Door' came on the radio. Dylan immediately switched the radio off.

'Hey, I like that song,' I said with a smirk.

'Ha-bloody-ha.'

Bob Dylan was a sore point with Dylan. His mum was a massive fan and named him after the singer. His school years hadn't been fun since everyone teased him about his name. Even now when he introduced himself, most people asked him if he was named after Bob Dylan.

As I reached to switch the radio back on, my mobile phone rang. It was Fergus. I told Dylan to keep quiet. I didn't want Fergus knowing I had someone with me. 'Hey, Fergus. What have you got for me?'

'Yeah. About that. I couldn't get the tape from the race. I tried. I really did, Aidy, but . . .' He trailed off.

'But what?'

Dylan flashed me a worried look.

'My dad put me in touch with a guy at the studio. I met with him and I thought things were OK.' Fergus stopped talking for second. 'Aidy, they put me in a room and grilled me. It was like a bad movie. They wanted to know why I wanted the footage.'

'What did you tell them?'

'Nothing. What do I know? You're the one with the ideas.'

'Did you mention me?'

'Of course not. I have to protect my sources.'

Fergus was taking the reporter thing way too seriously. Still, I owed him one for not mentioning my name, although I was positive they already knew. I'd hardly been keeping a low profile.

'Do you think they believed you when you told them you knew nothing?'

'I think so. They said the tape was gone. Destroyed.'

'Why?'

'By request.'

'Whose?'

'The family? I don't know. They weren't telling and I wasn't asking. I just wanted the hell out. Aidy, you're on your own.'

'I'm sorry, Fergus. If I knew this was going to put you in hot water, I wouldn't have dragged you in.'

'Yeah, well, the damage is done. I'm out, OK?'

'Yeah, sure thing. Look, if I find anything out, I'll give you an exclusive or whatever.'

'Sounds good, Aidy. Talk later, yeah? Gotta go. Bye.'

Fergus didn't sound like he wanted to hear from me even if I had the map to the Holy Grail. I couldn't blame him.

We arrived at Stowe Park around lunchtime. The circuit offices were dead, which wasn't surprising on such a grim and overcast day. Myles had called the night before to tell me Chris or Paul at Chicane's would be waiting for me.

I got out at Chicane's and went inside while Dylan drove the van over to the scrutineering bay.

Chris was packing parts into boxes for mail orders. It would be boom time for him until the next season got going in March. He saw me and called out to Paul.

'Aidy's here. Will you open up for him?'

A moment later, Paul appeared jingling a set of keys. 'Gotcha covered, Aidy.'

He ducked under the counter and led me out of the store. As he marched across the paddock, I struggled to keep up with his pace.

'Isn't it great about the collection for Alex? Mr Beecham says he's received over twenty thousand. I donated. I put in a race fee donation like most people.'

Paul was a sweet guy. There was no other way of saying it. He didn't make much money working for Chris and two hundred was a big deal. Luckily for the world, for every Derek Deacon, there was a Paul balancing out the scale.

'That's fantastic,' I said, then something suddenly occurred to me. Paul was a true fan. He filmed every race on his camcorder. Paul's coverage was often used for a montage at the end of season banquet. 'Paul, were you up at Barrack Hill at the time of the crash?'

'Yeah. I wish I hadn't been. Normally, I'd be over at Wilts, but it was too busy and I couldn't get a decent shot of the cars.'

'So, you filmed Alex's crash.'

'Yeah, terrible. I can't watch it. I wanted to record over it, but I can't. It wouldn't be right.'

'Could I see the tape?'

Paul came to a dead stop. 'Why would you want to see that?'

'To help me come to terms with Alex's death. We were chatting minutes before the race, wishing each other good luck, then he was dead. I can't really believe it. I want to see it with my own eyes. The telly didn't show the crash and if I could see it, it would help me say goodbye to him.'

I didn't like deceiving Paul. He was the most honest guy in motorsport and he believed everyone was just as trustworthy, even someone like Derek. Lying to him put me on thin ice with him. If he found out I'd betrayed his trust, I'd never win it back.

My dilemma reminded me of what Steve had said to me. If I kept digging into Alex's death, it wouldn't make me any friends. I was happy to lose people like Derek as friends, but not Paul. He might not thank me, but I hoped he'd understand what I had done.

Paul must have mistaken my distress for feelings about Alex. His expression changed into one of understanding and he patted me on the shoulder.

'Sure, I understand, Aidy, and it's OK. I'll get you the tape.'

'Thanks, but please keep it to yourself. I don't want people knowing. OK?'

'No worries.'

I pulled out my business card with my name, address and phone numbers. He took it and pocketed it.

A light rain had started coming down by the time we reached the scrutineering bay. Dylan jumped out of the van and jogged over to us.

'Hey, Dylan,' Paul said as he sorted through the keys for the one to the heavy padlock.

'How's it going, Paul?'

'Straight up and down with a swirl at the end.'

Dylan and I smiled at each other. Neither of us knew what that meant, but Paul always said it.

Paul found the key and removed the padlock. Dylan helped him pull the doors open. The scrutineering bay was empty.

Lap Ten

I couldn't believe it. The car was gone. I felt intense stupidity which quickly turned to anger. I looked at Paul. He just shook his head.

'Where's the car, Paul?'

'I don't know.'

I took two fast steps, putting me right in his face. Paul backed away from me into the scrutineering bay. I wasn't about to give him any breathing space and I followed him inside.

'C'mon, who's been here?'

I didn't need to ask. I knew. Derek had stolen the car out from under me, but I wanted someone to admit it.

'I don't know.'

'Don't lie to me, Paul. You're here all day. Nothing gets past you and Chris. Now tell me.'

Paul went to duck past me, but I blocked his path. 'I don't know, Aidy. Really, I don't.'

Dylan grabbed my arm. 'He doesn't know.'

Everyone kept their place inside the bay. The only sound to be heard was rain bouncing off the bay's roof. Hearing it took the sting out of me.

'I'm sorry, Paul. I didn't mean to take it out on you.'

Paul nodded, not saying a word.

'Who else has keys to this place?' Dylan asked.

'Mr and Mrs Beecham, some of the race officials and the Hansen brothers for the race school. That's it.'

I'd expected to hear Derek's name amongst the group, but I shouldn't have been surprised. Derek wasn't dumb enough to do this himself. He'd have someone do his dirty work to give him plausible deniability. He had Brennan to take care of his legal problems and he'd have someone here at the circuit to grab Alex's car for him. The question was who would have done it for him? Any one of the people Paul had named would buckle to Derek's demands if he showed up at their door.

Stupid. I'd screwed up. I had given Derek the opening he needed. I should have taken the car when I came for the press conference.

'Who's been here today?' I asked.

'No one besides us.'

I nodded. Paul wouldn't lie. That meant someone had claimed the car the night before.

'You need to go,' Paul said. 'I have to lock up.'

Dylan and I walked out into the rain and watched Paul lock the doors.

'Again, I'm sorry. I didn't mean to lose my temper.' I put out my hand. Paul hesitated before shaking it. 'You'll get me that tape, yeah?'

Paul nodded. 'I'll call you.'

The rain was coming down hard now.

'Get in the van. We'll drop you at the door so you don't get wet,' I said.

'It's OK,' Paul answered.

I didn't push the matter. I'd done enough damage. Dylan and I climbed into the van and watched Paul trudge back to Chicane's. I gunned the engine and pulled away.

'Where are we going?' Dylan asked.

'Myles's place. Nothing happens here without his say so.'

I'd been out to Myles's home only once at the end of last

season. He had everyone back for drinks after the championship dinner. He and Eva lived in a six bedroom house sitting on an acre of land in Corsham.

The house was set back from the road. I turned down the long gravel driveway and parked in front of the three-car garage. Myles wasn't giving me the slip.

'Keep a lid on your temper, Aidy. You can't blow up at Myles the way you did at Paul.'

'I know,' I said, and I wouldn't. Finding the car gone was a shock. Getting the runaround from Myles wouldn't be.

Dylan pressed the doorbell. The chimes sounded like Big Ben was being kept hostage somewhere inside. It was a long minute before footsteps approached and Eva Beecham opened the door.

'Hello, Aidy. I'm sorry. I don't know your friend.'

'This is Dylan.'

Eva smiled at Dylan. She made no offer to let us in.

'Can we speak to Myles?'

'He's not here.'

'When will he be back?'

'I don't know. What's the problem?'

'I came to collect Alex's car, but it's gone.'

The news failed to surprise her. I could tell without pressing her that she knew where Alex's car had gone. She had her thumb on the pulse of everything at Stowe Park just like Myles. It also meant she wouldn't be giving up information to me unless she and Myles had agreed to it.

'You'll have to take the matter up with Myles.'

'I will. Can I wait?'

'No. I don't expect him back until late.'

I could have kept pushing, but I was wasting my time.

'Just tell him I came by.'

'I will,' she said and closed the door before we'd even turned our backs.

In the van, I called Myles's mobile. It went straight to voicemail, so I left a message.

'We've got two choices,' I said. 'We either hang around on the off chance we'll get Alex's car or we go home.'

'The car's gone and there's nothing we can do about it. I say we go home.'

Dylan echoed my thoughts, but a part of me didn't want to

leave with nothing. Even if I didn't leave with Alex's car, I wanted to leave with answers. But I didn't see any point. Even if I camped outside Myles's house until he came home, he wouldn't tell me anything. A wall of silence was being built and this was just another section to keep me out.

I fired up the van and pulled onto the road. Myles's home put us in the middle of the Wiltshire countryside, miles from the motorway. I followed a series of winding, narrow roads barely wide enough for two cars to pass each other comfortably. It was slow going. It was going to take twenty minutes before we reached the motorway. Just to add insult to injury, I ran into roadworks. The car ahead of me made it through before a workman put his hand out and dragged a barrier across the road. He said sorry and directed me down a farm lane.

'Our day isn't getting any better, is it?' Dylan said as I followed the detour.

Hedgerows leaned into the road, narrowing it to a single lane track. If I was struggling, the moving van behind me had it worse. Its sides clipped the outstretched branches.

'Do you know where this brings us out?' I asked.

Dylan shook his head, broke out a road atlas and flicked through the pages. 'The bloody thing isn't even shown.'

A tractor reversed out of the field to our left and blocked the road. I slammed on the brakes. The van skidded on the rain-slick surface.

The atlas went flying out of Dylan's hands as momentum threw him forward against his seat belt. 'Jesus, Aidy. I would like to make it home in one piece.'

The tractor driver raised an apologetic hand. 'Sorry. Just need to get something.'

I rolled down the window and called back, 'It's OK.'

The tractor driver reached down to his right and brought out a double-barrelled shotgun. He aimed it straight at us.

Dylan reflexively raised his hands.

I jammed the van in reverse and checked my mirrors for the moving van behind. I hoped the sight of my reversing lights would inspire the van to do likewise, but they'd already made their move. Both driver and passenger were out of the vehicle, shotguns in their grasp. I took my van out of gear and raised my hands.

'Pull into the field,' the tractor driver said, gesturing with his shotgun.

I heard my pounding heart in my ears. I exchanged a glance with Dylan. He'd turned pale. No doubt, I had too.

'Move,' the tractor driver said.

I drove the van into the wet field. Derek Deacon was standing there with rain running off his wax jacket. He held a shotgun, broken, between his big arms folded across his chest. He stared directly at me and grinned. His eyes disappeared as his thick face squeezed them shut.

If I had any thoughts about hitting the gas and mowing the murdering bastard down, they ended when Derek snapped the shotgun shut and aimed it at me. I stopped the van a respectful distance from the gun's twin barrels.

'Come on out, Aidy. We need to talk.'

Both Dylan and I opened our doors. Derek swung the shotgun around in Dylan's direction.

'This is just between you and me, Aidy. Your grease monkey stays put.'

Dylan didn't have to be told twice and closed his door.

I stepped down from the van with my hands up. The two guys from the moving van jogged across the churned field. Not surprisingly, it was Derek's boys, Morgan and Strickland. They looked like brothers, both heavyset with bulldog builds, but they weren't related. Morgan stood out on account of his tattoos – a swallow on each side of his throat. He came up alongside me and pressed his shotgun under my chin.

'How's it going, son?'

He grinned when I didn't answer him.

'Jeff, make friends with the grease monkey,' Derek said.

Morgan climbed into the cab with Dylan. The shotgun was awkward within the tight confines of the van, but he made it work for him by jamming it against the side of Dylan's head.

'Box 'em in, Tommy,' Derek said.

The tractor driver eased the tractor forward and stopped inches short of the van's bumper. Strickland ran back to the moving van and completed the box manoeuvre by pulling across the open gateway and providing a convenient shield from passers-by. I clung to Steve's belief that Derek wouldn't kill me if I had a witness like a drowning man to a life preserver.

'C'mon, Aidy,' Derek said. 'Come a little closer. I won't bite, but I can't guarantee I won't shoot.'

The joke won him a round of laughs from his gang.

'Walk with me. We have a little misunderstanding to take care of.'

Using the gun, Derek gestured for me to join him. I dropped my hands and fell in alongside him. We looked like friends, except he cradled the shotgun in his arms, casually pointing it at me, his finger on the trigger.

We headed deeper into the field through the steady rain and further away from the safety of the road. I glanced over my shoulder. The field sloped downward from the road and Dylan and the blockade diminished from view with every step.

'Dylan won't come to any harm,' Derek said, 'if you listen.'

If. Had that been the ultimatum he'd issued Alex?

'I have to hand it to you, Derek. That was all very slick with the staged detour, the tractor and everything.'

'You liked that?' Derek said with a grin. 'It's very simple when you know how. All it took was a few friends and a heads-up that you were going to the track today. I've had someone on your tail since you came off the motorway.'

Considering all the choreography needed to sideline me, Derek obviously wasn't a stranger to this kind of work, but none of it would have been possible without one vital component – a snitch. He needed to know where I would be and when. It wasn't hard to guess who was on Derek's side. Myles was the only person who knew I was going to be coming to Stowe Park today. He could have told someone else, but his disappearing act put him at the top of the list.

'We have a problem, Aidy.'

'Do we?'

'Yes. You. You're our problem.'

Derek stopped. I took the opportunity to face him while staying out of direct line of the shotgun barrels. We were a long way from the edges of the field without anything for me to hide behind if I ran.

'You going around saying I killed Alex is upsetting me.'

'You did threaten to kill him and you were the closest person to him when it happened.'

Derek fixed me with a piercing stare. 'I didn't kill Alex.'

I nodded at his shotgun. 'And you're doing a bang-up job of demonstrating your innocence.'

I was being surprisingly ballsy considering how shit scared I was, but my remark worked, forcing Derek into a begrudging smile.

'Whether you like it or not, the police investigated Alex's death. They found no foul play. I was never a suspect.'

'Thanks to some influential friends.'

'It pays to have friends in high places.' Derek smirked. 'And in low places. It still doesn't change anything. I didn't kill Alex, despite what you may think.'

'OK, tell me this. Why is there this veil of secrecy surrounding Alex's death? Why is it no one wants to talk about it? And why is it, should anyone question your involvement, they get guns pointed at them in an open field?'

Derek shook his head. 'I don't know why. All I can tell you is that I'm well liked in these parts. People are willing to go out of their way to protect me. Nothing more. Nothing less. As to why Alex's death is being brushed aside, you're asking the wrong person.'

Something spooked a flock of birds from their roosts. They sawed into the air, squawking and crowing. Instinctively, Derek spun around with his gun. He followed their skyward progress, anticipated their move and fired both barrels. Two birds fell from the sky, dead.

'Vermin with wings,' he said. 'The only reason they exist is to be a nuisance and, left unchecked, they ruin people's lives. The problem is that they poke their beaks where they don't belong and destroy everything they touch. They have to be eliminated before they do too much damage. It's all for the greater good. You understand that, don't you, Aidy?'

It wasn't that hard to read between Derek's widely spaced lines and see his less than subtle point. 'Yes, I do.'

'Good. I'm glad we understand each other.'

A panicked voice squawked over the walkie-talkie in Derek's pocket. He ignored it, choosing to break the gun and eject the spent cartridges. He left the shotgun broken and unloaded. Seeing that, I knew Derek didn't plan to kill me. Not today, anyway.

'Is everything OK?' the voice yelled into the radio.

Derek removed the radio from his pocket. 'Everything's fine. I had to teach a couple of crows a lesson.'

The response quieted everyone. If discharging a shotgun panicked Derek's guys, I imagined the overdose of fear it must have sent through Dylan. I doubted he'd be so eager to help me after today. Derek switched the radio off and pocketed it.

'I have one piece of advice for you, Aidy. If you're going to mouth off, make sure you have some proof to back it up. Otherwise, I can't say how people will react.'

There was nothing to say. Derek had made his point very clear.

'Let's get you back to your van. Then you can go back where you belong.'

We headed back. The rise back to the road proved difficult to climb on account of the rain turning the earth into sludge.

'By the way, what are you doing here today?' Derek asked.

I wondered if this was a trick question. He knew why I was here. If he could play coy, so could I.

'I had some business at the track,' I said.

'Did you come for Alex's car? I heard you were going to have it crushed.'

Derek had robbed me of a piece of crucial evidence and now he wanted to gloat.

'I was, but it seems to have disappeared.'

'Is that right?'

We crested the rise. There was a look of relief on the faces of all the men waiting by the vehicles, those holding guns and those not.

I noticed the moving van. It had been a useful tool for boxing Dylan and me in, but it wasn't necessary. They could have easily pulled the same manoeuvre with any vehicle. So why the van? A vehicle of that size could easily carry a single-seater racecar without the need of a trailer.

'I've got a question for you, Derek.'

'Ask away.'

'Was this chat the only reason you pulled me off the road or did you have a secondary purpose in mind?'

'I don't know what you mean.'

I nodded at the moving van. 'Did you plan on hijacking Alex's car from me?'

Derek grinned. 'Maybe.'

Suddenly, nothing made sense. If Derek had grabbed Alex's car from the scruntineering bay, then he didn't need to snatch it from me.

Derek nodded to his boys and they scurried back to their vehicles and got ready to leave. Dylan shifted into the van's driver's seat.

Derek opened the van's passenger door for me and closed it when I got in. He peered over my shoulder into the back of the empty van. 'If you think I took Alex's car, you're wrong. We were both too late for it. You should look outside of the racing community.'

He signalled to his guy to make room for us. Dylan didn't wait to be told. As soon as there was a gap, he was back on the road and moving.

'What did that mean?' I asked.

'I don't care,' Dylan said. 'I'll think about it when I'm a long way from here.'

Lap Eleven

'We are so out of this,' Dylan said. 'We are so fucking out of this. Shotguns, Steve. They had shotguns. They weren't for show. One word from Derek and we would have been dead. No ifs, ands or buts. Dead.'

Being held at gunpoint had been a sobering event for me, but not for Dylan. In the hours since the hijacking, he'd been storming up and down the workshop, bouncing off the walls and work-benches like a pinball reliving Derek's roadside detour. I made no attempt to calm him. This was his way of dealing with the situation.

Steve had ignited Dylan the moment we got back to Archway when he asked, 'How'd it go?' Any chances of a calm and collected explanation went out the window.

Like me, Steve let Dylan rant. He wasn't interested in an account from Dylan. He was waiting to hear it from me.

When Dylan finally ran out of steam, Steve asked, 'You done?'

'No, I'm not done.'

'Well, I say you are. Take your foot off the throttle and get over here. I want to know what happened.'

Steve and I were standing around Graham Hill's 1967 F1 Lotus. Steve was restoring it for ridiculous money for a collector in

America. Dylan muttered something under his breath and trudged over to us.

'Right, then,' Steve said. 'What happened?'

'Someone took Alex's car,' I said.

'Tell him what happened after that,' Dylan chimed in. 'That wasn't the bad part.'

'I get that,' Steve said.

'Will you let me finish?' I said to Dylan.

Dylan put his hands in the air in surrender.

I filled Steve in. Dylan chipped in whenever I attempted to play down any part of our roadside encounter.

When I finished, Steve blew out a breath and ran a hand through his hair. 'What do you want to do now?'

It was a damn good question. I'd attempted to come up with some information quietly in order to help kick start the police investigation, but somehow my actions had gotten loud and drawn too many people's attention. People were shutting me out and I didn't even have the luxury of the police to run to for help. I was pretty much buggered. Trying to do the right thing had thrust me into dangerous waters that were washing me down river, far from safety.

'I can't let this drop. Derek's stunt has given me even more reason to keep pushing. I'm getting close to an answer. I have to be, or Derek wouldn't be trying to shut me down.'

'You're crazy,' Dylan said. 'You're going to get yourself killed and us with you. I'd be safer working on a ten-storey building in a gale than playing detective with you.'

'Alex was murdered. Are you OK with that?'

'Aidy, he could have killed us in that field,' Dylan shouted.

'But he didn't.'

'And that was our lucky break. I think we should embrace it and forget all about this,' Dylan said.

Steve called our bickering to an end when he pushed himself off the workbench he'd been leaning against and stepped in between us. 'OK. That's enough. Cool it. The both of you.' He turned to Dylan. 'You're panicking. You've got every right.'

'Damn right, I'm panicking. Aidy, you weren't stuck in that van with that animal. He played with the trigger to experiment with how much pressure it would take to fire the gun. A squeeze too hard and I was dead, Aidy.'

'Enough,' Steve barked.

Dylan sucked in a deep breath and released it. It slid from him in an untidy exhale. He crossed his arms tight across his chest and jammed his hands under his armpits.

'The two of you had a frightening experience, but it's over,' Steve said. 'You're safe now. Nothing can erase what has happened, but we need to move on.' Steve aimed his gaze directly at me. 'Are you sure about this? You want to continue?'

'I'm sure. I'll be damned if Derek will scare me off.'

Neither Dylan nor Steve showed any enthusiasm for my stance.

'Look, I'm not asking for your help. I don't want you getting hurt. I can do this alone,' I said.

'But you'd prefer help,' Steve said.

'Yes, I would.'

'Then you have mine,' Steve said.

Dylan spun the Lotus's front wheel. 'You've got mine too. I'd be a crappy friend if I didn't stick by you.'

'From now on, we work under the radar,' Steve said. 'We don't give anyone a clue as to what we're doing.'

'It'll force them to come out of the shadows,' I said.

Steve smiled. 'Good. Then it'll force them into mistakes.'

I have to admit, Derek's shotgun party had put me in a bit of a daze, but having Steve and Dylan say they were still with me brought me into sharp focus. I had direction and meaning again. I couldn't help but smile. All that was happening to my little group should have been breaking us up, but it was bringing us closer together. The more Derek tried to hurt us, the tighter our bonds. I felt confident for once.

Finding out what happened to Alex's car was my starting point. Derek had said to look outside of the racing community. That didn't help. I couldn't imagine who outside of the racing community would want the car. The cops? I didn't think so. If Brennan had taken the car on Derek's behalf, Derek wouldn't have been trying to hijack it for himself. The best person to pry an answer from was Myles Beecham. All roads led back to him. I called him twice on Sunday and once on Monday morning, each time getting voicemail. Obviously, he wasn't getting back to me until he was good and ready.

Myles rediscovered how to use the phone on Monday afternoon. He gave me a song and dance about why he'd been incommunicado, but I didn't much care about his excuses. I just wanted to know where to find the car and who took it. Myles gave me an address where I could find it, but warned me I'd have some explaining to do.

'To whom?' I asked.

When he told me, the reason why the car had been taken made a whole lot more sense.

So that night, I drove out to Ashford on the edge of London. It's a nice drive from Windsor along the Thames, past Runnymede and the JFK memorial. The light traffic and cool, still night left me feeling good about life. I had no real reason to feel this way after the events of the weekend, but I had the backing of my friends and family and I was on my way to collect Alex's car.

I followed the A30, the main drag into London from the south-west. An airliner glided into Heathrow airport to my left as I reached the outskirts of Ashford. I turned off the A30 into a residential maze and followed the directions Myles had given me until I reached a quiet street of semi-detached houses. The sizeable houses were bunched together on either side of a narrow road filled with parked cars. The cramped conditions made everything look smaller than it really was. I parked on the street a few houses away from the address Myles had given to me.

I picked up my mobile and called Steve. I wasn't to go anywhere alone, but this was an exception considering who I was meeting.

'Everything OK?' Steve asked.

'Yeah. No problems. I've arrived and I'm just going in.'

'Call me as soon as you're finished.'

'Will do,' I said.

After hanging up, I went up to the door and rang the doorbell. Alison answered.

'Come in,' she said and led me along a long hallway into the kitchen. 'I was making coffee. Want some?'

I said yes instead of asking why she'd taken Alex's car.

The kitchen was filled with the scent of a warm dinner being eaten. I liked the way the heat and smell wrapped itself around me. I sat at the dining table and watched Alison make the coffee. She wore jeans and a tee shirt, but they looked like so much more on her. She sat opposite me and slid a coffee mug over to me.

'I thought you lived in London,' I said.

'I do, but I don't have a garage at my flat. This is my parents' place.'

We were alone in the house. 'Where are your parents?'

'Out. Giving us space to talk.'

'About what?'

'About what you're doing.'

Myles had said I'd have some explaining to do, but I wasn't the only one. 'Why'd you take Alex's car?' I asked.

'For protection.'

'Whose?'

'Alex's.'

Her gaze was unflinching. Her eyes were the colour of storm clouds and shone bright under the kitchen lights.

'I'm not trying to hurt Alex or disgrace his memory.'

'How do I know that? I don't know you at all. And as far as I can tell, neither did Alex. So, I'm confused. You're taking a lot of interest in Alex's death and I don't understand why.'

'I told you at the railway station.'

'Yes, you did. You think Derek killed Alex.'

'Don't you?'

She was silent for a moment. The tough façade she was putting on cracked under the pressure of the belief we both shared.

'What are you hoping to get out of all this, Aidy? Your fifteen minutes? Your name in lights? A leg up in your racing career? Or are you trying to settle a score with Derek? Tell me.'

The remarks hurt, but she was hurting. She was striking out at the world for an injustice and I made a convenient target. I was going to have to take some body blows if I wanted Alex's car. I thought I'd made an ally in the railway car park, not an enemy. I felt my grip on Alex's car slip. 'I think you're being unfair.'

'Am I? I don't know, but I'm willing to listen. Explain to me why you're sticking your neck out for a person you hardly knew.'

'I just want to prove Alex was killed. That's all.'

'So you're on this crusade for justice?'

'I wouldn't call it a crusade.'

'Have you considered the damage your actions will have on the people who really knew Alex? Eric and Laura want to move on. You're not helping.'

'They only want to move on because they believe his death was accidental. Don't you think their attitude would change if they believed otherwise? You think Derek killed Alex. Do you just want to move on? Are you willing to let Derek go unpunished?'

She was silent for several moments. I'd gone too far and I regretted the remark.

'Alex meant the world to me. I want to remember him for who he was and not for the bad aftertaste left by others. If I asked you to drop it, would you?'

The incident with Derek in the field filled my head. 'No, I don't think I can. It's gone too far for that.'

'What does that mean?'

'The investigating officer in Alex's death is friends with Derek.'

Her eyes went wide and the hard as nails act collapsed. 'What?'

'When I tried to talk to him, I found him drinking with Derek. Then, on Saturday, when I went to Stowe Park to collect Alex's car, Derek forced me into a field at gunpoint and told me to stay out of his business, or else.'

'My God,' she said.

'People are doing their damnedest to prevent Alex's murder from coming to light. I can't let that happen.'

'And where does Alex's car fit into all this? Please don't tell me you just want it so that it can't be raced again, because I don't believe you. You don't get the car until I get a truthful answer.'

'It's evidence. I think the car could prove how Derek killed Alex. I've taken photographs of the crash site and, in combination with Alex's car, they'll paint a picture. It'll reopen the investigation.'

She stared at me. I didn't flinch from her gaze. I wanted her to see I was speaking the truth.

'No one asked you to get involved.' There was no malice or accusation in her remark.

'No, they didn't.'

'Then why do it?'

'It was the right thing to do. If any of us at The Chequered Flag that night had stepped in, Alex would be alive.'

'You honestly believe that?'

'I do.'

'OK, then I want to show you something. Hold on a second.' She left the table and returned a few moments later with a framed photo. She placed it before me. I expected it to be of Alex. It wasn't. It was of a girl in her early twenties. She looked like Alison, but it wasn't her. The hairstyle dated the picture back to the nineties.

'That's my sister, Jennifer. She died four years ago. I wish I could say she looked that happy when she died.'

'How'd she die?'

'Drug overdose.' She picked up the frame to stare at the picture more closely. 'Jen was Nick Jensen's girlfriend. Do you know who he is?'

I did. Nick Jensen was a Brit Pop superstar for all of two albums in the late nineties. I had both in my CD collection. He would have gone on to bigger and greater things if he'd stayed off heroin. When the drugs sang louder than his lyrics, a string of arrests and trips to rehab followed. Incoherent live performances and well-publicized fights at sell-out gigs killed his career. He tried a comeback a few years back, but the fan base wasn't there anymore.

'Nick and Jen went to school with each other. If I'm being kind, she got hooked on drugs when he did. If I'm being honest, Nick got Jen hooked on drugs and got her killed because of it. Our family tried to help her, but she wasn't interested. When Nick's fame deserted him, Jen didn't, but we deserted her. I understand loss and I understand guilt, just like you do. We could have done more. We should have done more. Sometimes, you have to accept you're not God. You can't save everyone.'

'Do you want me to stop?' I asked, still not sure that I could.

She shook her head. 'No. If you can prove Derek killed Alex, do it. I just can't help you. It's too much for me.'

I nodded. 'That's OK.'

'I want to stay informed, though.'

'Sure.'

She smiled and raised her coffee mug. She was close to tears, but her determination kept them from spilling. I guessed she'd free them after I left. Her strength moved me. I smiled back and clinked coffee mugs with her.

'Are you OK with answering some questions for me?' I asked.

She sipped from her mug. 'Ask away.'

'Tough one first, I'm afraid.'

'That's OK.'

'Did you see the satellite TV footage of the crash?'

Her hands tensed around her coffee mug.

'I hate to ask, but it was cut from the broadcast.'

'No, I didn't. Couldn't. The TV people assured me there was

nothing traumatic in their footage, but I couldn't watch it knowing I was watching Alex's last moments.'

'Did anyone see the film? Your parents?'

'Alex's dad.'

'Does he have a copy? I'm hoping the cameras caught the crash. That'll prove whether Derek intentionally forced Alex off the track.'

Alison shook her head. 'I don't know. I just want this to be over.'

'I do too and it will be soon. I'm sorry about this. I just have a few more questions. Is that OK?'

She nodded.

'I was told the satellite people destroyed the master recording by request. Any idea who asked for that?'

'Why would the recording be destroyed?'

'I'm guessing you didn't request it, then.'

'No, I didn't.'

'Could Mr Fanning have requested it?'

'I suppose, but I don't know. I'll ask him. But if the recording has been destroyed, there's no way anyone can prove Derek killed Alex.'

'Not quite. Redline wasn't the only one to record the crash. Do you know Paul at Chicane Motorsport?'

Alison shook her head.

'He records all the races and he captured the crash. He's going to let me see his tape. The quality won't be as good as the TV coverage, but I'm hoping it will be good enough for what I need.'

'I hope you're right.'

I'd pushed her to her limit for one night and I quickly finished up my coffee. 'Can I see the car?'

Alison pulled out a set of keys from her pocket and put them on the table. 'It's in the garage. I can't look at it.'

I nodded.

Alison picked up our mugs and took them to the sink. I took that as my signal. I walked out the back door and over to the detached garage towards the rear of the garden. I unlocked the doors and swung them open, then I flicked on the light. Alex's crumpled car sat on a pair of sawhorses.

A set of headlights lit up the garage and me. I put a hand up to shield my eyes from the light. A car rolled down the long driveway next to the house and stopped a car length from me. Alison's parents stepped into the light.

'You've come to take the car?' Mr Baker asked.

'Yes,' I said.

'I'll help you.'

'I'll check on Alison,' Mrs Baker said.

Alison's dad pulled his car back onto the street while I brought the van over. He guided me down the narrow driveway while I reversed the van up to the garage. A racecar isn't that heavy in the scheme of things, but shifting the wreck was tough with just the two of us lifting. Having the car on sawhorses helped. It was at the perfect height for the van's cargo bed. We slid the car off the sawhorses and manhandled it inside. We loaded the boxes of broken components and bodywork next. I wanted every scrap of the car so I could reconstruct it to prove what happened to it. Call it a crash post-mortem.

I closed up the van while Alison's dad locked the garage. We stood in the red glow of the van's taillights. I put out my hand to him.

'Thanks for your help, Mr Baker.'

He glowered at me instead of taking my hand.

'Now that you've got what you wanted, I'd appreciate it if you left my daughter alone. Is that clear?'

It was more than clear.

Lap Twelve

The following night was a big night for me. I was meeting Hancock to discuss and hopefully secure sponsorship for next season. I liked the proposal package I'd put together. It looked professional in spite of my limited resources.

Hancock understood I had a day job so he scheduled our meeting for seven p.m. in the lobby of the Brands Hatch Double Oak hotel. For him, the Double Oak was a twenty minute drive from the Hancock Salvage headquarters. I had to slog my way around the southern half of the M25 motorway during rush hour. Not a fun prospect.

Steve picked me up from work in the Capri and we swapped driving duties because I wanted something to do other than obsess about my meeting with Hancock. As we trickled along with our fellow commuters on the overpopulated M25, my mind played over the previous night's events. Mr Baker's angry face filled my mind. He wasn't the first hostile dad I'd encountered. I put his hostility down to a protective father looking out for his daughter. He had nothing to fear from me. I wouldn't be bothering Alison again.

A driver leaned on his horn when I let the Capri drift into his lane.

'Focus, son,' Steve said.

Steve was right. My train of thought needed to be on convincing Hancock to give me a budget for next season. The break from thoughts of murder would do me good. Alex's death was fast approaching an obsession.

'You want to go over what you're going to say?' Steve asked.

'Not really.'

'But you're going to anyway.'

I flashed Steve a begrudging smile. I went over my talking points and Steve reminded me of any I'd forgotten. We role-played, with Steve playing the part of Hancock. It helped kill the monotonous drive.

I arrived at the hotel with a few minutes to spare. The Double Oak is located outside of the Brands Hatch circuit's main entrance. I turned into the hotel's car park and parked. I reached for my document case and went through it to make sure I had everything.

'I remember going to meetings like this with your dad. Seems like yesterday.'

'Did he enjoy them?'

'Tell me what driver does.'

'None. Seeking sponsorship is glorified begging. It's never fun, unless you're already at the top. Then you have to beat their advances off with stick.'

'You want me to come in with you?'

'No, I'll be fine. You're only here as muscle to make sure no one takes me for a ride.'

He sighed theatrically. 'How tragic it is to be wanted for my body and not my mind.'

I laughed and double-checked I had everything before swinging the door open. 'I've got everything, so wish me luck.'

'No luck needed. What's your opening line to Hancock?'

I thought for a second. 'I am an asset to your marketing campaign. Now give me your damn money, Hancock.'

'Smart arse.' He jabbed a finger in my side. 'You're more than ready for this. Now get in there. You'll do fine.'

Heading into the hotel, I put on my game face. I was here to sell the benefits of motorsport sponsorship to Hancock. He might be a race fan, but at the same time, he was a businessman and I had to appeal to that side of him.

I looked around the hotel lobby and spotted Hancock amongst the sea of businessmen milling around. He waved and cut his way through the crowd.

'Have you eaten, Aidy? I've gotten us a table. Tonight's on me.'

He ushered me into the hotel's restaurant and we sat at a window table with a partial view of Brands Hatch. A waitress presented us with menus and asked us what we wanted to drink.

'Whisky,' Hancock said. 'Anything from your single malt range will do.'

'Diet Coke.'

'You can have a drop of the hard stuff,' Hancock said.

Booze sounded good. It would take the edge off, but tonight was too important to hand the reins over to alcohol. I wanted Hancock's sponsorship pounds and I didn't want to say the wrong thing because drink had gotten the better of me.

'No, Diet Coke is fine.'

After the waitress left, we got down to business. I'd brought copies of my proposal, but Hancock had the one I'd already sent to him. He flicked through its contents.

'This is very impressive.'

I'd gone to town on the proposal. I outlined the benefits of motorsport sponsorship, essentially cribbing from an article I'd found on the Internet. I included a profile of myself and my short racing career as well as one for Steve. His achievements added some legitimacy to my claims. I listed the activities I would assist Hancock's company with, things like corporate events, media appearances – all the usual guff. I added a nice little touch of a mock-up shot of the car in the company colours with the Hancock Salvage logo down the side. I'd Photoshopped the thing together in my lunch hour at work. Of course,

I ended with the ugly stuff: my budget needs. In the scheme of things, it was pretty good value for money. Steve would act as mechanic and engine builder for a full assault on the Formula Ford national title. My budget was a third of what it would cost to run with a top professional team, but, with Steve's expertise, we were just as good.

Hancock was smiling. I liked that. Smiling was good. Then he had to ruin it by speaking.

'From this, you're planning to take a shot at the national series.'

'Yes, I think it's time for me to stretch my wings.'

'Looking to follow in your dad's tyre tracks?'

'Yes,' I said with a nervous smile. I felt I was losing this guy.

'That's great. The thing is, I was looking to sponsor you as a replacement for Alex in the south-west.'

'Oh.' Crap.

'Considering all the great work you've done to honour Alex, I thought it would be good if we banded together in his memory and tried to win next year's championship for him.'

I didn't want another season in the Clark Paints series for two reasons. First, a race driver's career is short. Dad was twenty-nine when he made it to Formula One and that was old. Most F1 drivers enter Grand Prix racing in their mid-twenties. At twenty-one, I was a long way from having the skills and experience to race Formula One. Staying in a regional championship for another year wasn't going to enhance my career path. Second, I'd ruffled way too many feathers at Stowe Park. I'd lost a lot of friends over recent days and who knew how many I'd lose by the beginning of next season. By then, Derek might not be the only one willing to push me into a wall.

'I see,' I said.

'Would you be willing to stick around in the Clark Paints Championship for another season, for Alex's sake?'

He was trying to guilt me into this. Oh, that was a low blow. Especially when he was dangling money in front of me. I didn't like how Hancock was boxing me in, but it was business.

'I'll think about it.'

'Please give it serious thought. I was hoping to put out a two-car team next year.'

'Really?'

'Yes, you and Derek Deacon. Together, you'd make the perfect tribute to Alex's memory.'

Was he serious? Not only had Derek won the championship at Alex's expense, but he was also going to get Alex's sponsorship money. Where was the justice? I did well not to show my shock.

Hancock jerked a thumb over at the track. 'Are you racing in the Festival?'

Held every year at Brands Hatch, the Formula Ford Festival and World Cup is Formula Ford's only international event. Two hundred drivers from around the world take part in a knockout event held over three days. Dad won it in '93.

'No, I wasn't planning on it.'

'I want to reward your act of kindness towards Alex. He was slated to race, so I have a car leased for the Festival. I'd like you to take his place. Will you do it?'

I didn't have to be asked twice. 'Of course.'

'I know you want to race in nationals next year, but if you're willing to keep my offer open, then I'm willing to keep yours in mind. I'll make a wager with you. If you make the top ten in the final, I'll finance your national campaign. Don't, and you race in the Clark Paints series.'

It was a bet heavily weighted in Hancock's favour. The Festival is highly unpredictable. Usually the best driver wins, but there's no accounting for mechanical failure or just plain bad luck. Either way, just making it to the final grid of twenty six cars was going to be a hard enough prospect.

'Sure,' I said.

We shook on it.

Hancock insisted we celebrate after that. We ordered dinner and he went for a steak half the size of a cow, while I ordered the chicken, the cheapest thing on the menu. I didn't want to take advantage of the guy's hospitality, even if he was trying to manipulate me into staying in the Clark Paints series.

With our business seemingly out of the way, our conversation turned to motor racing. Hancock told me he'd been a spectator since he was a kid. As a Kent boy, born and bred, Brands was his local hang-out. He remembered seeing my dad clinch the Formula Three crown here by claiming second in the race. I remembered it too. I watched the race with my mum from a hospitality box. I'd thought days like that would never end. I was wrong.

As we finished our dinners, he insisted on after dinner drinks.

I never drank and drove, so accepting a drink meant I'd be stuck with Hancock for at least an hour.

When a pair of whiskies arrived, Hancock raised his glass. 'Here's to people always needing parts for their cars and making me richer.'

'Amen,' I said and clinked glasses.

'How much do you know about me?'

I knew what I'd read off his website. 'You operate the biggest car salvage and auction firm in the country.'

'Yeah, yeah, that's the business side of me, but what do you know about me?'

I couldn't dodge the question, not that I saw the point of it. 'Not much other than you're a race fan and you've sponsored a few people over the years.'

'Is that all?'

'Pretty much.'

'Well, there's a lot more to me than that,' Hancock said. 'Anyway, let's have a toast. To great friendships – past, present and future.'

I clinked my glass against Hancock's. 'To great friendships.'

'Alex was a good friend. I got to know him well over the years. His parents are great people and that Alison is a wonderful girl,' Hancock said.

'I agree.'

'You knew Alex well then?'

'Not well, but I thought he was a really nice guy.'

'You pointed out his broken exhaust pipe mounting during qualifying, didn't you?'

'That was nothing,' I said. 'Drivers look out for each other.'

I felt a shift in Hancock's mood. I didn't know if it was the booze talking or not. My whisky represented my only drink, but Hancock had been hitting the wine over dinner pretty hard in addition to the whisky he'd ordered before dinner. There was a need in his eyes, like he wanted something from me, but instead of coming out and asking outright what he wanted to know, he jabbed at me with question after question in the hope I'd spill the answer he was looking for.

'I saw you and Alex chatting just before the race.'

I realized he must have meant when Alex and I were in the men's room. Hancock hadn't been in there while we were, so he could only have seen us come out together.

'What'd you talk about?'

I remembered how happy Alex had been to give racing up for Alison. The memory hurt. 'The future, as sad as that seems now.'

'So you didn't talk about me?'

The question caught me off guard. 'No, why would we?'

He tried to brush his weird question away. 'No reason. Pit lane talk. You know. Your grandfather has an account with us,' he said, throwing a new wrinkle into the conversation.

'He does?'

'Yeah. Goes back years. I wasn't sure if you were discussing that.'

Hancock had lost me. I couldn't see how that could be a topic of conversation. 'No, we didn't talk about anything like that. Sorry.'

'No reason to be sorry. I just noticed that when you went your separate ways, you looked disappointed.'

This conversation had taken a very weird detour. Why the hell was Hancock watching Alex so closely? It was strange that first Derek, and now Hancock, had commented on my contact with Alex. More interesting still, both of them had read more into the encounter than really existed. What did they think Alex and I had discussed?

'I had a lot on my mind and there was a lot of drama going on in the paddock that day.'

This was my test for Hancock. I wanted to see how he would react. He wanted to squeeze something out of me about that day and I wanted to know what it was. I hoped my reply would provoke an admission.

Hancock waved a dismissive hand. 'That thing with Derek, he wouldn't do anything like that.'

He spoke as if he knew for sure Derek hadn't had anything to do with Alex's death. I almost believed him.

'You have Alex's car now, right?'

'Yes, I've got it.'

'I know you're planning to have the car scrapped, so I'd like to compact it. No charge of course. It's something I'd like to do for Alex.'

'Thanks, I appreciate it.' My appreciation failed to sound sincere, but Hancock's alcoholic state left him too dulled to pick up on it.

'I can send someone over to pick up the car tomorrow.'

'No,' I said. I needed an excuse. I couldn't say I was keeping the car for evidence. 'It wouldn't be convenient. I'm working and Steve won't be at the workshop for the next few days. And I know a few of the drivers want to be there when it's destroyed.'

'Just give me the nod when it's a good time and I'll have someone there.'

'Sure.'

With Hancock's bizarre questioning, I wasn't sure I wanted him to have the car at all. Looking at everything that had been said, I questioned the validity of his sponsorship offer. Was he dangling this carrot so that he could pump me for information?

Hancock finished his drink. The waitress took that as her signal to deliver the bill. He paid and I was more than ready to go. We headed out to the lobby, but he stopped short of leaving.

'I'm getting a room here tonight.'

'Good move,' I said.

He didn't say anything for a moment, just stared at me, as if examining me for answers. 'So you don't know much about me.'

'No,' I said.

He smiled. 'We'll have to change that.'

Lap Thirteen

Wednesday evening gave me and Steve our first chance to examine Alex's car. We hadn't had time to do more than unload the wreck from the van, get it on stands and cover it with a drop cloth since picking it up from Alison's on Monday night.

We stood looking at the remains of the car. The damage had robbed it of its elegance. It sagged under its own weight and its scars were ugly. In racing trim, it looked like a formidable piece of machinery. Now, it looked vulnerable, like an injured creature.

'What do you want to do?' Steve asked me.

'Reconstruct.'

We emptied out the boxes of buckled and broken parts which hadn't remained intact from the crash. I didn't want to reassemble the car. Couldn't. Many of the parts were too damaged to simply reattach them. Instead, we laid the parts out like an aircraft crash investigator with aircraft parts or a palaeontologist with a dinosaur skeleton. I hoped to see how the car had picked up its wounds. It was hard to tell which ones were a direct result of hitting the wall and which ones had caused the wreck.

The biggest broken piece was the right front corner, consisting of the upper and lower suspension wishbones, the push rod to the shock absorber, the wheel and tyre still attached to the upright. The impact had tied it into a knot, but it was all in one piece. Steve and I put it on the floor where it should have been attached. We duct taped the fibreglass bodywork in place and spent the next hour placing all the pieces of this skewed automotive jigsaw in their rightful positions until we had an exploded view.

We didn't have all the parts. It wasn't surprising, really. The car had crashed at high velocity. The tinier pieces would have been flung far and wide. Even if they weren't, they could have been lost when the recovery vehicle lifted the car over to scrutineering or during the car's transportation from Stowe Park to Alison's parents' house. One of the missing pieces was a bolt that connects the tracking arm to the mounting on the gearbox. The tracking arm is a tie-rod that adjusts the 'toe-in', the angle at which the wheels need to point in order for the car to travel in a straight line. Generally, all four wheels on any car point slightly inwards to make this happen. Considering the massive impact, the bolt had probably been sheared off.

I snapped photos of the car for later reference. I planned on keeping the car to use it as evidence, but I knew people expected it to be crushed, and soon. In case I lost the car before I was done, I needed a photographic record.

I made sure I had plenty of shots of the tyre burns on the right side of the car. The telltale black, circular scuffs strafed the bodywork behind the radiator pod. This proved Derek had manoeuvred his wheels inside Alex's. If I was right, there'd be corresponding tyre burns on the side of Derek's car. No wonder Derek hadn't wanted me getting my hands on Alex's car.

I picked up the envelope containing the pictures I'd taken of the crash site. I slipped them out and compared the skid marks on the track to the wrecked car in front of me.

Steve moved in behind me to peer over my shoulder. 'You know this doesn't prove anything.'

I'd come to the same conclusion, but I hadn't wanted to admit it.

'We can prove that Alex crashed into that wall,' Steve said, tapping the photo in my hands. 'We can prove that Alex and Derek locked wheels. What we can't prove is intent. All that we can prove is what everyone says; this was an accident. Nothing here says malice was involved.'

Every one of Steve's words was a kick in the teeth. I'd been threatened with a shotgun, warned off by the cops, burned bridges with people in the community and pissed off the grieving families. Now I was in serious danger of picking up a defamation charge if I said too much. And all for what? I couldn't prove a damn thing beyond the official story. I shoved the photos back in the envelope and tossed them on the work bench.

'I need the videotape,' I said.

'No, *we* need the videotape,' Steve said and patted me on the back. 'You're not alone in this. Has Paul gotten back to you?'

I shook my head. 'I'll call him.'

'Get that tape and you've got Derek over the barrel. Prove intent and the wreckage, skid marks, and photographs will mean something.'

The workshop doors rattled and then someone knocked. Steve looked at me for answers and I shook my head.

'Hello?' a familiar voice called out.

'It's Alison,' I said.

Steve crossed the workshop and swung open one of the large double doors. He smiled at her.

'Is Aidy here?'

'Come in, Alison,' I called out.

She smiled when she spotted me in the depths of the workshop, but her smile dropped when she saw me standing next to Alex's car. I reached for a drop cloth to toss over it.

'No, it's OK,' she said. 'I came to see what you're doing.'

'OK,' I said and put the cloth down.

'Aidy, I need to go out for a while,' Steve said.

This was his code for giving us some privacy. I almost frowned. What happened to I wasn't alone in all this? Actually, it was probably better that I talked to her alone. I got the feeling she wanted to talk and she might feel uncomfortable with Steve in the room.

Passing Alison in the doorway, Steve said, 'That boy is going all out for you and Alex. Let him know how much it means to you. He's got a good heart and he deserves thanks for it.'

She smiled at Steve's fatherly tone. 'I will.'

I blushed.

'Back in an hour, Aidy,' Steve said.

'That was embarrassing,' I said.

'But he's right.'

Alison hesitated in the doorway a fraction too long.

'We don't have to do this now if you don't want to,' I said.

'No, I want to,' she said.

She came over to the car and ran a hand over the shiny fibre-glass. It was a loving touch, as if she were stroking Alex's cheek. I looked away to give her this moment and picked up the envelope of photos.

'What have you found?'

I showed her the tyre burns down the side of the car. I slid the photos from the envelope, careful to hide the images from her. 'Now you might find these disturbing, but we can—'

'Stop trying to protect me,' she interrupted, frustration edging her words. 'Everyone is trying to wrap me in cotton wool and I want it to stop. I'm not that fragile.'

'I'm sorry. I'm not trying to.'

'Yes you are. You're just trying to be kind. And while that's nice, it doesn't help me. I'm going to get upset. I'm going to cry. But that's OK. I lost someone very close to me. It's only natural.'

Alison impressed me. She was a fighter. No wonder Alex was willing to give up racing for her.

'OK,' I said. 'I'll treat you like anyone else and I won't worry if you cry from time to time.'

She smiled. 'Thank you. You'd be the first.'

I smiled and showed her the photos. I explained their relevance, but also pointed out their lack of meaning without more proof.

'So you don't have anything.'

'I have pieces. I can show that Alex and Derek interlocked wheels. I have a room full of people who heard Derek say he was going to kill Alex. What I don't have is proof that he made the manoeuvre on purpose.'

'You need the footage of the race?'

I nodded. It was such a big part of the puzzle. 'Did you speak to Alex's dad about the film?'

Alison turned her back and nodded at the car. 'He told them to destroy the tape.'

'Did he say why?'

'Does he have to?'

He didn't. Who wanted their son's final, tragic moments immortalized for all time? But destroying the tape was such an unfortunate move. Those moments of tape, adding up to only seconds of time, would have answered so much. It would have been enough to nail Derek, but now it was all ashes. I just hoped Paul had captured the moment. All my faith was in him now.

'It's not too much of a setback. I'm still hoping to get Paul's camcorder tape.'

'Let's hope he's a good cameraman.'

We stood in silence staring at the wrecked car. Then I noticed something I hadn't seen before. I'd been too wrapped in looking for the big piece of evidence and I'd missed the significance of the little things.

Alison noticed me looking. 'What is it?'

'Nothing really. Just bad workmanship.' I pointed to the Allen head bolts holding the lower suspension wishbone on the right rear corner of the car. The two bolts connecting the wishbone to the brackets on the gearbox assembly were installed bolt head down.

'What's wrong with the bolts – wrong type or something?'

'No. The bolts were put in upside-down. You want the bolt head on the top so if the nut shakes loose the bolt remains in place. With the bolt head down, gravity takes over, the bolt falls out and the suspension falls off.'

'Won't the bolt come out anyway because of the bumping and bouncing?'

'Probably, but it's a lot harder and it will buy you a few laps before that all happens.'

I checked the other corners of the car. The bolts had been put in correctly. I supposed Alex and his mechanic had rushed at some point and made the mistake. It's somewhat academic these days which way the bolt goes. With Nyloc nuts, it's really hard for a nut to shake loose.

'It's an amateur's mistake,' I said. 'That's all.'

'Alex wasn't an amateur,' Alison said with a hint of irritation.

'No, but we all make mistakes,' I said with a smile. 'Can I get you something to drink? We've got some things in the fridge upstairs and I can make coffee.'

'Coffee would be nice.'

I put my private investigation on hold, tossed the photos back on the workbench and covered the car with the drop cloth again.

I led Alison up to the office. While I got the coffee going, she checked out all the pictures and posters hanging from the curved walls.

'Racing is really in your blood.'

I moved next to Alison. 'It's hard for it not to be. Steve, my grandad, worked the pits for Lotus during the golden age of racing and my dad raced. Whereas most kids grew up on fairy-tales about princes slaying dragons, I grew up on tales of great drivers like Stirling Moss, Mike Hawthorne, Jim Clark, Graham Hill and Nigel Mansell, all doing battle with Juan Fangio, Alain Prost and Ayrton Senna.'

'Do you have a favourite driver?'

'Jim Clark.' I pointed to a photo of Steve working on Jimmy's Lotus as he climbed into the cockpit. 'He won the Formula One world title twice, and the Indy 500. He started on pole five out of six races and won a third of his F1 races. But he raced in about everything from NASCAR to rallying. He just liked to race. It's hard to find anyone who'll say a bad word about him and Steve says he was the nicest guy in the pit lane. For me, he's the greatest driver who ever lived.'

I felt the heat of Alison's gaze on me. I turned to her. She was grinning at me. I blushed. 'I'm sorry. I didn't mean to go on.'

'It's OK. I know Alex talked about him. He died, didn't he?'

'Yes. April 7th, 1968 at Hockenheim in Germany. It was in a Formula Two race. There's a stone marker where he crashed.' I stopped myself then. I was crossing the bounds of sensitivity. 'Sorry.'

'It's OK.' She smiled. 'No cotton wool, remember?'

The coffee maker beeped and I filled two mugs.

Alison took her coffee and sat in Steve's chair. 'Why do you race?'

'I never planned on it. Considering all the sacrifices my parents made, my grandparents weren't keen that I follow on in the family tradition.'

'But you did.'

'I was in karts for a couple of years when I was a lot younger, but I grew out of it. I was happy to do something else with my life. Then, last year, something clicked. A Westlake gene fired or something and I wanted to race. I told Steve and he said he'd help me. Now, I can't see myself doing anything else with my life.'

Alison shook her head. 'I don't get you or Alex. I never saw the point of it, just going around in circles. I asked Alex and never really got a straight answer.'

The question stumped me for a second. I could describe the sensations – the thrills, the speed, the competition and the danger that came with it. But none of these justifications would have been worthy answers. Then, I had my answer for her.

I picked up a blank sheet of paper and a pen and placed it on the table before her. I handed her the pen. 'Draw me the most perfect circle you can draw.'

'What has this got to do with motorsport?'

'Indulge me. This will explain all. Trust me,' I said and tapped the paper.

She looked at me quizzically then drew a circle. It was pretty good. It wasn't perfect. It was more tomato-shaped than a true circle.

'What do you think?' I asked and nodded at her attempt.

'I can do better, but what's this—'

'Go on. Try again.'

She sighed and gave it another go. This time her circle was rounder, but it was still a long way from perfect.

Without asking me she drew a third and fourth circle. These were improvements on her previous attempts, but still none were perfect. She went to do a fifth and I grabbed the pen from her.

I tapped the paper with her attempts on it. 'That's motor racing. It's about the pursuit of perfection. For me to win the race, I have to go around the track the fastest. For me to go around the track the fastest, I have to put in the fastest laps until hopefully I set the lap record, but even if I do that, it's not good enough. I've set the lap record and now I have to break it again because for every tenth of a second faster I go, the better I am. But the kicker is, I can always go faster if I do better. So for all my attempts for perfection, I'll never attain it because I can always do better.'

Alison shook her head. 'You've described a fool's errand. If that's true, then racing is a futile pursuit.'

I grinned. 'But what exercise in futility has ever been so much fun?'

She laughed. It was nice to see. I couldn't imagine she'd laughed much over the last couple of weeks.

'Aidy, that's the closest I've gotten to a sensible answer, but it's still a bad one.'

I balled up the sheet of paper she'd been drawing on and tossed it in the waste-paper bin. 'Really? I thought it was pretty good.'

It was quiet in the workshop and there was no thumping baseline from the Jumping Bean. I was enjoying this intimate moment. It had been a long time since there'd been a lady in my life. Veronica was my last girlfriend and she'd dumped me when racing took over my life. I didn't blame her. Motorsport demanded everything from you and only the right kind of person would stick by you.

Alison stood up and hugged me. The move took me by surprise, but I hugged her back. Suddenly, she stiffened in my arms and pushed me away.

The about-face didn't shock me. I knew what had just happened. For a moment, she'd forgotten about Alex's death and indulged in a normal life. Guilt had crept up on her and held up a funhouse mirror to her. Here she was hugging me when her fiancé had only been dead for two weeks. There shouldn't have been any guilt involved. She hadn't done anything wrong, but it gets all distorted when you're grieving. I knew that from bitter experience.

'I should be going,' she said. 'It's getting late.'

Or way too early for something else, I thought, and watched her go.

Lap Fourteen

With Alex's car now in my possession, I needed an excuse to go back down to Stowe Park to see Paul about his recording. I could make another parts run, but I was pushing the limits of believability. Having the parts mailed to me was far cheaper than a two hundred mile round trip. But a reason presented itself in the form of Tony and Pete Hansen. They needed me to fill in as an instructor at the racing school.

Pretty much every circuit in the UK operated a school. The schools operated by the high profile circuits like Silverstone, Donington and Brands Hatch were well respected. Stowe Park's school wasn't in the top echelons, but that didn't matter. The majority of the people attending the classes were only doing it for one of those adrenalin-filled days they'd always remember.

On Friday, I drove down to Stowe Park. I liked being an instructor. It was a chance to play on the track and meet some new people while I got paid for my time. If I'm being honest, it was also good for the ego. I got to play racecar driver to people who didn't know any better and they revered me for it. Call me shallow, but it's nice to be adored once in a while.

Tony had called Graham Linden in to help out too. Tony had a sizeable class of twenty-five or so punters for the morning session and the same again in the afternoon. These were pretty good numbers for the Stowe Park school. I wondered if the bump in numbers had anything to do with Alex's death. It had brought the circuit increased notoriety because of the press coverage associated with the fund-raising, which probably explained my call up today. My presence raised the school's profile.

Tony gave the in-class instruction, but the on the track duties would be split between Tony, Pete, Graham and me.

While Tony went through braking, clipping points, and accelerating through bends, Graham and I helped Pete prepare the cars. The half day session broke down like this. They got thirty minutes of in-class instruction, then went out for a fifteen minute session on the track in a modified Ford Focus before getting ten laps in a Formula Ford. The three of us picked a Focus, made sure it had fuel and the tires were pumped up to the right pressure. The road cars are pretty self-sufficient and don't need much preparation. The Formula Fords are far more sensitive and need checking out fully before a novice driver gets behind the wheel.

I needed more people like Paul on my side to force the police into reopening the investigation. Graham's involvement made for an unexpected windfall. He'd had the closest view of the crash. He had to have seen something, despite what he'd said at Alex's funeral. He'd make for a powerful witness when combined with Paul's recording. I took a clipboard with the student scorecard attached to it and tossed it on the passenger seat. I grabbed my helmet and followed Graham over to the Formula Fords.

'How's it going, Graham?'

'Pretty good.'

'It's going to be weird getting back on the track after Alex's crash.'

Graham looked out across the track in the direction of the Barrack Hill bend and nodded. He went to climb into one of the Formula Fords when I stopped him.

'You know you told me about Derek's threat the night before Alex's shunt?'

I felt Graham retreat from me without moving. 'Yeah.'

'I know we've talked about this before, but you were behind Derek and Alex before the crash, right?'

'Yeah, I told you, I didn't see anything.'

'You were right behind them. Are you sure?'

'Of course, I'm sure.'

'Is it possible that Derek moved into Alex to put him out of the race?'

'They collided. That's all.' Graham's hands were balled into tight fists. 'Don't go trying to make more of it.'

'Everything OK there?' Pete asked from behind one of the Focuses.

Graham got an answer in before I did. 'Yeah. Just talking.'

'Well, get those cars on the track. Our clients will be out soon.'

Graham shot me a withering look and pulled on his helmet.

I guessed that was the end of that. This was a different Graham than the one who'd gloated to me in the clubhouse the night before the race. Despite his outburst, he was scared. He was a local, unlike me, and within Derek's reach. Derek had to know Graham was an eyewitness to what he'd done. He wouldn't have let that loose end go untied. Had Derek threatened him? Shoved a shotgun in his face? I could see it. Derek was bullying everyone into silence.

I torqued the wheels and kissed my mum's St Christopher before pulling on my helmet and belting myself into one of the Formula Fords. I guided the car onto the track and focused on driving. I pushed the car, but I wasn't trying to set any lap records. This was a quick check to make sure the engine, brakes and tires functioned properly. The engine is a minefield of potential problems from sticking throttle linkages to misfiring ignition systems. Tyres have a limited shelf life and, once it's reached, the grip degrades. Silicon brake fluid absorbs water and destroys braking

Just as I said my name, a shotgun blast punched a fifteen inch diameter hole in the door, spitting thousands of wood splinters at me. Dozens embedded themselves in my face. The shock sent me staggering back into the crudely constructed wooden safety rail. It gave way against my weight and I plunged over the side and stuck the soft dirt on my back. I just lay there, too winded to move.

Paul appeared at the doorway. He saw me, muttered something and disappeared back inside.

When he didn't emerge, I rolled over and I climbed to my feet. I picked splinters from my face and counted myself lucky it wasn't buckshot.

I was a little too dazed to comprehend how close I'd come to having my head blown off as I re-climbed the stairs. This time, I stopped short of the open doorway and pressed my back up against the buckshot-proof brick wall.

'Paul, it's me, Aidy. Can I come in?'

'OK,' a sheepish voice came from within. 'Sorry, Aidy.'

'That's OK,' I said, hoping that I could trust him.

I peered through the doorway before venturing inside, just in case Paul was still in the shooting mood. He sat on the corner of a single bed pushed up against the far wall with the shotgun spread across his lap.

Whoever had roughed him up had done a good job. His face was a painter's palate of reds, blues and purples. Swelling almost closed his right eye. I felt sorry for bringing this upon him.

'Do you want to put the shotgun down before it goes off again?'

He nodded and held it out to me. 'It's not mine. My landlord leant it to me.'

I took the twelve bore. I broke the gun open and removed the cartridges before setting the weapon against a wall.

'What happened?'

He looked up at me, disappointment moulded into his swollen features. 'He took the tape of the race.'

I'd guessed as much, but I wasn't prepared for the disappointment this news brought. One of the few pieces of hardcore evidence was gone.

'I came home from Chicane's late last night. It was dark. I didn't see anyone until someone smacked me across the back with a baseball bat.'

performance. Any deficiency in these three areas is dangerous. Any and all of these factors might send a student flying off the track. I settled into putting in some consistent laps to watch the oil and water temperature gauges rise and the oil pressure drop into safe running conditions.

I maintained a safe distance from Graham. He wouldn't have appreciated me hounding him on the track as well as off.

As I passed the pit lane, Pete joined the circuit behind me. Normally, he let the hired help like Graham and me handle the cars on the track while he worried about logistics. I put his presence down to the numbers of people we had to get through today. It also explained his pace. He was eating up the track behind me. He looked as if he was on a flying lap and not a warm up.

Seeing Pete catch up to me, my competitive streak kicked in and I upped my pace, but he still reeled me in. Ahead, Graham peeled off into the pit lane, but I stayed out for one more lap with Pete. With everything that had been going on, I needed to blow off some steam. A dogfight with Pete was just the remedy.

Pete wasn't the fastest of racers but he was outdoing himself. He was making mincemeat out of my speeds. He closed within fifty yards and my stomach dropped. I recognized the helmet design. It wasn't Pete's, it was Derek's.

If Derek wanted to tangle with me, I wasn't going to give him the privilege. I came off the gas a little.

Derek closed in behind me, so close that he disappeared in my mirrors. That meant he was a car length off my gearbox. The noise bleeding into my helmet confirmed it. The mirrors on a single-seater give limited rear-view vision and that's when a driver relies on his other senses. When two cars get within a car length of each other, the sound of a screaming engine changes. There are two engines and resonance comes into effect. In a race, it tells you you're about to be overtaken and it was no different this time. Derek moved out from behind me. My heart fluttered when he drew alongside me, slowing to match my speed. We were heading towards Barrack Hill and Derek inched slightly ahead of me then elegantly slipped his left rear wheel in front of mine. He was teeing me up for the same fate as Alex.

Carefully, I inched left and untangled myself from the web Derek was weaving.

Derek moved in again and looped his left rear in front of my right rear. I had nowhere to go. I was at the edge of the track. Taking to the grass run-off would be just as lethal. Derek and I were interlocked; our wheels inches apart. One wrong move could kill us both.

Our cars were so close that if Derek and I reached out for one another we could have shaken hands. I looked over at him. The only view I had of him was the letterbox slot in his helmet. Derek's eyes were dots where his cheeks were bunched up. The bastard was grinning.

We bore down on Barrack Hill and Derek made no move to untangle his wheels from mine. The turning point was seconds away. I couldn't do a thing. Derek held my fate.

We hit the turning point for Barrack Hill. We had no choice but to match each others' moves. For once, we worked as partners. If either of us got out of step or phase, we were both going off the track and into a wall. Derek turned for the bend and I turned with him. I synchronized my driving with his. It was all I could do. We exited the corner together and I released a relieved breath.

Derek eased his wheels out from mine. I glanced over at him. He flashed me the thumbs up then accelerated ahead of me.

I guess I'd just been threatened for the second time.

I kept to myself for the rest of the day, chatting with the punters instead of hanging out with my fellow drivers. I needed someone to watch my back and the punters were the best I could lay my hands on.

The Hansen brothers had used me. Today had been set up to teach me a lesson. They tossed me into the den with Derek so he could prove yet again he could get to me at any time. It was a point well made. Derek had friends down here. I couldn't trust anyone. No matter what I did, someone would be there to protect him. A curtain was being drawn around this circuit and its dirty little secret and I was on the wrong side.

When the last of the clients went home, I left Tony and Pete to put their cars away. I wasn't helping them. I changed and collected my cheque for playing patsy.

Derek had left before I came out of the changing room. Now that my fight or flight senses had been set off, I didn't take his absence as a good sign. It wouldn't surprise me if he was putting

together something else for me. I knew I wouldn't be foll
any detours on my way home.

I tossed my kitbag and helmet in Steve's Capri and jogged to Chicane's. I hadn't checked in with Paul yet in case D pulled a stunt like he did on the track and took the tape from It was best to get it from Paul on my way home.

Chris greeted me with a smile when I walked into Chicane

'Is Paul around?' I asked.

'He's at home, recovering.'

'Recovering from what?'

'Didn't you hear? He was mugged. The guy roughed him up real good.'

This had Derek Deacon written all over it. No wonder he wanted to show me his moves on the track today. He'd gone after Paul. Paul would have talked. I didn't blame him. Paul would have been outnumbered and probably outgunned.

'That's terrible,' I said. 'Where's he live? I'll drop 'round and see him.'

Chris looked at me suspiciously. 'Why would you do that?'

'I like Paul. He's been good to me. He did me a favour and I owe him a drink. The least I can do is give it to him after this.'

Chris's suspicion didn't ebb away, but he gave me Paul's address. I hoped Chris wasn't in Derek's circle of friends, but I had to assume that he was. It was too late to worry about that.

I drove over to Paul's place. He lived in a converted loft above a barn at a working farm on the outskirts of Chippenham. This wasn't some trendy affair, but the cheapest accommodation Paul could find on his small income.

The barn was a quarter mile from the farm itself. I liked that. It gave us the privacy I wanted. I parked and bounded up the wooden staircase to the loft door. There was no doorbell, so I knocked.

No one answered. I'd parked next to Paul's VW pickup that Chris had given him for making local pickups and deliveries. He was home.

'Hey, Paul, you in there?'

Paul didn't answer, but I heard movement. There weren't any windows, just skylights built into the roof. I tried the doorknob, but it was locked.

'Hey, Paul, it's me, Aidy.'

'Did you see who it was?'

'No, he was wearing a balaclava and before I could get up, he pulled a bag over my head. That's when he started beating me, punching and kicking. You think my face is bad, you should see my back.'

I winced in sympathy.

'How many people did this to you?'

'One, I think, but I'm not sure.'

'He took the tape?'

'Yeah. After he beat me, he dragged me inside here. He wanted the tape. I told him I didn't know what he was talking about. He beat me again when I said that. I wasn't trying to play dumb. I really didn't know. All I could think about was why someone was beating me. Then he asked for the tape of the race with Alex's crash. I gave it to him.' Tears leaked down Paul's face and he palmed them away. 'I had to, Aidy. I think he would have killed me if I hadn't.'

'That's OK. You did the right thing. I would have done the same thing myself.'

'It doesn't feel like the right thing.'

Even Paul was having doubts about Alex's death. No matter what Derek tried, he wouldn't be able to keep his crime a secret. It was going to come out. I wished Paul had watched the tape. It might have turned things around.

'Did you go to the police?'

Paul shook his head. That spoke volumes about who he thought was responsible.

'Did he tell you not to?'

Paul nodded.

'Do you know who did this to you?'

Paul didn't answer.

'Paul, he could have killed you. Who did this to you?'

Still, Paul didn't answer.

His lack of a reply told me all I needed to know.

Lap Fifteen

The Mygale car Hancock had leased for the Formula Ford Festival arrived at Archway on Saturday. The chassis was pristine in every way from the gleaming bodywork to the fresh rubber on the tires. It was all new. Untouched. Perfection. I buzzed with the kind of confidence that knocked half a second off lap times.

The engine Hancock had leased from Armstrong's had arrived the day before. Engines are a commodity of their own and they don't come with the car. Hancock must have pulled some strings to have gotten one built by Armstrong's. They were one of the top engine builders in the country and you just didn't get one by asking for it, regardless of how much money you had.

With the Festival two weeks away, I didn't have much time to get this car prepped and tested before it would be go time. Dylan came over to help Steve and me and the three of us jumped on the Mygale. With all of us working, it didn't take long to get the engine connected up to the chassis. Hooking up the pipes and wiring took a little longer. My plan was to have the car functioning on Saturday and set up in racing trim by Sunday night. I hoped to grab some track time the following week.

We broke for lunch around two. Seeing as I was taking up everyone's Saturday, I went and picked up lunch. We sat and ate around the car. None of us could take our eyes off the damn thing. This was a glimpse into the future where racing with the latest equipment and fresh engines built by the likes of Armstrong's was commonplace. It was a blissful moment and of course, someone had to break it.

'We're going to have to change tactics if we want to prove Derek killed Alex,' Dylan said.

I didn't want to talk about this, but it wasn't like deciding my next move wasn't a constant thought at the back of my mind. 'Change how?'

'Derek has done a nice job of shutting you out.' He counted off on his fingers. 'He's leaned on witnesses, he's got the cops on his side, he's got the tape of the race and he proved he can get to you whenever he wants. And what have we got?' He jerked a thumb at Alex's wreck hiding under a sheet. 'Alex's car and that doesn't tell us much.'

'So what do you suggest?' I asked.

'We focus on something Derek can't intimidate or eliminate. Derek himself.'

'That sounds a lot like trying to tame a lion by putting your head in its mouth.'

'Maybe, but it makes sense,' Steve said. 'You need to catch Derek in the act.'

In the act of what? The only thing I could see Derek doing was coming after me again. 'There's nothing to catch him in the act of. He killed Alex and he's got the witnesses, evidence and police covered. What else is there?'

Dylan frowned.

'You're assuming he's got everything covered. You don't know that,' Steve said. 'Derek might like to pretend he's in control, but his stunt on the track yesterday and beating up Paul are signs of a desperate man. Desperate men don't think straight. They over-think the situation and do dumb things. He could be making moves on someone as we speak or destroying something he believes is relevant. If we do nothing, then we'll never know.'

I tried to imagine a desperate Derek Deacon and couldn't conjure the image. All I could see was Derek with a shotgun and Derek grinning at me from under his helmet. Both of these versions of Derek were confident men, but Steve had a point. Everything Derek did was reactive, in response to something I did. My poking my nose in Derek's business got me a shotgun jammed in my face. My talking to Paul got him beaten up. Even Alex's murder was reactive. He saw Alex as a threat to his crown, so he killed him. Derek was like that on the track too. Despite his wins and championship titles, he never led from the front. He battled for the lead.

This trait worked in my favour. Derek would fight me every step of the way, but if I kept a couple of steps ahead, he'd never catch me. It was a nice theory that could work but it would be putting me and those close to me in harm's way.

'I think we should follow him,' Dylan said.

'Surveillance?' I said.

'Yeah. He won't be expecting that. Who's to say where he'll lead us?'

Dylan was getting far too excited.

'Dylan, his friends pulled a gun on you a week ago. You up for that again or worse?'

Dylan coloured and looked at his food instead of me. The shame of that day wasn't going away in a hurry.

'We're beyond the point of no return,' Steve said. 'Derek has you marked as a target. He can't trust you to forget this. He has only one option and that's to come after you. It's better you get something on him before he gets to you.'

The idea of being in Derek's sights scared me. He'd proved he could get to me any time. I wasn't safe. Not on the track and not away from it.

'Dylan's right. We should follow him. He won't be expecting it.'

I wasn't sure I agreed, but I didn't have any other ideas. 'We're going to need a car. He'll recognize the Capri and the van.'

'Don't worry,' Steve said. 'I've got that covered.'

Within a few hours, Steve had gotten us a Subaru Legacy wagon. It was a few years old and came with a couple of dents to prove it. It was the kind of car that blended in well with rural and urban settings, but had some power behind it to get us out of trouble should it present itself. Steve had borrowed the car from a client with a used car dealership. The guy didn't look like he had a pot to piss in, but it was all part of his act as a used car salesman. Steve maintained his collection of classic MGs.

Dylan and I set off after Derek, while Steve stayed behind to continue working on the new car. Even in an unknown car, I didn't like the idea of tailing Derek in daylight. The man was a predator, not the prey. We arrived in Wiltshire just after five. It was already getting dark and I liked that the cover of night added to our anonymity.

I didn't know how much Derek knew about me, but I knew little about him. I knew he raced, worked as a long distance lorry driver, was married and lived in Chippenham. I remembered his address from the initial fund-raising drive I'd done with Myles and Eva Beecham.

On the drive down, I remembered one other thing. His wife ran a stall at the Saturday market at the circuit. We arrived at the circuit too late for the market. It had closed. All that was left was the last of the stallholders packing up. Derek's wife wasn't one of them.

We drove on to Derek's house. He lived on a cramped housing estate where the houses were squeezed up against each other and cars were parked in front. There was no mistaking Derek's house with the big rig parked outside.

We pulled up in time to see him helping his wife unload her car. She was a heavy woman, but she came with curves. She must have been something twenty years ago. She seemed to put all her stock into her fluffy, over-bleached hair. She and Derek looked to be the perfect match for each other.

I'd seen enough. I turned down a connecting street, pulled a U-turn and headed out of the estate.

'Where are you going?' Dylan said.

'We're sitting ducks in there. We need something with a better vantage point.'

The estate was effectively a teardrop design with one road in and out. I parked in a pub car park across from the estate. It was half full with late afternoon drinkers and it overlooked the estate entrance.

'There's no need to watch Derek at home. We're only going to get something when he leaves and when he does, we're going to see him.'

Dylan looked at me. 'You're getting too good at this.'

We bedded in. Nothing happened. Derek's neighbours came and went, but Derek remained home. Sitting there was tedious. On the good side, no one bothered us from the pub.

Dylan reached inside his pocket and brought out his bag of sunflower seeds.

'Hey, not in here. This isn't our car, remember?'

'If you're expecting me sit around here for God knows how long, I need something to do,' he said and slung a handful of seeds in his mouth.

I was regretting my decision to bring Dylan along. 'Well, just don't get them all over the place.'

'Already got that covered.' He brought out a plastic bag and spat the shells into the bag.

'God, that's disgusting.'

'They're good for you. Don't knock them until you try them.'

'One day you're going to crap out a sunflower.'

'Haven't so far.'

'Let's hope for a change of fortunes.'

It was seven when Derek's big rig stopped at the entrance to the estate waiting for a gap in the traffic. Both Dylan and I sat up. I didn't know what hours a distance lorry driver worked, but starting his day on a Saturday night didn't seem normal.

'It's go time,' Dylan said.

I waited until Derek merged into traffic before starting the Subaru. The car came with the annoying feature of daytime running lights. If I'd started the car the moment I saw Derek, I would have hit him with my lights.

'Keep your eyes on him,' I told Dylan.

Derek had a sizeable lead on us, but that was OK. His big rig stood head and shoulders above everything else on the road, making him hard to miss and making my first surveillance job an easy one.

He headed north out of Chippenham. I expected him to turn towards the motorway, but instead, he drove into the countryside.

'Where's he going out here at this time of night?' Dylan said, echoing my thoughts.

Traffic thinned out in the country and I had to back off so he didn't spot the Subaru. I'd backed off so much I feared I was going to lose him until I saw the signs for Langley Hill. Then, I knew exactly where he was going and I backed off even more.

'You're going to lose him,' Dylan said.

'I don't think so.'

When I drove through Langley Hill, Derek's big rig stuck out in the street in front of the Green Man pub. I drove past, turned around and parked a safe distance from the pub, but with a clear view of anyone entering or leaving.

'A drink before work?' Dylan said.

'Not likely.' It didn't seem like a smart move for a trucker.

'What do you want to do?' Dylan said.

'Just wait.'

Dylan frowned. 'I want to go in.'

'He knows you.'

'I know. I just want to do a walk-by to see who he's drinking with.'

I didn't like it, but it was a good idea. 'OK. Go. Just be bloody careful.'

Dylan hopped out of the car and crossed the street. My chest tightened when he stepped inside and didn't reappear immediately.

'Don't push it, Dylan,' I murmured in the darkness.

As if he heard me, he reappeared. He walked at a normal pace back to me.

'He's in there alone talking to the barman,' Dylan said getting back into the car.

'Did you recognize anyone else in there?'

'Nah. What do we do now?'

'Wait.'

I cracked a window when the car started to mist up. We'd been waiting for an hour in the cold while Derek sat in the pub's warmth.

Dylan rubbed his hands together to get some heat in them. 'Al Capone knows how to spend a scintillating Saturday night.'

Derek wasn't entertaining himself. He wouldn't bring his big rig when he had the convenience of a car at his disposal. He was here to meet someone and we didn't have to wait much longer.

'Here we go,' I said.

'What?'

'The man going in is Detective Brennan of the Wiltshire Police Force.'

'Fan-bloody-tastic.'

Despite Derek's long wait for Brennan, their meeting didn't last long. Both men emerged from the pub fifteen minutes later and went their separate ways.

'What do we do now?'

'Stay on Derek. If Brennan's involved in something, he's not going to be too blatant about it. Besides, Derek didn't bring his big rig for nothing.'

Derek pulled away, heading towards us. Both of us ducked down out of sight. When we sat up, Brennan had pulled a U-turn and was heading back the way he came.

I gunned the Subaru and followed Derek. The heavy cloak of fatigue from sitting around for the last few hours lifted. We'd got what we came for. Action.

Derek circled around to join the M4 motorway and we did the same. He lived up to his name as a long distance driver. He followed the M4 all the way to the outskirts of London before picking up the M25 circular and taking the southern route around the city.

I wondered if he was picking up a load from an airport, but he failed to turn off at Heathrow or Gatwick. Suddenly, a sea port made sense. The junction for Dover was a few miles ahead, but when he passed the Dover junction, I stopped guessing and just settled for the fact we'd get to wherever we were going when we got there.

Derek got off the motorway in Kent and I wondered if he was going to Brands Hatch, until he drove into Gravesend. He turned into an industrial park. This was trouble for us. No one else was going there at this time of night on a Saturday. We risked being spotted.

I pulled over at the side of the road. 'Let's give him a minute to get to where he's going.'

Dylan nodded.

The good thing about the industrial park was it wouldn't be hard to find Derek amongst the buildings. The downside was we'd be just as easy to spot.

I turned into the park. It didn't take long to find Derek. He'd pulled into a Hancock Salvage facility. Hancock himself was there to greet him. He checked the street for prying eyes then closed the salvage yard's doors the second Derek was inside.

'A bit late for a sponsor meeting,' Dylan said.

'Maybe Derek does some off-the-books trucking work for Hancock,' I said. 'Derek wouldn't be the first driver to do a little extra-curricular work in return for his sponsorship cash.'

'Do you really believe that?'

'Let's just wait and see.'

'You're being surprisingly level-headed for once.' Dylan grinned. 'You know this is going to turn out dodgy.'

I said nothing and watched the entrance. Dylan was right. As much as this night time rendezvous meant nothing in itself, I found the association between Hancock and Derek curious. Why had Hancock decided to sponsor Derek? He must know about Derek's death threat. Maybe Hancock just didn't care who he sponsored as long as he had a winning driver. This late night meeting between Derek and Hancock put a fresh spin on Hancock's odd tone during my sponsorship pitch meeting. He'd been overly interested in my closeness to Alex. Why? Did Alex know something he shouldn't have? The petty motives behind his murder now seemed like a smokescreen for something far more insidious. Had Derek's death threat been a diversion to take attention away from the real motive? I didn't want to speculate any further. This could be nothing or it could be a whole bunch of something. I needed to see more. I drove past the yard and parked in the shadows between two buildings.

Spotlights lit up Hancock's yard, but the high fences and walls blocked our view. It was half an hour before all was revealed. Derek re-emerged pulling a commercial car transporter with six damaged, high-end cars loaded onto it.

'Transporting cars at this time of night?' Dylan said.

'Maybe Derek's trying to beat rush hour traffic.'

Dylan frowned at me. I smiled and gunned the engine.

We followed Derek back to the M25 and all the way back to the south-west. It looked as if Derek was going home. We were running low on fuel. I filled the tank at the M4 motorway services at Swindon. Once I had the car refuelled, I kept the accelerator floored to catch up to Derek. I needn't have worried. He kept to the speed limit and it didn't take long to catch him up.

We followed him all the way to Bristol. He threaded his way through the city to a street area filled with shabby and rundown industrial units. He stopped in front of an anonymous looking workshop with no company signs, but protected by a chain link fence. It was close to midnight, but a crew was there to receive him. They helped unload the cars off the transporter and into the workshop.

'Do you recognize those two?' I said pointing out Morgan and Strickland.

Dylan's expression turned angry at the sight of Derek's two shotgun buddies. 'Yeah,' he said. 'This is getting pretty intertwined.'

From the way Morgan was ordering Strickland and the others around, this was his place.

'What do you think they're doing – running a cut and shut operation?'

A cut and shut is a Frankenstein-style approach to car salvage. Say you have two identical car models but one has front end damage and the other has rear end damage. Instead of repairing both, the cars are cut in half and two good halves are welded together.

'I don't think so. Derek delivered six different cars and that place isn't big enough to hold another six matching cars.'

'He could be stripping them for parts.'

I shook my head. The cars he'd delivered were high-end and obviously handpicked based on their value. While their spare parts value was high, they were worth even more as the complete cars.

My mobile rang. I pulled it out. Steve's name appeared on the small screen.

'Hey, Steve.'

'Aidy?' Steve croaked.

Steve sounded sick.

'Steve, are you OK?'

'I'm at Archway. Come get me.'

'What's wrong?'

'Someone tried to torch the place.'

'Are you OK?'

'Just get back here.'

Lap Sixteen

The Subaru's headlights bore holes in the darkness. I chased the light with my foot planted on the accelerator, hoping to catch it.

Dylan had taken my phone and put it on speaker. 'How are you doing, Steve?'

'OK.'

Dylan and I shared a glance. He didn't sound it.

'Are you hurt?' Dylan asked.

'I took a bit of a pounding, but I gave back as good as I got.'

I was trying not to panic, just concentrate on driving, but I was failing miserably. Nasty images kept filling my head.

'Who came after you?' I asked.

'I don't know. The bastard was wearing a balaclava.'

It sounded like the same person Derek had sent to take care of Paul.

'Steve, have you called an ambulance?' I asked.

'No.'

'I'll call,' Dylan said,

'No,' he insisted. 'If you call an ambulance, they'll take me away and this place will be totally at Derek's mercy.'

Steve was right, but I wasn't about to lose him over Alex's car. I was going to nail Derek one way or another, with or without the car. 'Steve, if you're hurt bad, you need a doctor.'

'I'm OK for now. Just get here. How far out are you?'

'We've just gotten out of Bristol. We're at least an hour out,' Dylan said.

'I'll survive.'

Dylan covered the phone. 'He sounds bad, mate.'

'Keep him talking.'

Dylan nodded. 'What happened, Steve?'

'I was working on the car for the Festival. I'd put the ratios in the gearbox and was setting the car up with the factory settings.'

'We were going to do that tomorrow,' I said.

'I was enjoying myself and I wanted to get a jump on tomorrow. I heard a car pull up. I thought it was you coming back. I called out your name, but I didn't get an answer. Nothing happened for a minute. I called out again. This time the door opened and a man in a balaclava came in carrying a petrol can. He opened it up and started splashing it about. I rushed him and he knocked me down.'

'Jesus,' I said.

'He thought he'd dealt with me and went straight for Alex's car. He yanked the drop cloth off and started looking the car over as if he wanted something off it. When he didn't see what he wanted, he shoved it off its stands and came back for his petrol can. I think he was going to torch it, but that's when I got him back.' Steve coughed out a laugh. 'I lamped him with the adjustables. Got him good in the ribs. I had to have broken one. He turned on me after that, but that was just so I wouldn't follow him. Once he had me out of the way, he made off.'

Dylan kept Steve talking. He asked him how the Mygale was shaping up against my old Van Diemen and got little anecdotes out of him. Each story helped eat up the miles.

I kept my speed around a hundred. It was easy to do at that time of night. The first signs for Reading flashed by and my fear began to subside. We were only twenty miles away.

Steve was talking when he suddenly trailed off in the middle of a sentence.

'Steve?' Dylan asked. 'You there, Steve?'

Steve didn't answer.

'Shit, Steve, you're scaring me,' Dylan said. 'Talk to me.'

Still, Steve didn't answer.

Dylan checked the phone. 'The call might have dropped.'

We both knew he was trying to find an excuse not to scare us.

'Call him back.'

Dylan redialled Steve's number. 'I'm not getting through.'

'Call an ambulance.'

Steve punched in 999. The call got picked up after twenty long rings. 'Hello. Yes. I need an ambulance out to Archway Restoration, Six Goswell Arches. There's a man there. He's been assaulted. We had him on the phone and he lost consciousness. Thank you.'

'Christ, I hope he's OK,' I said.

'He will be.'

I pushed the Subaru to its limit. The speedometer needle hovered near the hundred and twenty mark. We were travelling at two miles a minute and it still felt slow. I wanted more out of the car, but I wasn't getting it.

'Aidy, slow down,' Dylan pleaded. 'You're going to get us killed. And what good would that do Steve?'

I shot him a glance. Dylan had purposely pressed one of my buttons and I bottled the urge to lash out at him. I had no tolerance for reckless driving because of my parents. I drove fast on the roads, but never stupid. I always left the high speed stuff for the racetrack. I took my foot off the gas and the needle dropped down to ninety. It was as slow as I was willing to go.

We covered the rest of the distance in less than twelve minutes. I threw the Capri into the service road behind the Archway units. The ambulance hadn't arrived yet. The Capri slithered on the loose surface and Dylan grabbed the handhold over the door to steady himself. I stamped on the brakes and the car slithered to a halt outside the workshop entrance. Dylan jumped out of the car before I did and yanked open the shop door.

The acrid stink of spilled petrol burnt the back of my throat the moment I raced through the doorway. A five gallon can lay on its side in a pool. It was a lethal hazard, but I ignored it.

Steve lay on the ground propped up against a workbench, a large adjustable spanner in one hand. He wasn't conscious.

Dylan got to him first, but I shoved him aside. I was sick with fear and my mind was in a panic. I didn't know whether to check Steve's pulse, lift him up, leave him where he was or kick a hole in the wall and I was too frightened to do any of these things in case I made it worse.

'Steve, it's me.'

He stirred. His eyes opened, searched the room, failed to lock onto anything, then closed again.

God, it was a relief to see even that small response. I got my arms under his shoulders to lift him.

'Maybe you shouldn't move him,' Dylan said.

'Steve, come on, mate. Wake up.'

He came around, this time more alert. He tried to sit up. I got behind him and guided him into a sitting position.

'Take it easy,' Dylan said.

'Are you OK?' I asked.

'Get me up,' he said. His voice sounded cracked and broken.

'An ambulance is on the way,' Dylan said.

'No hospital. Just get me up.'

'No, you're going to hospital, Steve,' I told him. 'You don't have a choice.'

'We'd better check you out,' Dylan said.

Dylan and I got Steve up onto his feet. He groaned.

'Just get me to a chair. Anything's better than being stretched out on a concrete floor.'

We carried him to one of the two ratty armchairs we kept in the workshop. They were dirty, greasy things we kept around for when we took a break from working on the cars. They were hardly the most sanitary place for an examination, but Steve would be comfortable.

I helped Steve to sit forward while Dylan helped him off with his shirt. His chest and stomach were mottled with palm-sized, red bruises. Many overlapped to make one big bruise. Steve looked so old and frail there in the armchair. He'd always seemed so invincible to me. It was frightening to see how easily he could be dethroned.

'I'm sorry, Steve. I'm so sorry.'

Dylan took over. He pushed me aside and looked Steve over as best he could. He was fantastic. I was useless. I was shaking, but I didn't know if it was from rage or fear. Probably both. Derek had struck too close to home. This was far too personal for me. Now

I understood why doctors rarely treated family members. It wasn't an ethical boundary, but one of objectivity. They couldn't view the patient as just a patient, or a set of symptoms or an injury that needed fixing. It was a loved one. One screw up on their part could make it worse. I stepped back and gave Dylan the space he needed.

Sirens wailed outside before becoming deafening.

'They don't need all the details,' Steve said. 'As far as the world knows, this was a bungled robbery. No mention of Derek, Alex or anyone. You got that?'

'Steve, no,' I said.

'Yes, Aidy. We can't trust the cops yet. This stays between us. Promise me.'

I didn't like it, but understood it. 'Whatever you say.'

'What about the petrol?' Dylan asked. 'How do we explain that? A burglar wouldn't be throwing it around.'

'Shit,' Steve mumbled. 'I'll tell them I used it as a weapon to scare the tosser off.'

Two uniformed police officers called out to us as they barged their way into the workshop. Naturally, the 999 call had brought the police.

'Here,' I said. 'Quick.'

They raced over and shoved Dylan and me aside to get to Steve while tossing out questions. I had no problem letting them take over. One of the officers gave Steve a cursory examination and asked him how he was doing.

The other officer distanced Dylan and me from Steve so his colleague could question Steve alone. He asked us who we were and what had happened then called for a detective and a scenes-of-crime team.

The ambulance arrived before we were through explaining. The paramedics rushed in. They worked on Steve for a minute before loading him onto a stretcher and into the ambulance.

The officer who'd checked Steve out said, 'I'm going with the victim to get his statement.'

Dylan and I went to leave too, but the second officer stopped us.

'I need someone to stay here.'

'I'll stay,' Dylan said.

I followed the first officer out. He pointed to his patrol car and I got in with him. He introduced himself as Officer Luke Pine. The ambulance roared off and we followed.

The ambulance took us to King Edward VII hospital in Windsor. The second we arrived at the hospital, the paramedics rushed Steve into the accident and emergency centre. The doctors pumped me for details and Steve's medical history, then eased me into the waiting room.

Officer Pine remained with Steve and the doctors but emerged a few minutes later. He was in his forties and he radiated the type of assuredness that came with experience. He sat next to me.

'Your grandad is going to be alright,' he said.

I exhaled. 'Thank God.'

'It'll be a while before the doctor is out to talk to you. OK if I get your statement?'

'Sure.'

'Any idea why someone would do this?' Officer Pine asked.

'Archway is well known. There are a lot of expensive tools there and the cars are valuable.'

Pine swallowed our cover story of a random break-in gone wrong and filled out an incident report. It didn't take long to get my meagre account down on paper.

When he had it all down, he said, 'Well, it sounds like your grandad gave the bastard a crack in the ribs. If he seeks medical attention, that's as good as a confession.'

I hoped the police did pick up balaclava man. His identity could prove interesting. Depending on who it was, it might put Derek in an awkward position.

Pine excused himself to report in and left me alone.

Knowing Steve was going to be OK dissolved my fear, but anger replaced it. Derek had actually done it. He'd come after me, but his thug had gotten the wrong person. Well, the stunt had backfired. Instead of destroying Alex's car, it was now under the police's watchful eye. There wouldn't be a second chance at the car. Not tonight.

The doctor came to see me after a couple of hours. She smiled at me as she approached.

'Your grandfather is going to be OK. Nothing's broken. He's just banged up. He took a pretty big knock to the head resulting in a mild concussion and because of that I'll be keeping him in overnight for observation.'

'Can I see him?'

'Of course.'

The doctor showed me into Steve's room. He looked drained, clinging loosely to consciousness. I pulled a chair up to his bedside and sat before picking up his hand and gripping it. He squeezed back and fixed me with a lazy stare. A tear rolled down my cheek.

'Hey, kiddo.' Steve's voice was thick with fatigue.

'You're a daft old bugger, do you know that?'

He smiled.

'Who do you think you are playing the sodding hero?'

'Steve McQueen. Everybody says we share a certain likeness.'

'You stupid git.'

'That's no way to talk to your grandfather.'

'I'm sorry.'

'I'm only playing, kid. Don't take it personally.'

'I'm not talking about that. I'm sorry because I nearly got you killed.'

'You didn't do anything. Don't you feel bad about this, OK? We knew this could happen.' He gripped my hand tight. 'No one comes between us. You know that, right?'

'Yeah, I know.'

'Good.' He closed his eyes. 'Now piss off, I want to have a dirty dream about that doctor.'

I palmed away a tear and left Steve to sleep. Officer Pine was waiting for me when I left Steve's room and he drove me back to Archway.

Dylan was standing in the doorway talking to a detective when we pulled up, while other officers and crime scene technicians gathered and catalogued evidence in the workshop. Pine introduced me to the detective and handed him my statement. The detective took me up to the crow's-nest and we went over the statement. Just like Pine, the detective accepted my account without question. He thanked me and rejoined his colleagues in the workshop.

Dylan came and joined me in the crow's-nest and we watched the police work.

'How's Steve?' Dylan asked.

'He's alright,' I said. 'He's got a mild concussion. They're keeping him in for the night.'

'That's good. It could have been worse.'

'Thanks for everything, Dylan. I don't know what I would have done without you.'

Dylan smiled. 'It's nothing. You know I'd do anything for Steve.'

We had things to discuss but we couldn't do it with the cops milling around, so we waited.

It was four in the morning when the police packed up and left. As the detective departed, he said, 'Don't worry, son, we'll catch this guy.'

I didn't believe him. I knew as well as he did that they didn't stand much chance of catching balaclava man. He'd had more than enough time to escape. The only way they'd catch him was if he screwed up, but Derek's people had proved themselves more than competent so far.

It might have been four in the morning, but I wasn't ready to go to sleep. With the police gone, Dylan and I set about cleaning up. We got Alex's car back onto stands and soaked up the spilt petrol with Oil-Dri absorbent granules.

Dylan scooped up a shovelful of petrol soaked Oil-Dri and dropped it in a waste bin. 'They'll try again.'

I finished checking out Alex's car and covered it with the cloth. The fall had damaged the wreck even further, but did nothing to hide what Derek had done. 'I know. That's why I'm not leaving here tonight.'

'Neither am I.'

'Thanks.'

'I hate to be the bearer of bad news here, but if they want Alex's car – and they do – they're going to come back for it.'

I sighed. 'I know.'

It was dawn before we had the workshop back in one piece and sleep was worming its way into us. We made ourselves comfortable in the office. I tossed a pillow and blanket at Dylan from a stash Steve kept in a closet. It wasn't the first time we'd pulled an all-nighter at Archway, but those were usually for better reasons than this. Dylan took the sofa and I dropped into my chair at my desk and stretched out with my feet on the table.

'Who do you think is the one in the balaclava?' Dylan asked.

'I don't know, but it wasn't Derek.'

It was one thing I knew for sure. The attempted arson was the perfect opportunity to pin blame on Derek and actually get him nailed for something, but our night time excursion only served to provide him with the alibi he needed. Derek had been busy moving Hancock's cars. It was a kick in the guts.

Derek must have turned to one of his crew. Morgan and Strickland had helped him unload the cars, so that put a spotlight on someone else. Whoever it was, he'd be nursing cracked ribs. That might give me the opening I needed.

'It could have been our friendly, shotgun-toting tractor driver.'

'Could be. We'll have to ask Steve.'

'Did you see the petrol can the firebug brought with him?' Dylan asked.

'No. Where is it?'

'The plod took it as evidence.'

'What about it?'

'It was a red five gallon can.'

I recognized the significance straight away. Everybody used the army-style surplus five gallon, steel petrol cans to refuel their cars. Motorsport suppliers sold them. They painted them to match their corporate colours.

'Was it Chicane's red?'

'Yes,' Dylan said. 'I even saw the Chicane's label on the bottom. Mr Balaclava is definitely a Stowe Park regular.'

At some point, we drifted off to sleep and awoke to the ringing of my mobile. The clock on the phone said it was after ten a.m. It was the hospital calling to say Steve was ready to be discharged.

I stretched and looked around me. The walls were draped in history. Each picture, poster and wreath was a reminder of a great feat in motorsport. Each image or memento was of someone I admired and loved, but all of whom were dead. The attack on Steve made me see the dead as victims, not heroes. This office had once been my favourite place in the world, but it was tarnished now. Goddamn Derek for ruining this place for me.

Lap Seventeen

On Monday, I went straight from work to Archway to finish the set-up on the new car. I'd booked a testing session at Brands Hatch on Wednesday to shake the car down. I was looking forward to it despite all that was going on.

Steve was hard at work on the Mygale. He'd bounced back

from Saturday's attack after taking Sunday off. The old man was tough.

When he saw me walk in, Steve grabbed a couriered package and handed it to me. 'You'd better take a look at those. They came from Hancock this afternoon.'

He'd already opened the large envelope and I slid out the contents. It contained the decals to put on the car. It was the usual thing, the corporate logo and the firm's name to go on the sides of the car as well as the nose. Sorting through the decals, I found the problem. Hancock had included two additional decals that proudly proclaimed, 'Hancock Salvage salutes Alex Fanning, RIP, please support the Alex Fanning Memorial Fund.' They were hardly sensitive under the circumstances.

'Is he serious?' I asked.

'He's just getting the bang for his publicity buck.'

'And milking it for every penny. Do you think he's told Alison or the Fannings?'

'I doubt it.'

'I'll call them.'

'Laura Fanning beat you to the punch. She left a message earlier. She wants you to drop by and pick up Alex's tools and equipment. She'd like you to have them.'

Great. Dead man's hand-me-downs. My feelings must have shown.

'Do this, please. It'll mean a lot to her.'

'OK. I'll go 'round.'

'Good lad. You want me to put the decals on?'

'Yeah. Do it. You going to stick around here tonight?'

'Yeah.'

Seeing Mrs Fanning created a dilemma. It left both Steve and me on our own. I felt safe visiting Mrs Fanning on my own, but I didn't like leaving Steve alone, not after the attack. We still had Alex's car, which meant I had something Derek wanted. Steve was no match for Derek's crew.

'If I go, I want Dylan here with you tonight.'

'Good idea,' Steve said.

I nodded and went upstairs to the office. I called Dylan to get him to come over then called Alison on her mobile. She sounded happy to hear from me.

'Something's cropped up that I need to talk to you about,' I said.

'It sounds serious.'

'Not really, but it's important. Can we meet up tonight?'

'Sure.'

'Is there a convenient place I can meet you?'

'I'll come over to your place.'

After the incident with Mr Balaclava, I didn't feel safe with Alison being here. She might get caught up in a second attempt. 'No, I'll come to you.'

We agreed to meet at a pub called the Frog and Whistle at nine.

I took Steve's van and drove home to change out of my work clothes before setting off to see Mrs Fanning. I cut across the evening traffic to Guildford and parked on the familiar street.

She welcomed me in like a long lost friend. I liked the night and day difference in her since the last time we'd met. She looked as if she was coming to terms with her son's death and possessed the strength to weather the storm of grief striking her. She sat me down in the kitchen after she'd made us coffee.

'I just wanted to thank you for what you're doing for Alex. I think the safety fund is a fitting tribute to him. I also want to apologize to you.'

'There's nothing to apologize for.'

'Yes, there is. I wasn't very friendly to you when you came over last week and I didn't even thank any of the drivers at the funeral. That was rude. None of you were to blame for my son's death.'

That was debatable. 'Apology accepted,' I said.

Mrs Fanning smiled and we clinked cups.

'I just wish it never happened,' she said.

'We all do.'

'Eric told me about your parents. It must have been tough on you.'

I didn't want to go down this road and I shrugged the comment away. 'It was a long time ago. I was really too young to understand.'

Mrs Fanning seemed to realize I didn't want to talk about my parents and nodded.

'I wanted to let you know that I'll be taking Alex's place in the Formula Ford Festival. It's part of the tribute Vic Hancock is putting together for Alex.'

'That's wonderful. I'll let Eric know. He's away on business at the moment. I'm sure he'll want to attend.'

I hoped they'd think it was just as wonderful after they saw Hancock's tactless decals.

Mrs Fanning finished up her coffee. 'Would you like to see Alex's things?'

I nodded and she led me to the garage. Amongst the usual clutter was Alex's racing gear, equipment and tools. He had a comprehensive collection of everything someone embarking on racing needed from setting-up equipment and specialist tools to essential replacement parts.

'Eric, Jo-Jo, Alison and her father emptied out Alex's rented garage. Is any of this of use to you? You don't have to keep it, but I'd like it if you'd take it.'

Obviously, she had a need to be rid of these final reminders of her son's death. I smiled. 'If I can't use it, I know someone who can. Thank you.'

'Please keep some of it for yourself. You deserve something for your time.'

She opened the garage door and helped me load the stuff into the van. I earmarked items I'd keep for myself. The wheels and tires were a must. Alex's camber/caster gauge was a more professional one than I owned. The collection of bearings and CV joints would also come in handy.

Just as we finished loading up the van and I'd divided what I'd keep and give away, something occurred to me. 'Where's Alex's petrol can?'

'I don't know,' Mrs Fanning said. 'I don't see it. Are you sure we didn't load it already?'

Another thought struck me, one that unnerved me. 'What colour was his petrol can?'

'Red, I think.'

The Frog and Whistle was a gastro pub not far from Alison's home in Richmond. I arrived at nine p.m. as arranged and she was already waiting outside for me when I pulled up in the van. She smiled and waved. I liked seeing her happy and being responsible for it.

'You didn't have to wait outside. It's freezing.'

'I wanted to. C'mon.'

The Frog and Whistle was busy and loud inside, which made it easy for me to speak freely. The barman handed us menus. Alison went for the chicken pasta. They had chilli con carne, so

I jumped on that. I'd developed a thing for Mexican food when Dad had flown us out to Mexico City for an invitational race the year before he and mum died. We'd gone out there as a family and I'd taken to the food like a burro to hard work. We grabbed a table next to the fireplace from a departing couple. The pub instantly melted the chill I'd gotten from driving the inadequately heated van.

'Why so serious?' she asked.

'Confession time.'

This failed to dampen her good mood. She just eyed me with a you'd-better-tell-me look. I liked this about her. She was simple and straightforward. It made a welcome change from all the confusion that surrounded me.

'Vic Hancock has asked me to replace Alex at the Formula Ford Festival and I've accepted.'

Alison's expression wobbled, but didn't fall. 'Why are you telling me?'

'The decals he wants on the car mention that the car is in memoriam of Alex.'

She said nothing.

'His gesture came over as a little insensitive.'

Alison sighed. 'Vic Hancock isn't exactly Mr Sensitivity.'

'So he hasn't been in contact?'

She shook her head. 'So you want my approval to go ahead?'

'I just wanted you to know. If you don't like it, I'll tell Hancock.'

'It's OK, Aidy. I'm fine with it. You don't have to ask. Look, you're a nice guy trying to do the decent thing. That means a lot to me.' Alison placed a hand on mine. 'You don't have to feel guilty about what's happening. You didn't kill Alex. Derek did. I'm happy to see something good come out of this.'

Our food arrived. I hadn't eaten all day and I tucked in. The chilli wasn't half-bad. Then again, I was half-starved. As I ate, the strange relationship between Hancock and Alex played over in my head and I wondered how far it stretched.

'Alison, was there anything going on between Hancock and Alex?'

'Like what?'

'I don't know. A rift? An argument? Something like that.'

'Not as far as I know. Why?'

'I met with Hancock last week. He thought Alex had told me

something about him or his company, like Alex had given away some secret.'

'Alex never mentioned anything. I know he didn't particularly like Hancock.'

I could see that. They were very different people. Alex was very self-contained. It hardly matched Hancock's brash nature. 'Did anything specific set this feeling off?'

'I don't know for sure, but I think something must have happened in the last few months.'

'What makes you say that?'

'In the past, Alex played nice with him, but since the beginning of the season, he seemed tense around him. It wasn't anything most people would pick up on, but I knew Alex. I tried asking why, but he wouldn't say. He knew I didn't like the racing world and he didn't want to bother me with things I didn't care about.'

'How did Alex and Hancock hook up?'

'Through Alex's dad. Eric and Hancock know each other.'

Mr Fanning and Vic Hancock came over as unusual bedfellows too.

'You should talk to Jo-Jo.'

'Alex's mechanic?'

'Yeah. He'd know better than I would. He'll be at the banquet on Friday.'

Suddenly, Alison lost interest in her meal, choosing to chase her food around the plate.

'Anything wrong?' I asked.

'Why didn't you want me to come over tonight?'

I hesitated too long before deciding on my answer.

'Has something happened?'

'It's probably better that you don't know.'

'I'll make my own decisions, thank you.'

As much as I didn't want to tell her, she was right. 'Someone tried to burn down our workshop Saturday night. Whoever it was wanted to destroy Alex's car.'

The colour drained from Alison's face. 'Was it Derek?'

'No, he sent someone on his behalf. The bastard was wearing a balaclava.'

'Was anything damaged?'

'No. Steve was there to stop it, but he took a beating.'

She shot a hand to her mouth. 'God, is he OK?'

'He'll be OK, but he gave as good as he got. Steve thinks he broke the guy's ribs.'

She shook her head in dismay. 'This has to stop.'

'It will when we prove Derek killed Alex.'

'No. I mean you. You have to stop. You can't get yourself killed over Alex.'

I expected this. It was the reason why I hadn't wanted to tell her. 'I think it's a little late for all that. People know what we're doing. They're going to keep coming after us now.'

'You keep saying *they*. Are there others involved besides Derek?'

'Derek has a lot of friends helping him. Look, I don't want to tell you more because I don't want to put you in danger. Let's talk about something else.'

And we did. We slipped into an easy conversation covering topics from music to movies and everything in between. It put distance between me and my problems, but it didn't make me feel any better for being with her. I was enjoying her company, but I felt I was not only taking over Alex's ride, but his girl too. After a second round of drinks, we called it a night.

'I can drive you home,' I said when we were in the van. 'It's late and it's going to take you forever to get home by train.'

She hesitated for a second before agreeing.

Again, we fell into a comfortable conversation. I made her laugh from time to time as she directed me to her flat. We were laughing so much that I overshot the turn for her street.

'Stop here,' she said. 'I'll walk back.'

I parked under a street light. It bathed her face in an orange glow.

'Thanks for tonight. It seems like forever since I last laughed and didn't feel guilty about it.'

'I'm glad I could help.'

She turned away and her face disappeared in the shadows. 'I miss him, you know. I can't stop thinking about what we had and what we should have had.'

'It's only natural. You'll always miss him, but it'll get better.'

She smiled. 'That's what I like about you, Aidy. You're honest.'

'I just know better, I guess. My mum and dad died over ten years ago. Not a day goes by that I don't think about them. They're my parents and I love them to pieces, but I don't miss them the way I did back then. I always wonder how life would have been s the question about whether the work going on kosher or not,' Dylan said.

n finished up his fag and wandered back inside. back to watching and waiting. Time slipped by with of a lazy summer afternoon. The dashboard clock dnight.

't know how long I can keep this up. Between these d babysitting Archway, this has become a twenty- That's fine when you're the cops, but we aren't. I work today. It's midnight and we're stuck out here.

n't have been on this quest if the police had done people had spoken up. If that had happened, Derek jail and we wouldn't be running around in the ime I tried to prove Derek's guilt, the more compli- mple task became. I liked to think I was doing ositive, but everything that had happened proved I ittle effect on the investigation. All I was achieving those people close to me. 'I'm sorry, mate. I didn't ould go this far.'

hat. I'm not blaming you. I'm just letting you know d.'

tand if you need to back out.'

you should walk away too. This isn't your fight.'

as right, but I'd made it my fight and so had Derek. 'I away. I have to follow it through now. I can't let Derek ith murder and what he did to Steve and Paul.'

ghed. 'I thought you'd say that.'

we'll stick around for another hour. If they're still we'll call it a night. Deal?'

Dylan conceded.

crew beat us to the punch by filing out of the workshop utes later. Their fatigue must have set in before ours. cked up while the rest of the guys left. I didn't move rove off.

s as if we're on,' I said.

was disappointment on Dylan's face. 'Let me come with

you to be my eyes out here.'

it ten minutes before leaving the car just in case anyone

different with them still around. Steve feels more like a dad to me than a grandfather now. He raised me for just as long as my parents had, and he's been there through all the hard times. It doesn't mean my parents mean less to me. It's just that I've grown to love someone else. And you will too in time.'

She leaned in and kissed me on the cheek. 'You're one of the good ones.'

She climbed down from the van and I climbed out too. 'If I'm one of the good ones, I should walk you home.'

It was cold and she leaned into me as we walked up the steps to her flat.

'You want to come in?' she asked.

'No, I have to get back to Steve. I can't have him doing all the work.'

'OK. Thanks for tonight. I had a lovely time.'

She made it sound like we were on a date. I wouldn't have called it that, but I wasn't about to disagree.

'When's the Festival?'

'It begins next Friday, but I'm out in the car Wednesday.'

'Can I come?'

Her request took me a little by surprise. I thought she'd seen enough of racetracks for one lifetime. 'Sure.'

'Good. I'll see you Wednesday.'

I waited until she was safely inside, then headed back to the van with her on my mind. I was really getting to like her and wanted something to happen between us, but it was too soon. Alex hadn't been dead two weeks. It was no time to think about dating his fiancée. If something were to develop between Alison and me, I'd let it happen in its own time. Alison was worth waiting for.

I didn't get far before someone called my name. I didn't know anyone in this part of town. With all that had happened, I should have been on my guard, but with my mind on Alison, my guard was down. Reflexively, I turned around.

It was only Alison's dad. I needed to be smarter in future. I waited for him as he caught up to me.

'Hello, Mr Baker.'

He nodded in the direction of Alison's flat. 'Seeing Alison home?'

'Yes.'

'Did you have a nice night out?' His sarcasm turned the question into something ugly.

'It's not like that. I just had some questions for her.'

'Oh, I see. Just questions. Look, I don't like the way you're trying to ingratiate your way into Alison's life.'

'I'm not.'

'Of course you aren't. You're doing all this for very selfless reasons. You're raising money for Alex, a man you didn't know. You want his car in order to give it a Viking funeral.'

'You've got it all wrong, Mr Baker.'

'I don't think so.' He stepped forward, invading my space and forcing me to step back. I stepped off the curb and fell against a parked car. 'My daughter has just lost her fiancée in a tragic accident. You're probably aware that she lost her sister to a similar tragedy. My daughter is in mourning. She doesn't need some lowlife like you trying to take advantage of it.'

'I'm not.'

He poked a hard, mean finger into my chest. 'I told you once already to leave my daughter alone. I won't tell you again. Do I make myself clear?'

His face was an angry shadow in the darkness. He waited for my answer.

He was wrong, but I knew how it looked. 'You've got it.'

'You make me sick,' he snarled, grabbed my arm and jerked me to him. 'Just stay away from my family. You're not welcome.'

'Dad, what are you doing?' Alison said, rushing towards us.

Lap Eighteen

'I don't like this,' Dylan said for the umpteenth time.

If he was hoping that repetition was going to change my mind, he was mistaken. It just served to turn me off, though I was inclined to agree with him. There was a lot not to like. The butterflies in my stomach told me I wasn't a huge fan of my plan either but I needed to make something happen. I kept my eyes on the road ahead and kept driving.

'You know what is really crazy about this?' Dylan continued. 'It breaks up the team. Here we are on our way to Bristol leaving Steve alone. Déjà vu, anyone? Anyone?'

I couldn't dispute thi
butterflies. Derek's team
vulnerable, especially
Archway Saturday night
been expecting anyone t
same mistake again.

The fragility of our te
on our side, but there wa
close to this had ties conn
have enlisted Alison's help
for her own safety.

'This isn't the way I war
when we're supposed to be
to test the car,' Dylan said.

I stayed silent and Dylan
we reached Bristol, I filled
long distance excursion, I di
drove back to Morgan's work
the cars and parked in the sa
using the same Subaru. I wou
car for another, but Steve's in
friends.

'They like to work late,' Dy

It was after eleven and I'd h
called it a night by now, but they
from the windows and the whin

'I just hope they aren't waiting

Dylan shook his head. 'I dou
cars. They're a small crew. How
It's Tuesday. They couldn't turn t
ready for more.'

We slumped down in our seats
guy I didn't recognize in overalls
from the workshop. He pulled the
and went to one of the three cars p
He grabbed a packet of cigarettes f

Morgan stormed out of the open
you want the whole world to see?'

I didn't catch the cigarette man's
the finger then slammed the roll-up

'That answe
inside there is
Cigarette m
Then we were
all the urgency
ticked past mi

'Aidy, I don
little jaunts a
four hour job.
fell asleep at
This is crazy.'

We would
their job and
would be in
dark. Every t
cated that s
something p
was having
was hurting
think this w

'I know t
where I sta

'I unders

'Maybe

Dylan w
can't walk
get away w

Dylan s

'Look,
working,

'Deal,'

Derek's
thirty min
Morgan l
until he d

'It loo

There
you.'

'I nee

I gave

came back. I looked both ways for any familiar cars before I trotted across the road.

I pulled out my mobile and called Dylan's number. 'Stay on the line,' I said when he answered.

'The same applies to you.'

It surprised me not to see some kind of alarm or security system. I put this down to the workshop trying to keep a low profile. A fancy security system alerts everyone to the fact that there's something worth stealing. It was a theory that worked as long as no one knew what went on here.

The chain link fence and gate surrounding the property weren't going to be hard to scale, but the spiral of razor wire fringing the top was. I tossed a floor mat from the Subaru over the razor wire and clambered up and over the fence without any problems. I yanked the mat off the wire and left it on the ground for my return trip.

'You're getting too good at this crap,' Dylan's voice came over the phone.

I didn't answer him and jogged over to the roll-up doors. Heavy padlocks locked them to the ground. I had a makeshift hacksaw, but I didn't fancy spending ten minutes in the open sawing through the lock.

I went around the side to the rear of the building. I had the choice of a couple of doors, but it meant drilling out the lock. I didn't think the noise would bring anyone, but I didn't want to put my theory to the test. I looked up for my best way into the building – the windows. If a chain was as strong as its weakest link, a building was as secure as its windows. The workshop had a row of narrow windows running underneath the eaves.

'How's everything look?' I asked Dylan.

I heard the crunching of sunflower seeds down the phone line. 'Good,' he answered.

'OK, I'm going in.'

I dragged a couple of rusted oil drums over to the side of the building. The building wasn't tall, just a single storey, and when I climbed on top of the drums, I was nose high to the windows. I thought I'd have to break one of them to get in, but the single-pane windows were old and the wooden frames were rotted. I slipped a screwdriver between the window and frame, then leaned on the screwdriver and the latch on the inside snapped, flying off into the darkness.

I pocketed my tools, grabbed the ledge and heaved myself up. The window only opened so far, making it hard for me to squeeze through. Dylan would have never fitted. I managed to worm my head and chest through the tight gap before I stopped. I pulled out my torch and snapped it on. Its beam fell on a workbench against the wall. No long drop for me.

I pocketed the torch and squeezed the rest of myself through. I made an untidy landing on the workbench, but at least I didn't break my neck doing it.

I found the light switches and flicked them on.

'I'm in,' I said into my phone.

'OK. Make it quick.'

Dylan had been right about the crew's work rate. Of the six cars Derek had offloaded here only three had been worked on and only one of those was close to completion. The car was a BMW 7-series. It had been metallic blue when Derek delivered it, but now it was black. The rear end damage had been repaired and the missing door replaced. The other two cars were going through similar transformations.

I had an idea as to what was going on here.

I pulled out my camera and snapped pictures of the cars, their number plates and vehicle ID tags. The vehicle ID tag on the BMW looked as old as the car, but the rivets holding the plate to the car were brand new. The BMW had another peculiarity. The number plate on the front was not the same as the one on the back. I found a stack of number plates in a box on the floor.

I wished I'd gotten pictures of the cars' particulars before any work began. It would have made proving what was going on so much easier. The BMW was a lost cause. I wouldn't be able to prove anything for certain, but the untouched cars were a different matter. I made a special effort to photograph every distinguishing feature of these cars. If I kept returning every couple of days, I could record their transformation. Then I would have something.

I wanted something else: paperwork. Pictures would prove one side of the story, but paperwork would tell it all. A makeshift office consisting of plywood and Plexiglas filled one corner of the building. Inside was a desk, a couple of chairs, an ashtray filled with cigarette butts, a couple of girly calendars on the walls and the *pièce de résistance*: a filing cabinet. The cabinet wasn't locked, so I went through the drawers. I didn't find anything connected to the six cars out there or Vic Hancock or Derek. It made sense that they'd be running a paperless operation where it counted. I slammed the filing cabinet closed and cursed.

'I've got all I'm going to get. I'm coming out,' I said into the phone.

Dylan said nothing.

I went around the workshop making sure I hadn't left anything out of place. I didn't think Derek's crew was the particularly observant type but I wasn't going to take any chances. I switched all the lights off and climbed onto the workbench to make my escape.

Using the rafters for support, I got myself onto the window ledge. I fed my legs through the window first so I would land on my feet instead of my head and squeezed my body back through the window. It was harder coming out than going in. My clothes kept snagging on the frame, but I made it through and lowered myself down.

I had a certain expectation as to where the drums were. Instead, my feet connected with air. I kept lowering myself and my feet still hung in the air. I looked down. The drums were gone.

Before I could do anything else, a fist drove itself into my left kidney. I yelled out, lost my grip on the ledge and came crashing to the ground. I landed hard on my feet. Pain crackled up through my legs and into my groin. I lost my balance and came down on my back.

A heavy shoe pinned me to the ground by my neck and a torch beam blinded me.

I wasn't going down like this. I grabbed the foot, lifted it up and twisted. My assailant wasn't expecting that and toppled back.

I flipped over onto my front then onto my feet, ignoring the tingling in my legs. I rushed my assailant then stopped when he spoke.

'Don't add resisting arrest and assault to breaking and entering,' Detective Brennan said.

Lap Nineteen

I helped Brennan up. He brought out a pair of handcuffs and made a circling gesture with his torch. I turned around and he snapped the handcuffs around my wrists. The seriousness of my situation sunk in when the clamp of steel bit into my skin. I'd screwed up. I was under arrest. God, I was stupid. My head dropped involuntarily.

Brennan leaned in close. 'This a new experience for you?'

I said nothing.

'Don't worry, you won't have to go through it alone.'

He didn't have to elaborate. He had Dylan. It now made sense why Dylan hadn't responded.

'C'mon, let's go,' Brennan said with pleasure and shoved me in the back.

He walked me to the main gates. I thought it was going to be interesting trying to get back over the fence while cuffed, but he simply opened the gate.

He grinned at me and jangled a set of keys in front of me. 'It helps when you have the keys to the castle.'

He scooped up the floor mat I'd used to get over the fence. 'Nice touch. Done much of this work?'

'Getting caught is a sign of my inexperience.'

He laughed.

He pushed me through, closed and locked the gate, then dug the torch in the base of my spine and walked me across the street. I looked over at the Subaru. It was still there, but Dylan wasn't. Brennan walked me over to an unmarked Ford Mondeo. I'd seen the anonymous looking car earlier, but hadn't considered it important. Dylan was in the front passenger seat with one of his hands cuffed to the steering wheel. We frowned at each other.

Brennan put me in the back while he re-cuffed Dylan. I looked around for any other cops who were part of this stake-out. I didn't spot any. Brennan should have had backup and shouldn't have had keys to the yard. Suddenly, I had more to worry about than a simple arrest.

He drove us to a nearby police station and walked us through the doors like we were his girlfriends, one on each arm. Besides us, the waiting room was deserted. From behind his protective glass barrier, the duty officer looked at Dylan and me, crossed his arms and twisted his face into a look of disapproval. 'Gifts? You shouldn't have.'

Brennan walked us to the counter and showed his warrant card to the officer. 'Could a travelling brother officer get the use of the cells?'

'Of course.'

The officer buzzed us in and Dylan and I walked through. We followed him to a room where another officer relieved us of our possessions, belts and shoelaces. Brennan's face lit up when my digital camera came out. The cops played up my having a screwdriver, a battery powered drill and hacksaw on me. Seeing the products of my stupidity paraded before me only highlighted the naivety of my plan.

'We have some lovely accommodations for you,' the custody officer joked.

Brennan kept a grip on me. 'I think I'd like to talk to this one first. Can I get use of an interview room?'

'Interview One is free.'

Brennan grabbed the plastic bag containing my possessions and dragged me off to the interview room. He pointed to a seat and dumped the bag on the table. We sat opposite each other in the cramped room.

A stack of sealed cassette tapes sat next to a clunky looking tape recorder at the end of the table. Brennan made no move to record the interview. Instead, he opened the plastic bag and spilled the contents on the table. He sifted through the items like a panhandler searching for gold. He picked up and examined the hacksaw blade with the masking tape wrapped around one end for a makeshift handle. 'I have to admire your persistence, Aidy. You're not one to give up.' He tossed the blade down. 'But it doesn't mean I have to like it. You want to tell me what's going on?'

I didn't. He had me fair and square, but that didn't mean I was about to say anything. I was more interested in how he'd known to stake out the workshop tonight. I put this down to a self-inflicted wound. When Steve had called the other night to tell me he'd been hurt, I hadn't been very subtle in my escape. Someone could have seen me and reported it back to Brennan. It was a pretty safe bet that I'd want a better look. I hated being the predictable one in this relationship.

'Not talking, eh? That's OK. I'll talk. I think it's better that you listen to what I have to say.'

Brennan separated the drill, the hacksaw blade and the screwdriver from the rest of my possessions. 'These I find interesting. Not exactly the tools of an expert burglar, but they're a nice starter kit. The way you got into that building was relatively neat and efficient for a novice. You deserve an A for effort. Where you deserve a resounding F is in what you took.' He poked about amongst my wallet, keys and loose change with the screwdriver. 'You didn't take anything. If you're going to go to all the bother of breaking and entering, you really should add theft to the equation. You deserve a reward for all your endeavours.'

Theatrically, Brennan's interest fell to the digital camera. He cast the screwdriver aside and picked it up. He switched it on and scrolled through the images. 'Hmm, very interesting. Judging by the pictures of you, this seems to be your camera. Why on earth would a thief want a camera at a job?'

Since I didn't have a choice, I endured Brennan's theatrics. He knew the answer already. He just wanted to flex his muscles and that was fine. He'd get around to the point eventually.

'There are some interesting images of vehicles captured here. Trying to get a jump on your racing competition? Except these don't look like racing cars.' He went suddenly wide-eyed. 'Oops. I seem to have accidentally deleted all the pictures you've taken tonight. Sorry, I thought I was scrolling through them. I really wish there was some way of making up for my mistake, but I think you have bigger problems than some lost photographs.' He put the ruined product of my hard work on the table between us.

It was a petty and obvious move on Brennan's part, but it struck a raw nerve in me. I was sick and tired of the mess around me. Cover-ups. Intimidation. Threats. Lies. Protection. Alex was murdered and that wasn't of prime importance to anyone, not even the police. It wasn't right. I lost my grip on my temper. 'You're a piece of work, Brennan.'

'That's Detective Brennan to you.'

'Well, for a detective, you're a pretty shitty one.'

'You watch your mouth, son,' he barked.

I'd gotten to him where it hurt. He boiled underneath, but he kept his rage contained. I shouldn't be pushing the likes of Brennan. He held the reins to my future. But at this point, I had nothing to lose. I'd lost already. I couldn't make it any worse for myself.

'You keep protecting Derek Deacon – why? He's a killer and you know it.'

'I told you already. Mr Deacon is no killer.'

'Yeah, stupid me for forgetting. He's a law-abiding citizen.'

'He is, unlike you. And I don't see what Mr Deacon has to do with the property you broke into. It doesn't belong to him.'

Brennan was baiting me. He was after what I knew. If I hadn't been on my guard, I would have told him about seeing Derek delivering the cars.

'It looks like I made a mistake then.'

'Not your first.'

I didn't like Brennan's smug look, so I removed it for him.

'What's it like being Derek Deacon's bent copper? And does anyone here know? I'm sure they'd be interested.'

Brennan lunged for me with both hands and yanked me across the desk, sending my possessions and my chair flying. I bounced off the floor on my back, my legs slamming into the wall. He kept me pinned to the floor with his foot on my chest.

'You really do need to watch your mouth.'

The door burst open and the duty officer stood in the doorway, stunned by the sight before him.

'Get him in a cell,' Brennan barked.

The play-acting ended there. The duty officer marched me down to the cells. There were no idiotic jokes or jibes, not even any conversation. It was all business. They put me in a cell, locked the door and presumably threw away the key.

The cell was a depressing box consisting of a stainless steel toilet and thin mattress covering a concrete slab jutting from the wall for a bed. I was alone. Dylan was in his own cell somewhere.

I didn't know what came next. A solicitor? A courtroom? A judge? It was a new and different world. I guessed nothing would happen tonight.

I dropped onto the rock hard bed. I should have tried sleeping, but I was too wired. Tonight's work was all for nothing. I had no proof and worse still, Brennan would feed it all back to Derek.

Worst of all, I was looking at a jail term. Probation at best. I leaned back and resigned myself to whatever came next.

The head of steam I'd worked up dissipated and engaged the gears in my head. I hadn't been cautioned. I hadn't been charged. I wasn't positive, but I thought that Brennan was supposed to have had a second officer in the interview room and he should have recorded the interrogation, for his protection as well as mine. Why did he bring us here to this police station and not his assigned station in Chippenham? The answer was simple. He couldn't get away with this in front of his own people. Too many questions would be asked.

Without my watch, I didn't know what time it was, but just as the first signs of dawn were showing through the narrow window, the cell door opened and a disapproving officer filled the doorway.

'C'mon, let's go.'

'Where?'

'I don't care. To whatever rock you crawled out from under. You're free to go.'

I sat there in stunned silence for a moment.

'C'mon, I don't have all day.'

I stepped out of the cell. Dylan stood in the hallway. We shared a sheepish smile.

They led us back to the booking area. All our possessions were returned to us. I was glad to see nothing had gone curiously missing other than my digital photos. No charges were being filed and we were free to go.

Brennan was nowhere to be seen.

The duty officer took us out to the waiting room. It wasn't a joke. We were free. This time, our smiles weren't so sheepish.

'Don't look too pleased with yourself. You should count yourself lucky that the detective decided to show you some leniency.'

'Where is the detective?'

The duty officer slammed the security door shut in our faces. I wasn't about to argue and we walked out.

Brennan stood outside waiting for us with a cigarette in his hand. 'I thought I'd cut you some slack. Let it be a reminder of how close you came to being on the wrong side of the law.'

We said nothing.

'Don't thank me all at once.'

'I won't,' I said.

Brennan laughed. 'Ah, the stupidity of youth. You don't know when you're being given a break. Seriously, don't squander this gift I'm giving you. I don't want you in my business or Derek Deacon's. Is that understood?'

'Why do you keep protecting him?'

The detective took a long drag on his cigarette then exhaled. 'I've got some advice for you and I want you to take it. Leave Derek Deacon alone. Forget all about him. You're interfering in things you don't understand and I can't protect you from getting yourselves hurt.'

'You're protecting us? That's a joke.'

'You look a little older and smarter than our friend here,' he said to Dylan. 'Maybe you can explain the facts of life to him.'

As Brennan walked over to his car, I asked, 'Are you going to give us a ride back?'

He laughed. 'You like to push, don't you, son?'

Lap Twenty

A cab returned Dylan and me to the scene of our botched crime. The Subaru sat parked in the same place, untouched and still intact. Brennan had had plenty of time to put a call into Derek's boys and I half expected to find a smoking husk as our punishment for poking our noses where they weren't welcome.

We looked across the street at the workshop. No one watched us from inside. The place had remained just as intact as the Subaru. Our little night-time escapade had failed to provoke a reaction. There'd been no dawn raid to clear the place out and cover their tracks. We hadn't caused them to lose a moment's sleep. I didn't know whether or not to be insulted.

'That proved to be a less than successful night,' Dylan said.

It was hard to disagree. We had nothing physical to show for our efforts, but a little more of the puzzle had been revealed. Derek was showing exactly how far his influence stretched. Maybe the stories about his links to organized crime were true. He did seem to have friends everywhere.

'Could have been worse,' I said and tossed the keys to Dylan. 'We could still be in jail.'

He snatched them from the air. 'Don't remind me. Let's get out of here before someone changes their mind.'

Dylan's bitterness was hard to miss. I was pushing our friendship to the limit. There was no point in apologizing. It would only be pouring petrol on a fire.

We got into the car and headed home.

I checked my mobile. Steve had left six messages. I woke him up with my call and filled him in.

'Jesus, I was worried sick.'

'I know. I'm sorry. If we could have called you, we would have.'

'I'm just glad you're OK. Now get your arses back here. You're meant to be testing today, if you'd forgotten.'

I didn't argue.

By the time we got back to Archway, it was time to leave for Brands Hatch. Steve had the van packed and ready, including my race gear. All we needed to do was load the car onto the trailer and connect it to the van.

I hadn't slept during the night and I was in no condition to even think about driving on a track, but I had little choice. The Festival was nine days away and I needed track time in the new car. Despite Vic Hancock's connection with Derek, I had an obligation to him as my sponsor to do well. I wasn't in a position to back out on him. It was pretty obvious after our sponsorship meeting he was suspicious of what I knew about his relationship with Alex. Pulling out on the Festival would only validate his suspicions.

We loaded up the car and headed out without a pause for breakfast, which wasn't such a bad thing. I was agitated. The last thing I needed in my stomach was food.

Steve drove. Dylan sat up front, but soon fell asleep. I bedded down in the back of the van with the tools and equipment and rested my head on my kit bag. I thought I was too wound up to sleep, but one minute I was thinking about Brennan and the next Steve was sliding back the van's side door and telling me to wake up, we'd arrived.

I slid from the van and checked my watch. I'd gotten an hour and a half of sleep and felt worse for it. The short nap left me feeling hung-over.

Dylan climbed down from the van.

'You look like shit,' I said.

'Back atcha, buddy.'

'Hey, enough,' Steve barked. 'You've had a crappy night. Big deal. Think of today as an endurance test. If this was a twenty-four hour race, you'd be feeling a damn sight worse. Aidy, you can wake yourself up by checking us in with race control.'

I jogged down the pit lane to get my blood flowing and flush the fatigue out. It didn't help. I wanted to throw up and I was a little bit wobbly on my legs, but I never felt good before I went out on the track, so it wasn't such a bad sign.

I cast a look down the pit lane. All the garages were full. I recognized most of the faces and teams. Of course, all the factory backed Formula Ford teams were present. A couple of the European teams were there getting in some early practice for the Festival. It was going to be a busy test session. Brands Hatch's short circuit, the Indy circuit, isn't much over a mile. Regulations restrict the number of cars on the track to twenty-six. We'd be divided up into timed sessions. It was a sensible approach and it prevented everyone from going out when they pleased. Normally, I found this a pain, but in my current condition it was a blessing. There were two groups and I was in the second group.

By the time I got back to our pit, Steve and Dylan had unloaded the car and wheeled it into the pit garage. They'd even gotten the timing gear out and all the tools set up. We looked professional and ready for action. All we needed was the driver.

I changed in the back of the van. The day was chilly and it felt good to have my flame retardant underclothes under my race suit to keep the cold out.

The officials sent the first group out for their timed session and I wandered out to the service road behind the pit garages and looked up at the sky. The forecast predicted rain, but the sky was relatively clear. It was cold, but if the weather held, it would make for a good day.

'Aidy,' a voice called.

From the far end of the service road, Alison was waving. She wasn't alone. Her father was with her. She was smiling. He wasn't. I groaned. I didn't need trouble before I went out.

I walked over to them and met them halfway. Alison gave me a quick hug and her dad shook my hand and not my throat.

'Thanks for coming out,' I said. 'You didn't have to be out here so early.'

'There's a reason for that,' Mr Baker said, looking embarrassed. 'I wanted to apologize for my behaviour towards you.'

'That's OK.'

'No, it isn't. Alison's told me about what you've tried to do for Alex and the resistance you've received. The last thing you need is me acting like a fool. This is a difficult time for everyone. Alison lost her husband to be and I lost my future son-in-law. But that's no excuse and I hope you'll accept my apology.'

'Of course,' I said and we shook on it.

Alison grinned.

'Part of my apology is that I'd like to offer my help to you. I'm good with my hands.'

'He is,' Alison said. 'He rewired my flat and redid the kitchen at home.'

I remembered Mr Baker's well-equipped garage where I'd collected Alex's car. If he used half the tools he had on the racks, he'd be useful.

'We can always use an extra set of hands. You'll have to do what my grandad says though,' I said with a smile.

'Deal,' Mr Baker said.

I led them back to our pit garage. Things were looking up. I had one less headache to worry about. It lifted my spirits and did more to revive me than a decent night's sleep.

I introduced everyone and Steve orchestrated the last minute tinkering consisting of retorquing the wheel nuts, checking tyre pressures and a spanner check to make sure every nut and bolt was tight.

Steve checked his watch. 'Fifteen minutes before the cars from the first session come in. It's time to fire it up.'

He inserted the key in the master cut-off switch and turned it, then flicked on the ignition. He nodded to me to press the start button. 'It's your car.'

I smiled, leaned in and pressed the starter. The engine turned over a few times before catching. Once it caught, it gathered strength and burbled with pleasure.

'Aw, listen to that,' Dylan cooed. 'That's a dirty, dirty sound. Automotive porn. Pure filth.'

The remark got a laugh out of everyone and for the first time, I was looking forward to today.

Steve left the engine running to get the water and oil temps up and the oil pressure down.

When the chequered flag came out to end the session and the cars began pouring back into the pits, I climbed into the car and belted myself in. Steve handed me my helmet and I pulled it on.

He knelt down next to me. 'Take it easy out there. Don't worry about times. Today is about getting a feel for the car and getting the set-up right for the Festival. Push the car, but don't *push* the car. Be smart. Got that?'

I nodded.

He patted me on the helmet. 'Good lad. Now go make me proud.'

I eased the car out of the garage and joined the line of cars waiting to be unleashed. The second the track marshal gave us the green flag my foot was on the gas. I joined the track, bursting through an invisible membrane separating racing from the real world.

As I came around to complete my first warm-up lap, Steve leaned over the pit wall with my pit board to show me where to look for my lap times. Alison was with him with a stopwatch in hand. I liked seeing her there.

At Steve's request, I took it easy for the first couple of laps. The Mygale was stiffer and more unforgiving than my Van Diemen. Having a fresh engine at my back made the cocktail even more volatile. I let cars overtake me to find a gap in the traffic. I wanted some alone time with the car to feel it out. Despite its skittish feel, it was predictable, so I went for it. I made a target out of the pack of cars ahead. While they got in each other's way, too eager for that flying lap, I steadily reeled them in. The lap times came down. They weren't mind blowing, but they were respectable. I came in at the end of the session to a row of smiles.

'You looked good out there,' Steve said. 'Where do we need to make improvements?'

Steve tinkered with the set-up, adjusting the anti-roll bar settings and ride heights. When I went out for the next session, he put Alison and her dad on the pit wall to record lap times while he and Dylan took up positions on different bends around the circuit to watch my performance on the corners. Their reports and the improved set-up brought the times down. At the end of my fifth session, I was consistently lapping a second and a half faster than my personal best around Brands. I didn't know if it was the new car, the new engine, the feeling of a solid budget behind me, sleep deprivation, or the support of my friends, but whatever it was, it was working.

By three o'clock, I was done. I still had one more session available, but fatigue had gotten the better of me. I brought the car in and found Vic Hancock in the garage chatting with Alison and her dad. He'd promised to drop by and while I needed him I didn't have the wherewithal to deal with him. I climbed from the car and pulled off my helmet.

Hancock held up my lap time log. 'These are good. I'm impressed. You are a chip off the old block.'

His praise was honest enough, but it sounded a little forced.

'It's been a good day,' I said.

'It's been better than good,' Alison said. 'Steve said you're only half a second off the times put up by the factory backed teams.'

Half a second doesn't sound like a lot, but over the course of the twenty-lap final, that's a ten second deficit. Around Brands, ten seconds equates to a little over a fifth of a lap which is around a quarter of a mile. Half a second was a lot to be off the pace, but it was promising after my first run out in the car.

Steve and Dylan wandered in from their watcher's posts.

'You looked a little shaky out there,' Steve remarked.

'I think I'm done for the day. Let's pack up.'

Mr Baker groaned as he picked up a toolbox.

'You OK?' Alison asked.

'Yeah. Just getting old. I'm not used to being on my feet this long.'

'It happens to us all. Let that be a lesson to you youngsters,' Steve said. 'How many laps did he get in?'

'Forty-nine,' Mr Baker said.

'That's a good number. You won't need that many next time out to dial this car in.'

I unzipped my suit and had started pulling it off when Steve stopped me.

'Stay suited up. The weather's closing in. I know you're tired, but if it rains, it'll be worth knowing how this car handles in the wet. You know there's a good chance it'll rain at some point during the Festival.'

It was good advice, but I just wanted a shower and something to eat.

'I'm pleased to see you're taking an interest,' Hancock said to Alison. 'I wanted to honour Alex as best I could.'

Alison stared at the decal dedicated to Alex on the side of the car. 'It's very nice and it's why I'm here to support Aidy. He's been so good to us.'

'Look,' Hancock announced, 'to mark the end of a successful day, I'd like to take everyone out to dinner. There's a great pub restaurant not far from here. What's everyone say?'

No one declined and I saw the opening I was looking for.

'One problem. I don't fancy the risk of parking the car on the back of the trailer in a pub car park and we can't leave the van and trailer here.'

'I could stay with the van while you eat,' Steve suggested.

'No,' Hancock said. 'I wouldn't want that. Tell you what, one of my salvage yards isn't too far from here. It's secure. You can park it there then collect it afterwards.'

I smiled. Fortune, bless her, was shining on me. It was about time I saw what Hancock kept on the other side of high walls. 'Sounds great.'

The rain didn't come, so I didn't go out again. While everyone loaded the car up, I washed up as best I could in the men's room. God love him, Steve had packed a clean set of clothes in my kit bag and they felt as good as an hour in the shower.

A message got back to my body that it wasn't needed for a while and it went into sleep mode. It had burned a lot of energy on the track and it was done. My legs weighed three times their normal weight as I trudged back to the pit garage.

The car was on the trailer and the tools in the van. Everyone was packed up and ready to go.

'You're going to sleep well tonight,' Steve said looking me over.

I nodded sleepily. I could have gone to sleep right there and then, but I had to keep it together for the next few hours. I needed access to Hancock.

Hancock led the convoy to the salvage yard. I rode in the van with Steve and Dylan while Alison and her dad followed in their car. Minutes into the drive, I knew we were going to the yard we'd followed Derek to. I smiled, pleased with this twist of luck.

Dylan saw it and frowned.

The yard was deserted by the time our convoy arrived. Hancock unlocked the gates and Steve drove us into the vast automotive graveyard.

'The car's in good hands,' Hancock said waiting for us at the gate. 'No one gets in here who isn't invited.'

The joke rang hollow.

Steve, Dylan and I got into Hancock's car while he locked the gates.

Hancock drove us into the depths of Kent to a place called The Long Barn. The place lived up to its name. It was a long, brick building with a steep gabled roof. It was easy to tell the place had been a barn a long time in its past. Above the tall door was a stained glass window where the hayloft must have been.

The pub made up the front half of the place with the restaurant in the rear. Both halves were packed. Hancock walked in like he owned it. He had a quick word with someone and we were immediately seated.

There was no Mexican food on the menu, but they did have a steak and Guinness pie and a good pie is my other Achilles heel. The food was great and so was the company. Hancock behaved himself by not drinking too much. He acted like the benevolent uncle I never had, telling impressive stories about himself, and as much as I didn't want to like them, I did. He was an endearing character. It helped everyone open up. Steve held court for a while with his stories about working for Lotus. Alison reminisced about Alex in a way that brought a smile to her face instead of tears. It looked as if her mourning period was passing. I hoped I'd helped in some respect.

'Aidy, what are your motor racing aspirations?' Mr Baker asked.

'Yeah,' Hancock said. 'Do you hope to emulate your old man?'

'I just hope to be half as good as him one day.'

'Don't sell yourself short,' Alison said.

'I'm not. Dad was an amazing driver, a rare breed – a natural. I'm not.'

'What do you mean?' Mr Baker asked.

'I remember when I was little and Dad took part in a Formula Three race at Spa in Belgium to cover for an injured driver. He'd never driven an F3 nor had he driven at Spa. The first time he set foot on the track was when he went out for morning practice, but he secured pole position.'

'And he won the race,' Hancock said.

I nodded. 'Put Dad in any car at any track and within five laps, he had the measure of both. I can't do that.'

'And your dad couldn't tell you how he did what he did,' Steve said. 'Rob was a great instinctual driver, but he was a terrible test driver. He had no idea how to help the pit crew make the car better. You're different, Aidy. You have a good engineering head on you. You know exactly what has to be done to improve the car.' Steve patted me on the back. 'You're not your dad, but you're just as good as your dad.'

'To the Westlakes,' Hancock said, raising his glass. 'Father and son, may they keep burning rubber.'

'To the Westlakes,' everyone said, completing Hancock's toast.

The dinner broke up after that. Hancock paid the bill after a swarm of protests and we filed out into the car park.

'We have to go,' Alison said.

'My wife will be wondering where we've gotten to,' Mr Baker said. 'We've had a great day and thanks for letting us help. We chatted in the car over here and we'd like to continue helping you. It would make for a nice tribute to Alex.'

'Sure. Of course,' I said. 'I'll probably test the car again midweek before official testing for the Festival. I'll let you know where and when.'

Everyone said their goodbyes and we watched Alison and her dad drive off before following Hancock back to the salvage yard. He opened up again and parked behind the trailer as we climbed from the car.

The yard was silent. Rusting hulks sat atop each other. Dismantled doors, bonnets, boot lids and hatchbacks hung off racks divided up by make and model. With all the surrounding businesses closed for the night, the silence stretched beyond the confines of the yard. I felt that if I screamed, no one would hear.

'Well done, Aidy,' Hancock said, 'and I'll see you soon.'

'Do you think you could give us a tour while we're here?'

'What, now?'

'We are here and it would help me. *Pit Lane* magazine is going to be interviewing me about the Festival.' They weren't but it was a plausible lie. 'It will be good if I can sound knowledgeable about Hancock Salvage.'

My appeal to Hancock's business side worked. He locked the

yard gates and led us into the offices inside a large warehouse. We stood in a spacious waiting room while Hancock disappeared inside the building to deactivate the alarm system.

'What are you doing?' Dylan asked.

'I want to see what happened to those cars Derek transported out here on Saturday. OK?'

'Last night almost had you on your way to prison,' Steve said. 'Can't you leave it alone for one day?'

I felt the weight of Steve and Dylan's disapproval squeezing me, but I wouldn't be dissuaded. 'This is different. We're not in Derek's territory. Brennan isn't acting as his eyes and ears. Hancock is the weak link out here. He's vulnerable and that's good for us.'

Neither Steve nor Dylan said anything. Their silence spoke volumes. They knew I was right.

'I won't need to do much. I just need to find something on those cars Derek transported. Just follow my lead, OK?'

'I'm with you,' Dylan said.

'OK,' Steve said, 'but on one condition. The second I don't like what's happening, I'm pulling us out.'

'Thanks.'

Hancock appeared in a doorway. 'Come through here and I'll show you how everything works.'

We followed him into an open plan office filled with workstations.

'Essentially, I buy write-offs from the insurance companies and low end trade-ins from car dealerships. I break the vehicles down for parts and classify them so individuals and repair shops can buy the parts. What can't be salvaged is crushed and sold for scrap.'

'You auction cars too?' Dylan said.

'Yeah. We act as auctioneers for dealerships, municipalities and individuals who want to offload their unwanted vehicles.'

'Do you ever auction the write-offs?' I asked.

'We have. Half the cars classified as write-offs are totally good cars. The damage is cosmetic but the parts and labour make it cost-prohibitive for the insurance companies to repair them. We can fix them up. The down side is we have to register the cars as recovered vehicles and we can never get their real value at auction. We do it from time to time, but not often.'

'Could you walk us through the process from write-off to salvage?' I asked.

Hancock didn't look keen but he agreed. He fired up a computer and launched an inventory program that logged the cars entering Hancock Salvage.

'Has anything good come through recently?' Steve asked.

'Got any 7-series BMWs?' Dylan asked. 'I've had my eye on one of them.'

I thought Dylan was pushing a little too hard to the point of cluing Hancock in to our motives, but he played along. He ran a search for BMW 7-series and four popped up. I looked for the one I'd taken pictures of in Bristol. It was there, third one on the list.

'Take your pick,' Hancock told Dylan.

'I like that one,' Dylan said and pointed to a red one and not the one I'd seen. 'Complements the colour of my eyes.'

Hancock double-clicked on the red BMW's details. It listed all that had happened to the car since Hancock had received it. 'It's gone, my friend. You wouldn't have wanted it. It was a wreck according to this.'

I didn't want to fixate on the BMW too much or we might alert Hancock. 'So what happened to that car then?'

'This way,' Hancock said and led us out of the office and into an area of the warehouse with clean and well-equipped service bays. 'The car would have been brought here and my guys would have stripped it for everything we could get – engine, headlamps, mirrors, seats, steering wheels, bumpers, doors. Basically, anything that wasn't damaged. The small stuff goes into our warehouse and the big stuff goes out in the yard. You saw the racks with doors and bonnets on them.'

Hancock ran a very smooth operation. It was easy to picture the salvage business as a dirty business run by guys covered in grease and dirt, but Hancock had a twenty-first century grasp on the business. He'd taken the supermarket approach to selling scrap. It was pretty impressive.

'That's how you deal with the meat,' Dylan said, 'but what do you do with the bones?'

'We crush them.'

'You have a crusher here?' Dylan asked with boyish enthusiasm. 'I've always wanted to see one of those things.'

'Well, let's go see it. It's not anything special, so don't get too excited.' Hancock walked over to one of the bay doors and hit a button. It rolled up into the roof.

'Don't spoil it. It must have some awesome force to squash a car into a three foot cube.'

Dylan played the dopey friend to a tee. It gave me the opening I needed.

'I'll give it a miss,' I said. 'Can I use your toilets?'

'Sure. They're back in the office, next to the reception area where I brought you in.'

The second Hancock, Steve and Dylan were out of sight, I sprinted back to the offices. I ignored the men's toilet for the computer Hancock had left on. I closed the file he'd opened and double-clicked on the dark blue BMW I'd seen Derek drive out of here. The notations on the file said the car couldn't be salvaged and was crushed in 'as-purchased' condition.

I searched for the other cars I'd seen transported from the warehouse. They all had the same notation: Unsalvageable condition. Crushed in 'as-purchased' condition.

I stared at the innocuous sounding statement. It sounded so believable. But none of it was. It was a deception. Was I looking at the information that got Alex killed? If I was, then I'd just made myself a bigger target.

'You're a big fat liar, Vic.'

Lap Twenty-One

On Friday night, Steve, Dylan and I got dolled up in suits and ties for the Clark Paints Formula Ford Championship banquet. The banquet was being held at the Priory House, a fairly plush hotel a few miles from the Stowe Park circuit. The championship trophy was being officially presented along with the other awards. As a top ten finisher in the overall standings, I would be receiving an award and prize money. Also, Myles was going to announce how much money had been raised for the safety fund. These were all good reasons to attend, but I had a different reason for going. I wanted to dangle a fresh carrot in front of Derek to draw him out. It had to be something big enough to lure him out from under the umbrella of Brennan's protection. It was about time he came after me on my terms.

We took the Capri. Steve drove with Dylan alongside him while I rode in the back. Nobody talked. We were getting to the sharp end of things and we knew it. Everybody was lost in their own thoughts, which was fine with me. I wanted to think and I spent the drive staring out the small window on my side.

Hancock had been on my mind since we'd visited his scrap yard. He'd given me another piece of the puzzle. He was fixing up high end cars written off by the insurance companies, then selling with new identities. Derek was transporting the cars and his mates were doing the makeovers. Brennan provided protection. The last part of the puzzle was how these cars were getting sold. For that, I needed to follow the cars when they left Morgan's workshop.

I wondered how much money was at stake. A lot, if this operation was a regular thing. If Alex knew what I knew, it could be the reason Derek killed him. Hancock couldn't afford to risk his business empire. Brennan had his career to lose. So, if Derek was the bullet, who'd been the trigger man?

Steve pulled into the hotel's car park.

'Everybody knows their cover stories?' I asked.

'You realize how dangerous this is going to be if Derek goes for this?' Steve said.

'I do.'

'Then we just get in there and do it before I lose my bottle,' Dylan said.

'Then let's do it. We have a job to do.'

The banquet was being held in the hotel's ballroom and we followed the signs to it. It was a big room that contained a stage, thirty or so circular round tables, dance floor and a bar. A banner hung above the stage announcing, 'Congratulations on another great year of racing.'

We'd arrived early, but the room was already bustling with people. I recognized not only drivers and mechanics, but their wives and girlfriends. Circuit officials, timekeepers, scrutineers and marshals were also in attendance. It was fun to see these people decked out in suits and evening dresses. You won't see anyone in their Sunday best on race days. I never thought they could clean up so well.

Some had taken to the dance floor where a DJ provided suitable mood music and commentary from his setup. Some had taken their seats, but most were clustered around the bar set up in the far corner.

Myles was on the stage arranging the trophies with his wife, Eva, when he spotted me. He jumped down, cut across the room and snagged my arm. 'OK, I have you and your guests at table four in the front. I need you close for announcements.'

He didn't give me a chance to answer before rushing off to bend someone else's ear.

'I don't see Derek around, so let's mingle,' I said, 'and spread the word.'

I set my sights on the bar and cut across the dance floor. Dylan took a lazy route to the bar, while Steve headed towards the tables to hit up people there. I scanned the faces for someone to home in on, but I checked for the enemy too. I didn't see Derek or any of his friends, making it the perfect time to get the word out.

I wasn't planning to confront Derek directly. Instead, I thought I'd take a page out of his book and let the community do it for me. The viral effect worked well for him when he wanted to spread gossip and incite rumour, so it should do the same for me.

I spotted Paul standing at the bar and I worked my way over to him. He looked pretty good compared to the last time I'd seen him. The swelling had gone down and his bruising had faded to a sickly yellow-green, which the muted ballroom lighting hid well. The barman placed an open bottle of Guinness and a brandy in front of him and he handed over cash.

'Hey, Paul. How are you doing?'

Paul told the barman to keep the change and walked away without acknowledging me. I guessed he'd be somebody else who wouldn't be sending me a card this Christmas.

I asked the barman for a lager that I didn't want and watched Paul walk over to Chris. Chris took the brandy and listened to Paul before cutting me a nasty look and ushering him away. I wouldn't be receiving the friendly service I was used to getting from Chicane's anymore.

Graham Linden moved in next to me. Graham was the perfect person to get a rumour going. He'd been oh so eager when Derek wanted everyone to know about his intention to kill Alex. I expected him to show me the same level of affection he'd showed me at

Stowe Park when Derek appeared, but he was the first person to show any signs of being pleased to see me. He patted me on the back.

'Good to see ya, Aidy,' he said and ordered a round of drinks.

'You seem happy.'

'I am. Got a new sponsor today, so I'm back in business for the new season.'

'Very nice.'

The barman lined up Graham's drinks and I helped him carry them through the crowd.

'I've got some news,' I said, more than a little conspiratorially, but Graham failed to pick up on my tone. He seemed to be riding a beer haze.

'Really? Good for you.'

'I've got a tape of the race.' I didn't have to say which one.

The remark caught him off guard and he pulled up short. 'What?'

People slid past us, not listening, just in a hurry to get to the bar.

'I put the word out that I was after a recording of Alex's crash and some spectator sold me the tape. It cost me fifty quid, but I don't care. I've got the tape. I know what happened.'

It was all lies, of course. There was no spectator with a recording. I just needed word to get back to Derek. Being the bull that he was, he'd come charging for me without thinking and I wanted that. I needed him to incriminate himself. Once he did that, the wall of silence he, Brennan and Hancock had put up would come crashing down.

'If you want to talk about what you saw, Graham, I want to listen. It's OK. Nothing will happen to you when I take the tape to the police next week.'

Graham went white. 'I don't want anything to do with it. Give me those.' He snatched the drinks from my hands, slopping some of the contents on the floor. 'I told you before I didn't see anything and I'm not saying anything.'

That wasn't completely true. Graham wouldn't say anything to me, but he would to everyone else. He wouldn't be able to help himself. He'd tell others and it would get back to Derek. I watched him scurry off in the direction of his wife and presumably, his new sponsor.

I also managed to slip the videotape story to a marshal before

Derek arrived. Derek walked through the doorway with his wife, his usual trackside cronies, Morgan and Strickland, and Vic Hancock. I expected Hancock to be a little subtler than that. But maybe he didn't have to be anymore.

'Now the party can really start,' he called out and got a rumble of cheers and applause.

I caught Dylan's eye and we regrouped with Steve. 'How'd you do?'

'OK,' Dylan said. 'I told the Hansen brothers.'

'I told a couple of mechanics,' Steve said.

'I got to Graham and a marshal. Hopefully, that's enough for now,' I said. 'Let's not be so blatant now that Derek's here.'

A couple of minutes later, Myles climbed onto the stage, grabbed the microphone and told everyone to find a seat.

We worked our way across the room to table four. Name cards marked where we'd be sitting. We were sharing the table with Vic Hancock, the Fannings, and Alison and her dad. Myles had seated me between Steve and Alison.

The Fannings arrived with Alison and her dad. All of them looked somewhat sad, but they were also smiling. The mixed emotions made sense. This was a proud, yet melancholy moment for them all. We shook hands, Mrs Fanning and Alison hugged me and we all sat down.

Alison looked stunning in her cocktail dress. She'd put her hair up, which revealed a slender neck and highlighted the elegance of her face. I noticed she still wore her engagement ring and I felt guilty for admiring her.

She looked at me and smiled. I felt her warmth, but Hancock ruined the moment with his arrival. He went around the table pumping everyone's hand. 'Nobody has to put their hand in their pocket tonight. This is a special night and Hancock Salvage is picking up the bill. OK?'

Hancock wasn't afraid of splashing cash around like it didn't matter, but in his case it didn't.

Myles remained on stage waiting until everyone had found their seats. 'We've got a lot to get through tonight and we will. I just want everyone to relax and enjoy the proceedings. We'll start with dinner and over dessert we'll make the presentations. So enjoy.'

Myles left the stage to applause and took his seat. His table was next to ours, consisting of his wife, a couple of his right hand people from the track, and representatives of Clark Paints. On the other side of us was Derek's table. I didn't know if it was coincidence or intentional, but he sat with a direct view of me.

Dinner was served. It was pretty good for a catered event. Just as the dinner plates were being removed, Myles returned to the stage and the DJ killed the music.

'Before we get down to the awards tonight, we have a couple of announcements. As we all know, Alex Fanning died tragically at the last race.'

I looked over at Alison. Her head was down.

'Something good came out of Alex's death and that was the safety fund. We're announcing the total tonight.'

There was a round of applause.

'Can I please have Alex's parents, Alison Baker and Aidy Westlake to the stage?'

We joined Myles. Mr Fanning stood proudly. Mrs Fanning wiped a tear from the corner of her eye. Alison looked small and vulnerable and I wanted to hold her and tell her it was going to be OK. Mrs Fanning clasped hands with her husband and Alison, then Alison reached over and took mine.

Camera flashes caught us in the face. I recognized the photographers from *Motorsport News* and *Pit Lane* magazine.

'This safety fund is the brainchild of Aidy Westlake, no stranger to the racing world and the tragic price it sometimes demands. I'd like him to read the amount raised.'

I stepped forward and took the envelope from Myles. I ripped it open and read the handwritten figure on the card. I couldn't believe the amount. I cast a look Myles's way and he nodded to confirm the total.

'The amount raised so far is fifty-two thousand, seven hundred and twenty-five pounds,' I said into the microphone.

A cheer erupted around the room. The Fannings hugged each other and Alison. I couldn't disguise my joy. So much could be done with that money. Some serious improvements could be made to paramedic crews at the track. It was just a shame at what cost.

Myles took the mic from me. 'I like how he says, "so far".' We're still taking donations and I would love to see that figure double by the beginning of next season.

'Seeing as you've started this, Aidy, I think you should finish it. I hope you will oversee how these funds are administered.'

'Of course,' I said.

Myles and Mr Fanning shook my hand. Mrs Fanning engulfed me in a hug that I didn't think I could recover from. Alison kissed me on the cheek.

Mr Fanning took the mike from Myles. 'I just want to say thank you to everyone who contributed. Nothing will make up for losing my son,' Mrs Fanning slipped an arm around her husband's waist, 'but you people, this community, have gone a long way to filling the gap in our hearts. I want to thank you all.'

We walked off the stage to a standing ovation and deafening applause. Many in the crowd were palming away tears.

Mr Fanning slipped an arm around my shoulders and whispered. 'Thank you so very much, Aidy.'

I didn't deserve my thanks until Derek was behind bars.

'OK,' Myles said. 'Let's get down to this year's championship.'

Myles talked up the championship before announcing Derek as the winner. He lifted the trophy off the table as Derek climbed the steps to the stage. Derek took the trophy and hoisted it into the air before taking the mic from Myles. 'It's great to claim my tenth championship, but I wish I hadn't won under such sad circumstances. I would give this title up for another year to compete against Alex.'

The room cheered for Derek. He was the hero again, after all he'd done and said. The man was a killer and people were chanting his name. I glanced over at Alison. She was clapping, but she didn't appear to be buying the lie Derek was selling, judging from the disgust on her face.

Myles handed out the awards for the top ten finishers. Mr Fanning went up to collect Alex's second place award and I collected my sixth place award. I stared at the certificate acknowledging my achievement and the sealed envelope with my prize money inside. I should have been proud, but the recognition felt empty.

'OK, now,' Myles said. 'This year's spirit award goes to the person who gave their all for the championship. This can be given to a driver, a team member or even a course official. The winner this year was decided by myself and a small panel and we thought it fitting that the spirit award went to Alex Fanning. He is one person who gave everything to this passion we call motorsport.'

At Mr and Mrs Fanning's urging, Alison went up to collect the award. Myles handed her the trophy and the mic.

'Thank you very much for this. I think Alex would be very proud to have received this, but I think he would have agreed he didn't deserve it. I'll be honest. I've never understood motor racing. Going around in circles never made any sense, until now. His death has shown the true character of the motor racing people.' Alison's gaze aimed like a gun barrel on Derek. The man didn't even flinch. 'They will reap all they deserve.'

I stood up and applauded for completely different reasons than everyone else in the room. Alison was magnificent. Not even someone like Derek scared her. It made my decision to follow this to the end more important than ever.

'Great speech,' I said when she sat down.

'Thanks,' she said.

Myles called up Mr Fanning to show off the trophy for the Alex Fanning Memorial Trophy race and explain the rules for it. Then the formalities were done and Myles told everyone to enjoy themselves.

The room broke up after dessert. The music returned. People switched tables to chat, hung out around the bar and the more adventurous danced.

Quite a few people came over to the table to shake hands with the Fannings, Alison and me. A huge group crowded around Derek. Dylan went off to the bar and I saw him chatting up one of the timekeepers. Hancock got entrenched in conversation with Myles. I had the feeling Myles was trying to sell him the idea of taking over as the series sponsor. I'd heard rumours Clark Paints might not be next year's sponsor. The Fannings got up on the dance floor and Alison and her dad soon joined them at Mr Baker's insistence. It was weird watching the four of them up there. This event could have been mistaken for a wedding reception. It was an image of an event never fulfilled.

Steve leaned over to me. 'You like her, don't you?'

I didn't know if he wanted to make me squirm but he was doing a great job.

'She's a great girl. Smart. Young. Pretty,' he said. 'But she's just buried her fiancé. Awkward.'

That was the understatement of the decade. I liked Alison a lot, but what kind of person would I be to make a move on her? Even if she didn't mind, it made me look like an opportunist.

'I get the idea she feels the same about you as you do about her,' Steve said. 'Give it some time. She'll come around when it's time to move on. Just don't blow it. I think she's a girl you should keep in your life.'

'I know,' I said, but it didn't make me feel any better about the situation.

To make matters worse, the music switched up to something a little too up-tempo for the older set and everyone returned to our table. Mr Fanning made some crack about the music and that I should be up there with Alison.

'Great idea,' Steve said.

'No, it's OK,' I said, standing. 'I was just going to get a drink. Can I get anyone anything?'

'No,' Mr Fanning said. 'I'll get the drinks. You dance.'

Alison held out her hand. 'Dance with me.'

'I'm not a dancer.'

'And I'm not interested in excuses. I want to dance.'

I couldn't refuse. She led me out onto the dance floor. I looked over at my table. Everyone looked happy to see us, except for Alison's dad. I didn't blame him. I knew how it looked.

The song changed to something much slower. Alison moved in closer. There was no way of not holding her.

'You need to relax.'

'Sorry.'

'Don't be sorry. Relax.'

I tried, but I felt the gaze of everyone watching us. She caught me looking around.

'Don't worry about them.'

'I don't want anyone to take this the wrong way.'

'Yes, people dancing. I've known it to start riots.'

I smiled.

'See. You are human.'

'I'm sorry.'

'You say sorry again and I'll make you do this all night.'

I felt her smile penetrate me and I said, 'OK.'

'You can't worry about what others are thinking. Everyone has been kind and that's wonderful, but I don't need to be handled like fine china. Remember, no cotton wool.'

Her words took the steel rods out of my back.

'See, you can dance. You liar.'

'OK, I'm a spaz. Can we leave it at that?'

'OK.'

We danced for a minute before we both spotted Derek watching us from the centre of his group, which included Hancock. He studied us with a predator's gaze.

'I liked what you said up there,' I said.

'Do you think he got the message?'

'He got it. Whether he felt anything is a different matter.'

'I can't wait to see that bastard pay.'

'It won't be long.'

'I want him to beg me for forgiveness. I'll never give it, not to the person who killed Alex.'

'Derek's days as a free man are numbered.'

She came close to stopping me. 'How sure of that are you?'

'Very. His secrets can't be kept much longer.'

The song came to an end.

Alison waved at someone behind me. 'You wanted to talk to Alex's mechanic, didn't you? He's here.'

Jo-Jo stood in the doorway. Alison walked me over to him and hugged him. 'You're late.'

'I couldn't get away.'

'Aidy wanted to ask you something, is that OK?'

Jo-Jo shrugged.

'Can we talk outside?'

Jo-Jo shrugged again and I followed him out into the hallway before ushering him into the hotel's lobby bar. I bought him a drink and sat him in a quiet corner of the bar.

'I wanted to ask you about Alex and Vic Hancock.'

'What about them?'

'Their relationship. How did they get on?'

Jo-Jo fixed me with a suspicious stare. 'Why do you want to know?'

'Hancock is sponsoring me for the Festival and he's interested in sponsoring me next season. I just wondered if there was anything I should know.'

'Bollocks. Don't lie to me. I'm not stupid. I know what Derek said that night and I know what you've been up to. If you have a question, ask it, but don't bullshit me.'

This made things easier. 'OK. Hancock wanted to know if Alex had told me anything about him and his business. I didn't have a clue what he was talking about it, but he kept pressing me.'

'Hancock has been sponsoring Alex since he raced karts. Money was never a problem, until about eighteen months ago. Then checks bounced. The money always arrived eventually, but Alex was acting as Vic's credit line in the meantime.'

This wasn't the Hancock I knew. Money had been flowing thick and fast since he came to me. Then again, I knew where he was obtaining his secondary income. 'He doesn't seem to have money problems now. He's been splashing the cash around me.'

'Maybe so, but I know for a fact he struggled paying Alex when he was supposed to.'

'Did Alex know why Hancock was having problems?'

'Maybe, but I didn't know.'

'He never looked into his businesses dealings or financial accounts?'

'No. What makes you say that?'

'I know Alex was an accountant. I thought he might have checked Hancock out.'

'I don't know.'

I was going to leave the questioning at that but I remembered something. 'I've got Alex's car and I've been looking it over.'

Jo-Jo shifted awkwardly in his seat. 'Yeah?'

'I noticed something. The bolts on the rear suspension were bolt head down.'

'What are you saying?'

'Nothing. I just noticed the bolts were mounted the wrong way.'

'Are you saying I screwed up? That I caused Alex's crash?'

'No. I just thought it was strange.'

I spotted Morgan wandering about in the lobby. He hadn't seen me, but he would. My time was up.

'Thanks, Jo-Jo,' I said, rising. 'I really appreciate the talk. Let's get back to the party before we miss all the fun.'

Jo-Jo grabbed my arm. 'Do you know something?'

'Maybe. I don't know. We need to get back.'

Morgan trailed us back to the ballroom. Jo-Jo kept pushing me for answers, but I didn't give him any. I thought it was going to be a problem with Morgan nearby, but Mr Fanning saved me by pulling Jo-Jo to one side for a chat.

It was a relief to sit down with Steve and Dylan. They failed to look as happy as I did.

'What's wrong?'

'Derek,' Steve said.

Derek still held court over in his corner of the room. Graham and the Hansens were with him. The thirty or so people far outnumbered the three of us at our table.

'Do you think Graham or the Hansens talked?' Dylan asked.

'I think someone did,' Steve said.

Derek was laughing and joking, but his gaze was locked on me. He knew. The rumour had gotten to him. Now I would see how he would react.

Lap Twenty-Two

The next morning, it was business as usual for a Saturday. Steve and I worked on the new car and finished checking the set-up. It might seem like overkill but every time the car comes off the track, it needs to have its toe-ins, camber and ride heights checked. Clip a curb and it's more than likely that the alignment has been knocked out a fraction. There's also some general maintenance stuff to make sure nothing's leaking, bent or broken. The car was in good shape and ready for its next outing.

I tried booking another test at Brands Hatch for the coming Wednesday, but they were fully booked. It wasn't surprising. Qualifying for the Festival began on Friday. All the foreign teams would be in town by Wednesday and fighting for track time. I should have booked earlier but all my sneaking around had gotten in the way. All I could do was test elsewhere. It wasn't a great alternative, but better than nothing.

I called around the circuits and didn't have any luck. Except for the Festival, the racing season was over in the UK. The tracks were mothballing operations until the spring. Even Stowe Park had closed its doors for the winter. My only option was Knockhill in Scotland, but that was too far to be practical with the time available.

'Have you called the Hansens?' Steve asked when I explained the situation.

'No. Why?'

'If they've got a track day on, ask them if they'd let you have a run between their student classes.'

After the little ambush they'd sprung on me last time, I wasn't so keen, but I didn't have much in the way of options. I got Tony Hansen on his mobile. He had his last track day of the year on Wednesday. As a favour, he could give me twenty laps. And Tony being Tony, that favour came at the price of two hundred pounds. I wasn't in a position to argue and accepted his generous offer, in spite of the fact that he was probably on the phone to Derek now telling him when and where to find me. I'd have to be extra careful.

'Hello,' a voice called from downstairs. 'Anyone home?'

Steve and I were up in the office and we looked down into the workshop. It looked like my worries about Wednesday were pointless, considering Derek Deacon was wandering through the workshop.

'Stay here,' I told Steve. 'I want you as a witness.'

'To what – your beating? No way.'

'Yes. I'll need someone to call the cops.'

Steve grimaced, but he nodded his agreement.

'I'm here,' I called out and descended the stairs.

By the time I walked into the workshop, Derek was rooting around, picking up tools and putting them down and examining the cars Steve was restoring for his clients. He patted Graham Hill's Lotus.

'You've got some nice wheels here.'

'They aren't mine. They belong to Steve's clients.'

Derek nodded then his gaze fell to my new Mygale. He walked up to it. If he was hoping to scare me, he was doing a good job. He crouched to study the car's lines up close and smiled at what he saw.

'This the car for the Festival?'

The Mygale looked so vulnerable on its stands. One hard shove would send it crashing to the ground.

'Yes.'

'Nice.' He looked around then paused for a second. 'How many Formula Fords do you need?' He laughed. 'It sounds like one of those light bulb jokes. How many racecar drivers does it take to screw in a light bulb? None. Their pit crew would do it for them.'

He laughed. I didn't.

He sidestepped the car to take another step towards me. 'You didn't answer my question, Aidy.'

'I've only got the one.'

'But I see three.'

'I only own one.'

He nodded again. 'That's right. Vic Hancock leased this one for the Festival. And that one,' he pointed at Alex's car under the drop cloth, 'doesn't belong to you.'

He brushed by me to jerk the drop cloth off the car. I didn't bother stopping him. He wanted to make a point and I wanted him to make it. The more he talked the more he incriminated himself.

'Why do you have Alex's car?'

'I'm going to have it destroyed.'

'That's what I've heard, so why do you still have it? It's not that hard to get it crushed. I heard Hancock offered to do it, but here it is. You're not thinking about cannibalizing it for parts before selling it, are you?'

'Christ, no. Of course not.' I didn't pretend to hide my disgust.

'So if you're not stripping the car, then why are you keeping it – to prove I killed Alex?'

There was no point in playing coy anymore. 'Yes.'

Derek rubbed a hand over the tyre burn. 'So, you thought if you kept the wreckage, you'd be able to piece together how I did it. Was that the idea?'

I said nothing.

'How's that working out for ya?'

I still said nothing.

'That good, huh? For that to work, you need my car to line up all the telltale marks. The problem with that is it still wouldn't prove that I pushed him off. You'd need something more substantial to back it up. Wouldn't you?'

'If you say so.'

'I do. I would say you'd need a recording of the crash to prove it.

'That would be helpful.'

Derek grinned. 'I stuck a shotgun in your face and told you to forget it and still you keep clinging to your belief.'

'No shotgun today, I see.'

Derek opened up his jacket to let me see he was unarmed. 'Physical threats don't work with you. I'm hoping that talking to you will make you see reason.'

'So convince me.'

He put the bravado to one side and looked me in the face. 'I didn't kill Alex.'

If that was true, he shouldn't have been frightened of me or what I knew, yet here he was. It looked as if my story about having a tape had worked.

'So it's coincidence that ever since you said you'd kill Alex, people have been protecting you.'

'I have a lot of friends.'

'Friends who go around beating people into silence.'

'I don't know what you mean.'

'Did you see Paul last night? Someone beat the living crap out of him.'

'That wasn't me. I have no reason to hurt Paul.'

'Coincidence again?'

'It wasn't me.'

Derek picked up a five pound mallet, examined it then swung it as if he was limbering up before exerting himself. I held my ground.

'I heard a rumour about a tape of Alex's crash. Do you have it?'

'That's become a rare commodity. The people at Redline destroyed their original. Paul had his copy taken from him after a good kicking. Anybody who has seen it won't talk about it. It's like no one is supposed to see this footage.'

Derek stopped swinging the mallet and gripped it tight in his fist. 'Again, you've not answered my question. I'm trying to be polite here as an apology for the whole shotgun thing. Do you have the tape?'

'Why?'

'Have you seen it?'

'Does me having it make you sweat?'

Derek grinned and the mallet went slack in his hand. 'You haven't seen it. What's the problem – is the person with it asking too much?'

'What makes you say that?'

'If you had the tape, we wouldn't be having this conversation and you wouldn't still be holding on to Alex's car. You'd know the truth.'

'And what's that?'

A crash from the other side of the workshop doors cut off

Derek's answer and shouting followed. I recognized Dylan's voice and glared at Derek. I should have known he would have come mob-handed. When talk didn't work, force had to take over.

I shoved past him for the doors. Derek dropped the mallet and raced after me. I threw the door open. It slammed into Morgan, sending him crashing to the ground. The full shotgun crew was here. Tommy and Strickland held Dylan down. I hurled myself at them, taking both of them down.

Dylan broke free, jumped to his feet and threw a punch at Derek. Derek blocked it and laid Dylan out with a punch of his own.

Tommy put me in a headlock, cutting off my breath, while Strickland drove a fist deep into my gut, dropping me to my knees. Tommy laughed and dragged me to my feet to line me up for some punch bag duty. Strickland duly obliged. I clenched my stomach muscles up to protect myself, but collapsed when he buried a fist low into my gut. I sagged in Tommy's grasp.

Dylan tried to get back onto his feet. We both knew from too many school playground fights that you had to keep on your feet. Stay on the ground and you were prime meat for a kicking party. Derek knocked Dylan back down and pinned him to the ground with his weight.

It left Morgan with no one to fight. He brought out a flick knife and snapped it open. 'We should have taken care of you back there in the field. No one would have found you.'

Tommy and Strickland got drunk on the idea. Tommy rearranged his hold on me, hoisting me onto my toes. Strickland tore open my shirt, exposing my stomach to Morgan's knife.

'Have you ever seen your intestines?' he cooed as he approached.

He didn't get far. Steve burst through the open doorway with a quick-lift jack handle in his hands. The four foot length of pipe made for a useful street weapon.

'No,' Derek yelled out.

Steve brought the handle down on Morgan's forearm, breaking it. Morgan screamed and dropped to his knees, the flick knife slipping from his loose grasp. Strickland gathered up the knife and went for Steve.

The jack handle was big and heavy, making it unwieldy. It would take Steve time to tee up another swing, far more time than it would take Strickland to stab him. I knew it and so did Steve, but he had nowhere to go.

'No,' Derek yelled again. 'Leave him.'

Strickland ignored Derek and kept going. Steve swung the handle to protect himself. Strickland sidestepped his swing.

Derek didn't hesitate. He jumped off Dylan and charged at Strickland and Steve. He dropped his shoulder and slammed into both of them, smothering the attack and driving them both to the dirt.

Tommy loosened his grip on me and my feet touched the ground again. I drove my heel down his shin. He screamed out and doubled up, but didn't release his hold. I drove my elbows into his stomach and he finally let go of me.

Dylan was up and both of us charged into Derek and Strickland who were still piled on top of Steve. Strickland wriggled from under Derek's grasp. He didn't have the knife in his hand. I grabbed him by the shoulders and jerked him back, sending him crashing into Morgan.

Tommy slammed into my back, sending my head snapping back before driving me into the ground.

Derek pulled himself to his feet with the flick knife in his fist. Dylan went for it, but Derek slapped him aside. He grabbed Tommy and peeled him off me, then put the knife under the chin of his own man.

'Enough,' he growled to all of us.

Tommy raised his hands slowly above his head. Derek pushed him away.

Dylan helped Steve to his feet. Despite the pounding they'd taken, they looked OK.

I slowly got to my feet. My neck ached and I felt lightheaded.

Derek pointed the knife at me. 'I didn't come here for this. I just came to talk. Stay away. I don't want to hurt you, but you're giving me no choice.'

There was plenty I wanted to say, but I didn't. I'd gotten the reaction I'd hoped for, but not the result.

Derek threw the knife with frightening skill. It buried itself in the dirt at my feet. 'We're going. Remember what I said.'

Derek gathered up his gang. He half-carried Morgan to his car. Tommy got behind the wheel and drove them away.

'Bloody hell,' Dylan said with an exhale.

With the danger gone, my hands started to tremble.

'You two OK?' I said.

They both nodded.

'You need to get home,' Dylan said. 'They got to the house too.'

I locked up. Steve wanted to stay. I didn't want any of us being there alone, just in case Derek planned on coming back. If he wanted Alex's car, he could have it. It was of no use to me at this point.

Dylan drove us to Steve's house and took us around to the back door. It had been forced open and not too efficiently. Whatever tool had been used to bust the door open had left deep gouge marks in the door and frame.

I pushed the door open and ventured inside. I didn't have to fear anyone lying in wait. They'd been and gone. The place had been turned over. Everything Steve and I held precious lay on the floor – some of it in pieces.

'Christ,' I murmured.

'I came over to see you and found the place like this.'

Steve brushed past me and picked up a picture of him and Gran. There'd be plenty of other mementos in just as bad a condition.

No wonder Derek knew I didn't have the tape. He'd already been here and searched for it.

'I'm sorry, Steve. I didn't think he'd do this.'

'But we should have expected it.'

'All this for nothing,' I said.

'Not for nothing,' Dylan said.

'What?'

'I know when they're moving the cars. I overheard Derek's boys discussing it.'

'When?'

'Tomorrow night.'

I grinned. 'Let's return the favour and crash his party.'

Lap Twenty-Three

The following night found us back in the south-west. The three of us came to a halt two streets from Morgan's workshop. We meant business this time. There wouldn't be a second shot at this. Once the cars were delivered, who knew when another shipment would arrive? We were going to follow the cars to their next point of call, then phone it in to the local police. Brennan's protection only went so far. He might be able to shelter Derek on his turf, but not on someone else's. If all went well, it ended for them tonight. I tried not to think about what would happen if it went badly for us.

We'd driven down in three fresh cars. All our vehicles were known to Derek and his guys. Steve had returned the Subaru and got a Vauxhall Vectra and a Renault Laguna as replacements. Dylan had borrowed his dad's Honda Accord. All three cars were pretty anonymous, but powerful enough to keep up with most things on the road, especially Derek's car transporter. Having three cars gave us lots of options when it came to surveillance. If the shipment of vehicles was hauled over a long distance, one car was going to get noticed, but with three cars we could rotate the tail.

I slid from my Vauxhall into the cold, dank night. I waved Steve and Dylan over. We huddled up in front of my car.

'Everybody still up for this?' I asked.

'I've got my sunny seeds,' Dylan said tapping his jacket pocket.

'I'm serious. Last chance for anyone to back out.'

'We're doing this,' Steve said. 'End of subject.'

'OK,' I said. 'You ready, Steve?'

He nodded and put on his mobile phone headset. I called his number and he picked up the call.

'You're all set,' I said. 'Stay in touch.'

'I will.'

Dylan and I got into my car as we watched him walk towards Morgan's workshop. My heart skipped a beat when he turned the corner and disappeared from sight.

Steve was checking for lookouts. We weren't going to get caught in Brennan's surveillance trap like last time. Out of the three of us, Steve was the only one Brennan didn't know.

I set my phone to speaker so Dylan could hear. 'Anything?' I asked Steve.

'Nope. Nothing so far. No one sitting in cars or hanging around. I'm coming up to Morgan's place now.'

Dylan tracked Steve's progress on a street map with his finger. The map showed the street as being only a few inches long. It looked like nothing, but anything could happen in those few inches.

'OK, Steve?' I asked.

'Fine, son.'

Dylan glanced my way. 'He'll be OK. Don't worry.'

I wished I shared his optimism.

After three agonizing minutes, Steve reported, 'All clear. There's no one out here.'

I breathed easy again. 'How about the workshop?'

'Sunday night is just another work night.'

'Is Derek there?' Dylan asked.

'I don't think so. I don't see anything to transport the cars either. I'd say he hasn't arrived yet.'

'Where are you?' I asked

'At the end of the street.'

'OK. Come back.'

'Steve, don't double back,' Dylan said. 'If you go right and then take your next right, you'll end up back here.'

'See you in a few,' Steve said.

When Steve returned, he knocked on Dylan's window. I powered the window down.

'It looks as if we're good to go, so let's do it,' he said.

Dylan asked, 'What do I do if I need a pee?'

'Use a Coke can,' I said.

Dylan grinned.

'Don't forget,' I said, 'if the can's warm, don't drink it.'

The joke gave us the spurt of energy to get on with the job. The three of us moved into position. I drove the Vauxhall to the workshop and parked in a spot that gave me a clear view. Steve watched from the north end of the street and Dylan covered the south. If anyone entered or left Morgan's workshop, we had it covered.

As soon as I was parked, I called Steve and Dylan to give final instructions. Everyone was to stay off the line unless they saw anything.

My phone sat silent in my hand for a long time. The hands on the dashboard clock inched from seven through to eleven. In all that time, I had nothing to report other than the lights were on inside the workshop and Morgan's people were working. Of course, I doubted Morgan was doing much in the way of actual work after Steve had broken his forearm.

'I hope it hurt like a bastard,' I said within the confines of the car.

I checked in with Steve and Dylan every thirty minutes to make sure they were staying awake. The long wait failed to eat into us. We'd prepared for this night. After the break-in, we spent time putting the house back in some semblance of order, then ordered a takeaway from a local Indian restaurant. We hatched out our plan while we ate. We went to bed late, but slept in late, so we were ready for a long night.

Sitting in the silence of the car, something Derek had said scratched at the back of my mind. He'd said, 'If you had the tape, we wouldn't be having this conversation. You wouldn't be still holding on to Alex's car. You'd know the truth.' I'd know what truth? That Derek was innocent? I didn't believe that for a second. What was bothering me was that he believed in the tape's existence. To him, its existence wasn't a possibility. It was a fact. He hadn't demanded that I tell him who the source of the recording was because he already knew. So my phantom tape story was true after all. It made me wish I really did have the tape. I wondered who was in ownership of the recording and why Derek hadn't kicked down their door to get it. He didn't have any problems doing it to mine when he thought I had it.

My mobile rang, jerking me from my thoughts. Steve's name came up on the small display.

I answered the call. 'What's going on?'

'I've got an empty car transporter coming my way.'

Good, the cars were being transported together. That gave us the advantage. It kept us together and, for once, we outnumbered them.

'Is Derek driving?'

'I can't see yet. Hold on. He's just passing me.' The sound of an approaching diesel engine dominated the background noise coming from the phone for a minute. 'Yes, Derek's driving.'

'OK. Tell Dylan what's going on and I'll call you both back when I know what's happening,' I said, then hung up on Steve.

The engine I'd heard on Steve's phone cut the silence on the street. I powered down my window in the hope of eavesdropping and slumped down in my seat so as not to be seen.

Derek stopped the transporter outside the workshop's gates. The noise of his arrival brought people out to greet him. Morgan was amongst the group of familiar men to emerge from the workshop. His arm was in a cast and a sling. Strickland and Tommy were among the group of mechanics I'd seen before.

Tommy opened up the gates and Derek pulled the truck forward to manoeuvre it into the yard before turning it around. His headlights lit up the parked cars across the street, including mine. I threw myself across the passenger seat before the headlights lit me up.

I stayed down and listened to the grind and growl of Derek changing gears as he manoeuvred the truck into position. I heard voices guide him in. I sat up the second the headlights were off me and I heard the clang of the gates closing.

Light spilled out from the workshop as the roll-up doors retracted. While Derek lowered the loading skids, car engines roared into life from within the workshop. The noise bounced off the silent buildings on both sides of the street. It was enough to draw the attention of the neighbours in a normal neighbourhood, but this part of town was dead and no one came running to complain about the late night disturbance.

I called Steve and brought him up to speed then told him to pass the message on to Dylan.

The cars filed out of the workshop and carefully climbed onto the transporter. They were the same six cars I'd seen before, but now in different colours and sporting number plates and no doubt the documentation to back it up. These cars were reborn the same way people with bent identities were reborn. Illegally.

It took a little time to load the cars onto the transporter and tie them down. Derek and his boys worked well and showed no signs that they were expecting trouble. Not that they would be with Brennan clearing the way for them.

My pulse quickened when a couple of the mechanics started

shutting the workshop down for the night. This was it. This was where Derek put his head through his own noose.

I called Steve then Dylan and told them. 'They're getting ready to go.'

Derek, Morgan, Tommy and Strickland huddled around the truck's cab for a team talk. I couldn't hear them over the rumble of the truck's engine.

The team meeting didn't last long and Derek climbed into the cab of his truck. The others went over to a fairly old C-class Mercedes. Morgan opened the boot and Tommy and Strickland removed three shotguns.

'Shit,' I murmured.

Strickland jogged over to Derek's truck with a shotgun in each hand and climbed up into the cab with Derek. They shared a smile before Strickland put the guns behind their seats. Tommy put his gun in the back of the Mercedes before getting behind the wheel. Morgan got into the passenger seat alongside Tommy.

Derek eased his truck out of the workshop with the Mercedes behind. Both vehicles turned in Dylan's direction.

I jumped on the phone straight away. 'Dylan, Derek's coming your way. There's a green Mercedes following behind. Strickland is riding with Derek and Morgan and Tommy are in the Merc.'

'You want me to follow them?'

'Yeah, but be careful. They're armed.'

'Shit. Why am I not surprised?'

'I'm going to stay here and wait for the mechanics to leave. Then I'm going to catch you up. Call me if you hit any trouble.'

'Don't worry, I will.'

I hung up on Dylan. I called Steve and told him Derek was on the move and Dylan was following, but I needed him to stay put.

The minutes ticked by slowly as the mechanics locked the workshop down for the night. With their work done, they weren't in a hurry to leave. They laughed and joked with each other as they switched off lights and closed doors.

'Come on, come on,' I urged. I didn't want Dylan on his own any longer than necessary. Derek and his boys had him outnumbered and outgunned. It wasn't like my presence would stop them from shooting at him, but it would make it harder for them if they had to shoot at two targets.

The last man out closed and locked the yard's gates then climbed into an old Rover SD1 with the other three mechanics. They pulled away in Steve's direction and I called him.

'A Rover SD1 with a dented rear passenger door is coming your way. Follow it.'

'I see it now.'

'They're the mechanics. I don't know if they're going to meet up or not, but stick with them.'

I heard Steve gun the Renault's engine. 'Will do.'

'I'm going to catch Dylan up. Derek's guys are armed.'

Steve didn't say anything for a long moment. 'Be careful.'

'I will,' I said and hung up.

Lap Twenty-Four

The second I hung up on Steve, I hit the road. Naturally, there was no sign of Dylan or Derek when I turned onto the next street. In this maze of streets with all its different turns, I'd never catch up with them. I punched in Dylan's number and waited for him to pick up.

'Where are you?' I asked when he answered.

'I'm on Newfoundland Way getting ready to join the M32.'

I made a left to get me heading towards the motorway. The M32 was essentially an arterial road from the M4 into Bristol. If Derek picked up the M4 he was either heading east to London or west to the M5. That would take him either south-west into Devon and Cornwall or north to Birmingham.

'Where's Derek?'

'He's about three hundred yards ahead with the Merc behind him. They just got on the motorway.'

'Have they noticed you?'

'No. I've had a pretty clear view of them so I've hung back.'

'OK, I'm on my way. I'm a few minutes behind.'

'Where's Steve?'

'He's following the mechanics.'

It took me ten minutes to reach the M32. Dylan called back twice to tell me they had first joined the M4 going west then the M5 going north. That narrowed down Derek's potential destinations.

Once I got on the motorway, I caught up to Dylan pretty quickly. Half a mile ahead of him, I picked out the car transporter and Morgan's Mercedes. The traffic was light, but heavy enough for Dylan and me to blend in.

I called Dylan. 'I'm behind you.'

'I see ya. How do you want to handle this?'

'Stay as we are. If the traffic thins out, we'll take turns being behind Derek.' My mobile bleeped, telling me I had another call. 'It's Steve. I'll call you back.'

I switched over to Steve's call. 'What's happening?'

'Nothing. These guys were just going home for the night. The driver is the only one left now. I'm following him home.'

'OK. Ditch him and catch up to us. We're on the M5. I've just passed junction fourteen for Dursley.'

'I'll see you soon,' Steve said and hung up.

Knowing Steve was on his way helped settle my nerves. With the three of us back on Derek's tail, we had the flexibility to handle whatever came next.

Steve caught up with us between Stroud and Gloucester. We took turns at being the lead car behind Morgan's Mercedes. I didn't get the feeling that our game of leapfrog alerted Derek or his crew. They seemed to remain blissfully unaware, both vehicles eating up mile after mile, not adjusting their speed or course.

It looked as if we were heading into Birmingham, but Derek led the procession off the motorway into Redditch.

My arms and legs tingled with anticipation and fear. We were a long way from home and I didn't know what to expect next. I just hoped we weren't out of our depth.

I put my nerves on hold and coordinated my next move with Steve and Dylan. Dylan and I were to keep close to the transporter. Steve was to hang back. If Derek stopped, we would blow by and let Steve pick up the action while we waited for his update.

The streets narrowed and Derek slowed down to compensate. We soon ended up on streets where traffic was non-existent. Dylan and I were beginning to stick out, especially since Dylan had been directly behind Morgan's Mercedes for some time. I jumped on the phone to him.

'Pull over. I'll take the lead for a little while. Tell Steve the latest.'

'OK.'

Dylan pulled into a petrol station and I took his place behind the Mercedes.

I felt very alone. Suddenly, it was me versus four scumbags who, together, had killed one person, assaulted and threatened several people, tried to burn down Archway and held me at gunpoint. If they caught me now, I doubted anyone would hold off from pulling the trigger.

Steve called me. 'I just passed Dylan. I'm in the two spot. Dylan's going to take over as tail end Charlie.'

Derek flicked on his indicators to make a left onto a narrow street. 'They're turning off onto Ladbroke Street. I'm letting them go. Pick up my lead.'

'Ladbroke Street it is.'

Derek navigated the tight turn with the Mercedes close behind. I kept going straight. The second they were out of sight, I turned my Vauxhall around and stopped.

Steve came into view moments later. He flashed his lights at me and made the turn.

I stayed on the line with Steve and he talked me through a series of streets. I waited for Dylan to catch up, then we followed Steve's directions. Within a couple of streets, the complexion of the neighbourhood had changed from residential homes to industrial. Address after address was home to ancient factory buildings, but some of the factory sites had been demolished and replaced with modern prefab units.

'Shit,' Steve said over the phone. 'We have a problem.'

'What is it?'

'They've arrived.'

'Where?'

'You'll see. Turn right at Harrington Road and it's two hundred yards on your left. I can't stop. I'm driving by.'

I turned onto Harrington Road in time to see the tail end of Derek's transporter and the Mercedes disappear between a pair of gates not much shorter than the transporter. Only the top of the factory building could be seen from the street. Along with the solid gates, ten foot high brick walls hid the goings-on from the public eye. But none of that mattered. The familiar Hancock Salvage logo covered each gate. Shit was right.

I parked my car a hundred yards down the street from the yard's main gates. Dylan drew up behind me and got into my car. I set my mobile to speaker so Steve could hear us.

'I can't believe we've come all this way and we can see bugger all,' Dylan said.

'Steve, can you see any low points?'

'No, that wall goes all the way around.'

'Let's call the cops in,' Dylan said.

'And tell them what?' I said. 'We don't know what's going on inside there.'

To rub our noses in the fact, security lights lit up the yard hidden from us.

'We're going to have to go over the wall,' I said.

'Are you touched?' Dylan said.

'No.'

I'd been looking at the wall. It was a product of its time. It was brick and several layers thick with foundations that probably went halfway to China. I doubted a tank could bust through it without firing a few shells first. A coil of barbed wire ran across the top. It was more like a fortress than a security or privacy wall. But it wasn't impossible to breach. The brick and mortar surface gave me foot and handholds. The barbed wire wasn't such a big deal and I didn't see any security cameras.

'Those walls aren't that tough to climb. We'll find a couple of safe spots to get over. We'll sneak up on them and as soon as we see something go down, we'll call the cops.'

'And who exactly is we?' Dylan asked.

'You and me.'

'And what about me?' Steve said.

'You're our safety switch. You stay on the outside. If anyone catches us, you call the police.'

'This is crazy,' Dylan said.

'But we're going to do it.'

'Of course we are.'

Dylan went back to his car and looked for an entry point. We decided to enter from two different points just in case one of us got caught. I turned the car around and looked for my entry. The factory provided a huge blind spot. It blocked the illumination from the security lights and potentially blocked anyone's view of me.

I drove up onto the pavement and parked the car up against the wall, then powered down the window and climbed onto the car's roof.

I could just see over the top of the wall. I couldn't see anyone, which meant they couldn't see me. I grabbed a tow rope from the Vauxhall's boot and hooked it over a bracket set into the top of the wall for fixing the barbwire. I climbed back down into the Vectra and parked it on a neighbouring street. As much as I liked having the car as a convenient stepladder, I couldn't leave it parked against the wall.

I scurried back, carrying a floor mat from the car. I stuffed the mat inside my jacket and climbed the tow rope. When I reached the top, I laid the mat over the barbwire. The technique had served me well at Morgan's workshop and it did again this time. I tossed the rope over the other side of the wall and slithered down. I touched down on soft dirt behind a pile of discarded tyres.

'Please don't let there be dogs,' I said to myself.

I called Dylan. 'I'm in. Are you?'

'Now I am. It nearly killed me getting over that sodding wall,' he whispered.

'OK. Stay off the line. Call Steve if something goes wrong. OK?'

'OK,' Dylan said with a sigh and hung up.

I edged my way towards the glow of the light. I used everything and anything to hide behind, from oil barrels to the factory building itself. Even though I was sure I wasn't being watched, I didn't take any chances. The last thing I needed was to walk into one of them taking a leak against the wall.

Unlike the facility Hancock had shown us back in Gravesend, this Redditch facility was far from a showpiece. The place was made up of a mammoth factory building and a storage shed big enough to store half a dozen double-decker buses.

As I got nearer, the sound of voices got louder.

I pressed my back to the building and peered around the corner. Derek's transporter sat at the centre of the yard surrounded by dozens of wrecked cars. Some had been stripped bare. Most hadn't. An ancient car crusher sat off to one side with a crane for hoisting the wrecks into it.

I groaned inside. Derek and his boys weren't alone. Six heavily-built, nightclub bouncer types examined the cars on the transporter. Vic Hancock stood next to a much taller man leaning against an Audi A8. I didn't see any guns, but if Derek had come tooled up, these guys would have too.

The man with Hancock was obviously Hancock's partner here.

He dressed to impress with his designer suit and topcoat, but his severe crew cut jarred with the designer clothes. The Audi and the gold on his hands said he was a man of means, but none of it looked right on him, as if he'd borrowed his expensive trappings for tonight's event. To rub that fact in, he was gaunt to the point of emaciation. His skin looked vacuum-sealed to his skull and his pallor was just as sickly – a sun-starved grey. There was also a quickness to his eyes. While he chit-chatted with Hancock, his gaze never left the target – the cars. There was no arguing he was the alpha male here.

I waited until everyone had their back to me before I darted over to a group of four wrecked cars awaiting processing. I scurried underneath a Range Rover with front end damage. It was about as close as I could get without being seen. I was still two hundred feet from the exchange, but it was good enough to hear what was being said. Voices carried on the still night air.

'Unload them,' Hancock ordered and everyone unloaded the cars off the transporter. As they rolled off, the bouncer types each took one and lined them up in a fan formation for inspection.

The man with the crew cut inspected the cars with Hancock and Morgan. He checked out the engines, examined the paintwork and the finishes.

'Nice work, Morgan,' he said in a heavy Russian accent. 'What happen to arm? You drop a car on it?'

Morgan squeezed out an anaemic laugh. 'No, no. Just a small problem that got out of hand.'

The Russian grabbed Morgan's cast and smashed it across his knee. Morgan screamed and fell to the ground clutching his arm.

Neither Derek nor his friends came to Morgan's side. Hancock looked terrified. The demonstration proved who was at the top of the food chain here.

'Jesus Christ, Valentin,' Hancock said. 'There's no need for that.'

The Russian whirled on Hancock. The move startled him and he stepped back, bumping into the Audi. The Russian closed in until he invaded Hancock's personal space.

'My friends call me Valentin. You call me Mr Rykov.'

Hancock nodded.

Rykov turned back to Morgan and jerked his hair back. 'I pay good money for no problems. Got that?'

Morgan nodded, unable to speak.

'I cautious man. I do my homework. My sources tell me you've been getting a lot of attention.'

'It's being taken care of,' Hancock said.

Derek helped Morgan to his feet. 'The problem won't be a problem after next week.'

Rykov turned towards Derek and grinned. 'Really?'

'Really.'

'I like confident man. Do I have your word?'

'Yes.'

Rykov smiled. 'I have your balls if wrong.'

'I won't be.'

'Good. Let's get this shit done.'

Hancock followed Rykov over to the Audi and handed him a bunch of paperwork. It looked like the documentation belonging to the cars. Rykov handed him a thick envelope that had to be cash.

We had them now. It was time to call in the cavalry, so I fished for my phone.

Rykov's mobile rang and he removed the phone from his pocket. He didn't talk; he just listened. He snapped the phone shut and pocketed it, then snapped his fingers at one of his people and pointed at the gates. The bouncer ran over to them and swung them open.

It had to be another delivery. I guessed the cars were worth about a hundred grand, which wasn't a lot in this day and age. With the number of cars Hancock turned over through his yards, this operation he had going with Derek was probably being replicated all over the country.

Instead of another transporter, a single car drove through the gates. It was a Renault Laguna with Steve at the wheel. The man in the passenger seat held an automatic against his head.

Lap Twenty-Five

I didn't move. Couldn't move. The sight of seeing Steve being dragged from the car by two of Rykov's men bound me as tightly as ropes.

Steve was silent. Defiant. I wanted to race in there to save him, but I knew him well enough to know he wouldn't want me to. We couldn't give ourselves away, not yet.

The Russians dragged Steve over to Rykov and threw him to the ground. One of them grabbed him by the hair and hauled him up into a kneeling position.

Rykov pulled out a gun from his overcoat pocket and pressed it to Steve's forehead. 'Who's this?'

'Part of our small problem,' Hancock said.

Derek stepped forward to join Rykov at his side. 'He's Steve Westlake. Aidy Westlake is his grandson and the bigger problem here. If Steve's here, Aidy's here too.'

Rykov snapped his fingers at his men again. The Russians, along with Derek's crew, spread out to comb the yard for me. I lay flat on the ground amongst the dirt and shadows and crawled under a buckled and twisted car. They'd find me eventually, but not fast enough, I hoped.

'Forgive me, Steve,' I murmured while I called Dylan. 'Dylan, they have Steve. Get out. Get the cops.'

'Jesus, Aidy,' was all he could say.

'Go,' I growled. 'But be careful. They're combing the yard for me.'

Derek held his hand out to Rykov. The Russian smiled and handed the gun over.

'You always were a piece of shit,' Steve said.

'And your son would have never made it in Formula One.'

'Fuck you.'

Derek backhanded Steve across the temple with the gun. Steve crumpled, falling to his side. Derek moved in and dropped a knee in Steve's side, pinning him to the ground. He pressed the gun to Steve's eye.

'Jesus Christ,' Hancock said.

'You'd better come on out, Aidy,' Derek bellowed. His voice crashed off the building and wrecked cars. 'You wouldn't let this defenceless old man die for you, would you? That's pretty cowardly, even by my shitty standards.'

I wanted to get in there and give myself up, but the second I did, it was over. Rykov would have Derek put a bullet in each of our heads. I had to give Dylan time to call the cops and get them to mobilize. How long would that take? Five minutes? Ten? Did we have ten minutes? I didn't think so. I might, but Steve didn't. I had to buy him some time.

'Aidy's not here, you arsehole,' Steve growled.

'Nice try, Steve, but I don't believe you. Aidy, do I have to hit him again?'

Derek paused for a second before smashing Steve again with the gun, then pushed himself to his feet, using Steve as an aid. Steve rolled away and struggled into a sitting position. Blood streaked his face. He looked old and haggard. He wouldn't stand up to too much more.

My hands were angry and frustrated fists. I was breathing hard and fast, but I had to keep calm. I couldn't let my emotions get the better of me.

'Aidy, you're really testing my patience. I think I'm going to have to shoot him.'

Theatrically, Derek pointed the gun at Steve and put out his hand to protect himself from splatter.

It was a farce. Derek wouldn't do it. He just wanted me to give myself up. He was arm-twisting. Nothing more. Then he pulled the trigger. A harsh, flat crack split the air.

I jolted as if the bullet had struck me. White noise filled my head and I forgot how to breathe. Only one thought replayed itself in my head. You killed Steve. You killed your grandfather.

'That was a warning shot,' Derek shouted.

Derek dragged Steve up into a half-sitting position and propped him up with his knee. Steve was unharmed. The shot had left him dazed and confused, but alive. I felt a whole new pain in my chest.

'OK, Aidy. No more warnings. No more second chances. Steve dies if you don't come out now.'

Anger twisted Steve's face into something I'd never seen before. 'Don't do it, son. He'll just kill us both.'

'At least I know he's here and I'm not talking to myself.' Derek put the gun to Steve's temple. His finger slipped over the trigger. 'Last chance, Aidy.'

'OK, OK, I'm coming out,' I yelled.

Steve's head sagged in defeat. He would have died for me, but I couldn't let him.

A couple of Rykov's men zeroed in on my voice. Before I had a chance to clamber out from under the wrecked car, they dragged me out. One of them hoisted me to my feet while the other stuck a gun in my face.

'Don't fuck around,' he said.

They shoved me out into the open. I walked slowly with my hands up towards Derek, Steve, Rykov and Hancock. I'd lost all sense of time. Everything was coming at me too quickly. I couldn't tell ten seconds from ten minutes. I just wanted to give Dylan as much time as possible to get the cops here. A gun barrel to the back of my head quickened my step.

Rykov's men and Derek's crew wandered back to the centre of the yard. They exchanged grins. This was fun for them. It was a chance to uncork their violent sides. Tommy and Strickland looked somewhat out of their depth. They no longer held their shotguns like they intended on using them. They were oversized toys they didn't want anymore. Morgan was different. This was payback for his busted arm. He was unable to carry a gun, but his leer said he was more than happy to live vicariously through everyone else.

They clustered around Derek, Steve, Rykov and Hancock to make an unwelcoming welcome committee. It all looked to be too much for Hancock. Before, he'd looked frayed, but now he was coming apart at the seams. He pressed a hand to his forehead and kept shaking his head.

Derek stood with the gun loose at his side. I was tempted to throw myself at him, jam the damn thing under his chin and pull the trigger. My hate showed on my face, but Derek gave me nothing in return. He didn't care if I lived or died.

A hard shove in the back sent me onto my hands and knees. I went to get up but Rykov pushed me down.

'You stay there,' he said.

'You OK?' I asked Steve.

He nodded.

'You the little problem, yes?' Rykov said.

I didn't answer.

'I think you more than little problem.' He shot Hancock a disgusted look. 'I need to know how much damage you do to me.'

The Russian had unknowingly thrown me a lifeline. He wanted to talk. I didn't mind talking. Talking kept me alive and gave the cops time to arrive. I pictured them speeding over here.

'What you know?' Rykov said, leaning into my face.

'And what do you think you know?' Derek added.

'They don't know anything, Mr Rykov,' Hancock said.

'Don't be bullshitting me. They here because they know something.'

'OK, but don't do anything stupid,' Hancock said.

The glare Rykov sent Hancock's way looked as if it could pierce armour plating. 'I never do anything stupid. Everything I do is calculated. Got that, Vic?'

Hancock blushed. 'Yeah, you're right. I'm sorry. You know what you're doing.'

Rykov took the gun back from Derek and put it in my face. 'What you know? And do not be lying. I do not hand out warning shots.'

'Don't tell him anything,' Steve said.

Rykov's grip tightened on the gun.

'No, I want to talk.'

'I am glad one of you has brains in family. Now, talk.'

'You're making over high end cars written off by insurance companies. Vic here buys them from the insurance companies. He separates the wheat from the chaff and hands them over to Derek. His crew makes the cars over with new identities. I don't know how it's done. Someone must have some useful friends in the DVLA and the car plants because the new paperwork isn't forged and the vehicle ID tags aren't fakes. Then the cars come to you and you sell them.'

Rykov looked impressed with me, but he didn't volunteer any information to fill in any gaps in my knowledge. 'Interesting. What else you know?'

'I'm guessing you went to Vic with this project.'

Rykov laughed. 'Why you say that?'

'This looks like your operation. Vic looks way out of his depth.'

Hancock balled a hand into a fist, but he didn't even have the courage to take a swing at me.

Rykov laughed again. 'I like you. You smart boy. Tell me, why do I partner up with spineless prick like Vic?'

'There's a lot of money in salvage, but it's a margins business. There's a lot of capital expenditure needed for it. He's overextended and can't keep up with the loans and mortgages. He needed some extra income to cover his debts.'

'How do you know all this?' Hancock demanded.

I shrugged. 'It's not hard to work out.'

'Why you care?' Rykov asked. 'Why put your life in danger?'

'I'm not interested in you. I'm only interested in Derek. He killed a racecar driver I know. That's all I care about.'

'That fantasy again,' Derek said.

'Not fantasy. It's fact.'

Rykov's eyes flicked to Derek then back to me. He was intrigued by this. I thought he might have ordered Alex's murder, but it was obvious this was all news to him.

'You really don't know what you're talking about,' Derek said.

'I guess it helps when you have a cop covering your trail for you.'

'A cop?' Rykov asked. The question was aimed at Derek, not me.

'I have a friend on the force and he's not averse to some additional income.'

'He knows about this enterprise too,' I said. 'He had to if he was going to cover up the killing.'

I thought I saw a glint of fear in Derek's eyes. The odds of my survival weren't good. It would sweeten the outcome if Derek took a bullet along with me.

'Does cop know this?' the Russian demanded.

'Yes, but he protects the operation in Bristol. He's in my pocket. He's not a problem.'

'Every cop is problem, especially dirty cop. They would sell out mother to save ass.'

I'd ignited something in the Russian. Gears were turning in his head. He had a problem that needed fixing. My talking had bought Steve and me time, but also guaranteed our execution. I didn't have high hopes for Detective Brennan after tonight.

'Is that everything?' Rykov snapped at me.

'Yes.'

'Who else know?'

'Just Steve and me.'

Rykov put the gun to Steve's head. 'I kill him if you lie.'

'He's going to kill us anyway, Aidy,' Steve said.

I thought of Dylan and was glad one of us had gotten away. I repeated myself. 'Just Steve and me.'

Rykov lowered the gun. I took that as a sign of belief.

His mobile burst into song and he answered it. He spoke in Russian and his face darkened.

I assumed a lookout had spotted the cops. I strained to hear for sirens, but heard nothing. There wouldn't be sirens anyway. They wouldn't want to spook the Russian and his pals. I hoped the cops were close.

Rykov said something in Russian then snapped his phone shut.

Moments later, I heard scuffling, followed by a cry. My stomach went into free-fall. I knew what was coming.

Out of the far corner of the yard, another of the Russians emerged from behind a stack of ruined cars. He shoved Dylan ahead of him. Dylan's nose was bleeding and his left eye was closed up.

Rykov's man threw Dylan down on the ground between the Russian and me.

'You insult me with lies,' Rykov said. 'You disappoint me.'

'I'm sorry, Aidy. I didn't get the call out. He got me first.'

There it was. No cops. No rescue. No chance.

Lap Twenty-Six

'Bind them up,' Rykov said.

The bouncer who'd shoved a gun in my face said, 'Put out hands.'

I put my hands together as if in prayer and he wired them together in front of me. He repeated the process with Steve and Dylan.

Rykov tossed out a bunch of instructions in Russian. Whatever he said got a laugh out of his fellow Russians. The English speakers looked on dumbly. Actions would have to speak for themselves.

'Aidy, what the hell is going on?' Dylan asked. Panic roughed the edges of his words.

'Nothing yet. He won't try anything here.'

One of Rykov's men rushed over to Steve's Renault and got behind the wheel. He brought the car over. Three of the bouncer types pulled us to our feet and shoved us in the car. Steve and Dylan went in the back. They pushed me into the front passenger seat.

They weren't going to kill us here. Rykov wasn't dumb. He'd kill us somewhere else so as not to leave any physical evidence.

Steve leaned over close to me and whispered. 'We'll take this prick on the road. He won't be able to handle three of us at once.'

I nodded. It was the only option open to us. We didn't stand a chance at the salvage yard.

The Russian behind the wheel looked at the three of us and reeled off a stream of Russian then laughed like he'd told the world's funniest joke. He sat behind the wheel with the engine running but made no move to drive off. He just kept laughing and pointing at us.

Another of Rykov's enforcers ran over to the crane and fired it up. I saw a sea of blank faces from the English speakers. What the hell was Rykov playing at?

Hancock put a hand to his mouth. 'Oh, no. Oh, no,' he kept repeating.

Then I understood. 'Oh, God,' I murmured.

'What's going on, Aidy?'

I couldn't bring myself to utter the words.

The Russian behind the wheel snapped his fingers and pointed at me. Then he laughed again. 'You get now, yes?'

'What?' Dylan said. 'What's going on?'

The Russian drove the Renault over to the crane and the car crusher. His compatriots thought it was the funniest thing in the world. They banged on the car's roof as it went by. The Russian stopped the car and slid out. He waved at us and said in jagged English, 'Bye, bye. Have good trip.'

'Jesus Christ, they're going to crush us, aren't they?' Dylan said.

I wanted to deny it, but I couldn't. My silence was all the confirmation any of us needed.

Dylan bolted from the car. He got ten feet before one of Rykov's men pistol-whipped him across the cheek. The blow chopped his legs out from under him. Two Russians picked him up and tossed him back in the car with us.

I looked at Steve. He looked a thousand years old.

'Everything will be OK,' he said.

I so wanted to believe him.

The crane rotated on its base and I closed my eyes when its magnetic plate crashed down on the Renault's roof, then lifted the car off the ground.

Christ, this was it. We were going to die. My stomach clenched so tight it forced me to bend over. I wanted to see my future stretching years in front of me, but my mind blotted out the images, instead screaming you're going to die, again and again.

The car swayed in the air and it gave all three of us a clear view of the crusher's mouth. There were no teeth, just three independent hydraulic rams capable of reducing any vehicle to a cube and us along with it.

The sight of the crusher's open maw stilled me. The fear didn't leave me, but it no longer paralyzed me. I didn't know if there was a way out, but I'd be damned if I was just going to sit there and do nothing because Rykov decreed it. I saw life beyond the next five minutes.

'I can't believe I'm going to die,' Dylan said.

'You're not. At least not today,' I said.

Dylan met my gaze.

'We're getting out of here.'

'Are you mental?' Dylan said.

'No, he's not,' Steve said. 'It'll take minutes to crush this car.'

'And we only need a few seconds to get free.'

'Then what?' Dylan said. 'Rykov isn't going to let us walk.'

'Then we do something else. I'm not letting Rykov get the better of us. I'll die first.'

'You might get that wish,' Dylan said, 'but I'm with you.'

Rykov barked an order and the crane operator lowered us into the crusher.

The Renault hit the crusher's loading trough hard enough to toss the three of us around. Steve yelled when he smashed his head off the roof of the car. I smacked my head on the gear shift, which left me dazed, but only for a second. The cold realization that we were going to be crushed alive snapped me out of it. We had to get out. This was no joke. No test. Rykov was going to kill us. I reached for the door handle with my bound hands and opened the door. A gap of no more than three inches opened up before the door slammed into the side of the trough.

A cackle of laughter from Rykov and his boys came back at me. They, along with Derek and his crew, lined the edge of the crusher for a front row view of the action.

'Try the other doors,' I yelled.

The three of us tried the remaining doors with the same result.

Without the ignition key, the power windows were dead. 'Kick out the windows.'

Rykov had made a mistake binding our hands in front of us. We still had mobility and the ability to grab things, albeit it in a handicapped fashion. I scrabbled across the seat and kicked at the driver's door window. The glass flexed against the impact, but absorbed the blow. I kicked again and again. I wouldn't be stopped. 'Break you bastard, break.'

Steve and Dylan fought for space in the tight confines of the car's back seat in order to get to a window. They manoeuvred around until they were back to back to give each other room to kick. We gave it everything we had. Each of our blows reverberated throughout the car.

Steve's window went first, then mine. Diamond-sized splinters of glass went everywhere. I crawled across them to climb through the window. It was a squeeze, but I wormed my way through. Glass shards gashed my arms and chest in the process.

One of Rykov's men climbed into the crusher and kicked me hard in the ribs. The kick took my breath away, easily immobilizing me. He shoved me back through the busted window, then jammed his gun in Steve's face to halt his escape. Dylan pulled Steve back into the car.

'No escape for you,' he said and jumped off the crusher.

I looked at my grandfather and my best friend. They were terrified. I'd put them in this danger. I wanted to say, 'We'll survive this. We'll get out,' but the lie wouldn't come.

'Help. Get us out of here. Help,' Dylan screamed. His voice bounced off the car's interior.

'Stop,' I said. 'Don't waste your energy. There's no one here who can help us.'

Dylan just looked at me, his face devoid of all emotion.

'I'm sorry,' I said.

Rykov leaned over the edge and peered directly into the car at me. He grinned at me, revelling in my misery. 'Hancock, come. You see.'

Hancock was conspicuous by his absence. When he didn't respond to Rykov's immediate beckoning, one of Rykov's goons dragged him over.

Rykov slung an arm around Hancock's neck and drew him close. 'You see, Vic? This is how you deal with problem. I show you to teach. Next time, you do same and make problem disappear like a bad dream. Yes?'

'Oh God,' Hancock murmured. All the colour had drained from his face.

'No gods here,' Rykov said. 'Only devils.'

He repeated the joke in Russian for his compatriots, judging by the laughter that followed.

He waved at his man closest to the crusher's controls. He went to the control panel and kick-started the crusher into life. The roar of the engine and whoop of the hydraulic compressor winding up turned my insides to water.

'Oh my God,' Dylan murmured. 'This is it. They're really going to do it.'

'Keep it together,' Steve said. 'Don't give them the satisfaction.'

It was a nice sentiment, but I felt my grip slipping on the notion. Just the idea of the hydraulic rams squashing the car and us along with it swept away any possibility of bravery. We were going to be crushed to death. We wouldn't last long, which was a blessing, but those final moments before the end came would last a lifetime.

'Your grandfather is right,' Rykov said. 'I am going to kill you.' He moved over to the controls. 'I cannot say it will not be fun.'

Derek snatched the Russian's arm. 'Don't do this. Let us deal with it.'

'Why take risk? Kill birds with one rock while we can.'

Derek didn't correct Rykov on his poor telling of the phrase. But who would?

'You'll literally leave a trail to Hancock's door. Do you want that?'

Rykov thought for a second then shook his head. 'I do not think so. I have done before. Very clean kill with little blood. It easily washes away and body is burned up when car is smelted. There will be no trail.'

'I can take care of them just as cleanly,' Derek said.

A distrusting smile spread across Rykov's face. 'You sound like friends.'

'It's not that. I screwed up and you're fixing it for me. I don't want that. I fix my mistakes myself. I want to make up for it,' he nodded at us in the crusher, 'so I don't suffer the same fate.'

I didn't know why Derek was going to the trouble of staying our execution. Rykov was right. This was a very effective and clean execution. Wasn't this what Derek had wanted all along? Maybe it wasn't. From his expression, he wasn't deriving any glee from this. Maybe Rykov had crossed a line Derek wasn't willing to cross.

'You don't worry,' Rykov nodded at the crusher. 'You, good soldier. You I trust,' Rykov said, removing Derek's hand from his arm. 'But if make you feel better, you start machine.'

Derek hesitated then nodded.

Rykov stepped aside for Derek. He barked at his men and they trained their guns on us in case we tried escaping again.

'I think I'd prefer to take a bullet than to go out in here,' Steve said.

'I don't want either option,' Dylan said.

'None of us do,' I said. 'Everyone stay put.'

Something about Derek's personality shift gave me hope. He wasn't the same man who'd played up killing Alex in the clubhouse. This was a human. He wouldn't let us die this way. He wouldn't press the button. He'd do something to help us. I didn't understand it, but I felt it. My panic melted. I hoped I could believe in my gut feeling.

'We won't talk,' I yelled. 'No one knows what we know. Anyone I've tried to tell hasn't believed me.'

Rykov smiled. 'I believe you. That big problem. If I believe, others believe. Is not good for me. Can't take risk. Derek, please continue.'

Derek looked at me. I looked into his eyes for hope, but it wasn't there. He pulled a lever on the control panel and the crusher burst into action.

The crusher's engine roared and the first ram moved in from the side. It eased along its path with slow, deliberate speed, sweeping the Renault along. The tyres squeaked as the car slid on the metal bed. There was nowhere for the car to go except inward. The ram pinched the car against the opposite wall. The door panels popped and banged as they buckled under the pressure.

My breath shot in and out in fast, untidy pants. A scream was building in my throat.

Even though it was futile, the three of us yelled for help. Rykov patted Derek on the back as he operated the controls and his Russian buddies pointed and laughed at us. Some mocked us by putting their hands to their faces and pretending to scream back. I wished we could keep our screams in, but we just couldn't help ourselves.

dn't. I just knew how close I'd come to dying. Another seconds and the crusher would have squeezed all the free from inside the Renault. When the crusher opened up, we erged into a war zone. While Steve, Dylan and I thought we living our last moments, four of the Russian's men had lived . The armed response team had killed them. They lay in us, untidy piles riddled with bullets. It looked to be touch go for another of the Russians. Blood pumped from a big d in his chest and the cop working on him struggled to stem ow. Derek and his boys were OK and in cuffs. Hancock was . The police had slapped a bulletproof vest on him, put him car and taken him out of there before Steve, Dylan and I had n cut from the crippled Renault. Rykov had been wounded, not seriously. Uniformed, plain clothes and armed police littered salvage yard in large numbers.

When Brennan had brought me to the station, he stuck me in interview room and left me for an hour before attempting to to me. The backlash of almost dying a nasty death was phoria. I was amped up on the simple notion that I had a norrow and another one after that. My emotions pinballed off ch other. I went from laughing one second to crying the next. nce the elation burnt itself out, Brennan came for my atement.

There was no pantomime or messing around with procedure his time. Brennan went by the book. He recorded the interview. another detective sat in the room with us while I spilled everything o Brennan from the night before Alex died to the police's eleventh our arrival. Brennan had to change the tape twice before I was inished.

The other detective left with the tapes to get them transcribed. Now Brennan and I could really talk.

'Did I get any of it right?' I asked.

Brennan cracked a small smile. 'Not much, but I'll give you marks for originality.'

'You could have made things a lot easier by telling me what you were up to.'

'Yeah, like I was going to confide in you about a six month undercover operation. I tried to be as clear as I could that you were on the wrong track and you needed to back off. You chose not to listen.'

The ram's progress slowed then stopped when it squeezed against the Renault's tough chassis. I wanted the crusher to chip its tooth on the French made car, but no. Derek cranked up the power and the ram resumed its path. The chassis resisted the overwhelming pressure for just a moment before giving way. The exterior of the car collapsed with a shriek of buckling steel. The confines of the car's cabin shrank and we instinctively shifted to the centre of the cabin where there was still space. It was a futile gesture. We were only buying ourselves seconds. But there was no control over our need to survive. We tried to hold onto life for as long as we could.

The front and rear windscreens split then burst under the pressure, spraying us with glass.

Steve pointed to the gaping holes. 'Out through the front and back.'

I scrabbled out over the bonnet. Two bullets thudded into it inches from my left hand.

'What we say about escaping?' Rykov shouted over the din. 'Get back in.'

The Russians opened fire on us, driving us back into the Renault. They laughed as we disappeared back inside.

'We're so dead,' Dylan said.

'Not yet, we aren't,' I said.

I jumped on the car horn and learned on it. It blared. The annoying sound spread far and wide. I hoped it would draw someone. No one would put up with that noise for long. The car shifted by another inch and something inside the car broke, killing the horn.

'Nice try,' Steve said, 'but a little late.'

Steve was resigned to his death. I wasn't.

'Keep moving,' I barked. 'Don't get trapped.'

The floor pan buckled and collapsed beneath us. The roof popped and peaked. We might have been losing width, but we were gaining headroom.

'Get in the middle,' I said, clambering between the two front seats.

I had the front of the car to myself. Steve and Dylan had to share the back seat and were losing space. Dylan tore out the parcel tray from the boot with his bound hands and tossed it through the windowless hatchback. He clambered into the boot space.

'Now what?' Dylan demanded.

'We keep fighting.'

The back seats snapped off their mounting. One seat smashed into Steve, knocking him over. He yelled out, stuck in the well between the front and rear seats. He had seconds before he'd be pinned down. Dylan lunged for him and when he yanked him back up, blood streaked half my grandfather's face. The front seats crushed the centre console and armrest as they came together. Other pieces of the interior sheared off and struck us as the car continued to shrink. Dylan yelled out when he got his hands trapped between a seat back and the car's frame. He worked them free, but the damage had been done – two broken fingers on his right hand. The injury didn't stop him. We all contorted our bodies in an attempt to find an inch of space, tossing anything and everything that was no longer affixed out the busted windows for that vital extra cubic inch of space.

Suddenly, the ram stopped. The crusher had squeezed the car to a third of its width and we were still alive. Sweat streamed down my face and burned my eyes, but my hands and feet were ice cold. I looked at Steve and Dylan. We grinned at each other like idiots. Our lives were coming to an end, but we were grinning.

'I'm sorry,' I said to them.

Steve reached across the front seats and grabbed my bound hands with his. 'Don't be sorry. You didn't do anything wrong. You're a good kid and I'm proud of you.' He turned to Dylan. 'I'm proud of both of you. Got that?'

A new hydraulic whine wiped away our smiles. The crusher had only completed the first stage of the process. The second ram, a hinged affair, folded over to crush us from the top like a giant, metal clamshell.

I looked up at the gallery of faces watching us. The Russians were egging the machine on to do its job. Hancock had turned away. Tommy had lost all the colour in his face. Even Morgan had lost his bloodlust. Only Derek met my gaze. I saw compassion, which wasn't the reaction I expected to see. The top ram closed over the car and everybody disappeared from sight. Tyres burst, the suspension collapsed and the roof buckled and lunged at us.

Now in total darkness, my fear spiked. The collapsing car was

a lot more frightening in the dark. The pit
to find a pocket of space based on sound an
geography changing every second, it was e

Our actions were futile, but life had becom
We no longer cared about the noise from the s
the shriek and moan of collapsing steel or I
didn't care because none of it mattered. Living
We'd fight to survive for as long as we coulc

Over the noise of the compressor, the hyd
buckling steel, I thought I heard something
Loud noises. Harsh snaps. Sounds that didn't fi
brain processed them and delivered an answer.

'Gunfire,' I said.

Steve and Dylan didn't hear me. They were t
find the last pockets of space to save themselves

I heard shouting, then the crusher stopped. Th
oping us was silent.

I was shaking. It had to be a joke. Rykov wan
our deaths for his entertainment.

'Get that bastard thing open,' a muffled voice
outside.

The voice had authority and moments later the c
up. I stared out through the slit of the windowless
Detective Brennan looked back at me.

'Get them the hell out of there,' he barked.

Lap Twenty-Seven

For the second time, I was alone with Brennan in
interview room in the early hours of the morning. T
I was being held at the divisional headquarters in Kidde
He'd sent Steve and Dylan to hospital to get checked ou
statements could wait. Mine couldn't. I was tired and I wa
see Steve and Dylan to say sorry, thanks and tell them it wa
but I couldn't leave without giving Brennan some answers

'Do you know how bloody close you came to ballsing u
operation?' Brennan asked.

'You didn't do a very good job.'

Brennan swung his arms wide. 'What can I say? Guilty as charged.'

I wondered how guilty. That smile said a lot. Brennan could have done more to set me straight, but he'd let me believe in the myths surrounding Derek, concoct my own theories and charge off on my fool's errand. My misguided beliefs had done him a favour. It worked to his advantage to have me as a fly in everyone's ointment. My interference made things happen.

Suddenly, I became aware of my stink. I reeked. I'd sweated through my clothes. First, from fear, and then from my survivor's high. I wouldn't bother washing them. I was burning the lot. Brennan had to have noticed and it was kind of him not to mention it. I wrapped the blanket the paramedics had given me at the salvage yard even tighter around me.

'If I'm going to be your star witness, you have to tell me how wrong I've been.'

'Valentin Rykov is Russian mob. He's been in the UK since the nineties. Glasnost did wonders for the Russian mob in Western Europe. They set up shop running drugs, girls, protection, human trafficking, loan sharking and anything else you care to name. Rykov had his fingers in a lot of dirty, yet traditional, criminal pies. The trading in phantom cars was just one string to his bow.'

'Phantom cars?'

'One of the few facts you were right about. The conversion of insurance write-offs into new cars.'

'He couldn't have made much off each car. The depreciation must have killed most of the profit.'

'That was where Vic Hancock came in. You guessed right about his money troubles. He was stretched thin, forcing him to secure funding outside the High Street banks. Rykov provided Hancock a way of paying back his debt and making some money. The great thing about Hancock was he gave Rykov the complete network to exploit. What you saw was one of two dozen operations. They might only make five to ten grand a car, but when dozens of cars are going through his dealerships every week, it stacks up.'

'At least we know the British car industry isn't dead.'

Brennan laughed. 'It might be after tonight.'

'So this is a pretty big coup for you.'

'Only if we can get a conviction. That's been our problem in the past. Witnesses tend to disappear before they see a witness box.'

'Hancock is going to make a pretty big witness.'

'He's massive. Landing him was as important as catching Rykov in the act.'

It explained why Hancock had been the first person out of there when Brennan and his swarm of cops raided the place. Rykov might have had his hooks into Hancock, but that was to the police's advantage. Hancock was so entangled in Rykov's operations that his testimony would destroy the Russian and probably a large chunk of the Russian mob.

'The hope is that bringing Rykov down on this front will give witnesses the courage to come forward to testify on his other business dealings.'

'And you owe all this success to Derek Deacon.'

'Afraid so. He proved to be a great informant.'

I couldn't believe Derek was a police grass, but it explained his behaviour tonight. Taking Rykov's gun from him when they captured Steve probably saved Steve's life. Rykov would have put a bullet through Steve's skull to make his point. Derek's pleading to take care of Steve, Dylan and me himself was another attempt to save our lives. He might have operated the crusher, but he'd slow-played it in order to buy us time. I had to give it to Derek, he was a good informant.

However, his informant status wouldn't do his reputation any good with Morgan, Tommy, Strickland or any of Morgan's mechanics. He was selling them down the river along with Hancock and Rykov. At this point, they didn't know it was Derek who'd screwed them, but they'd find out in court.

'I suppose Derek's going to be under lock and key for a while.'

'Good news for everyone in racing, Derek won't be around to defend his title for a year or three.'

If at all. Brennan didn't have to say it. I knew Derek would be going into a witness protection program. Even if Rykov went down for life, there'd always be a price on Derek's head. No matter where the police sent him, he'd never step foot on a race circuit again. It would be the first place Rykov's people would look. It meant Derek's tenth title would be his last. His motor racing career was over. I almost felt sorry for him.

'How did you recruit Derek anyway?'

'Our intelligence pointed to an association between Rykov and Hancock. Our guys picked up Derek on a delivery run. We made him an offer he couldn't refuse.'

This was where I'd been completely wrong. Brennan wasn't Derek's bent cop. Derek was Brennan's informant. Brennan couldn't stop laughing when I explained during my statement what I thought I'd witnessed at the Green Man pub.

'I guess I owe you an apology over the bent cop remark.'

Brennan smiled. 'Not really. When Derek told me what you thought, I told him to play it up. It was a nice misinterpretation that worked in my favour.'

'When you busted Dylan and me, you weren't looking out for Morgan's workshop, were you?'

Brennan shook his head. 'You were becoming a bigger and bigger pain in the arse. I was protecting my investment. Derek saw you staking out the place when he dropped off a shipment. I knew you'd come back and I needed to stop you from screwing up my good work. I hoped the bad cop act and a night in the cells would scare you off. It might be a good idea if you dropped the Boy Scout act in future. It's going to get you killed.'

'I wouldn't have had to if you'd helped out there. You left it a little late with the rescue.'

'You brought that on yourself. Tonight wasn't our night to spring the trap on Rykov. Derek spotted you while en route and called in with the panic message. We had to scramble to put together a rescue mission. It takes time to assemble an armed response team. We didn't want a fire fight. We couldn't lose Derek, Hancock or Rykov.'

'Or us?'

'Or you and your friends.'

Yeah, me and my expendable friends. 'So that's that,' I said.

'Pretty much.'

'As far as the official story goes.'

'And what's that supposed to mean?'

'Derek took his undercover status a little too far, don't you think? He busted up my grandfather's business and tried to burn it. He turned over my home. He beat the crap out of the poor bastard who works at Chicane's.'

'We won't mention your criminal acts such as breaking and entering or your grandfather breaking someone's arm.'

'Don't try to scare me off.'

Brennan put his hands up. 'OK, I'll talk to Derek. It sounds like he crossed a few lines. Get me a list of damages and I'll see what I can do about making amends.'

'And Alex Fanning?'

'Drop it.'

'No. Your man killed someone. He might be your star witness, but I'll be damned if I'll let you sweep Alex's murder under the carpet.'

'You don't know what you're talking about,' Brennan said.

'Don't I? We both know what he did, but no one will say it. It's going to look pretty bad if your star witness is also a murderer.'

Brennan stood up. 'You're tired and overwrought. We've booked you a hotel room for the night. I'll have someone take you there. Your friends will be waiting for you.' Brennan checked his watch. 'The hospital should have discharged them by now.'

Brennan stood and crossed to the door. I jumped up and blocked his path. 'You're not going to brush me aside that easily.'

He grabbed my arm to usher me out the door. I shook it off.

'Time to let it go, Aidy.'

'No.'

Brennan got up in my face, then sighed. He settled on the corner of the table and pointed at my chair. He waited for me to sit down. 'OK, you win. I'm going to give it to you straight. One, because you deserve the truth and two, because I'm tired of your sodding crusade. It's about time you saw something.'

Brennan led me out of the interview room and into a briefing room. Rows of tables and chairs lined the room facing a dais and whiteboard. A large, wall-mounted TV peered down at the empty seats.

'Find a seat and wait,' Brennan told me. 'You'll want to be up front for this.'

A minute later, he returned with a videotape. I didn't have to ask what was on the tape. He loaded it into a player.

'This is the unedited feed of the race. It's the raw footage shot by the cameras that captured the crash. OK?'

'I thought the tape had been destroyed.'

'It was. Redline destroyed the tape at Mr Fanning's request out of respect for his son. I kept a copy because I thought I might need it.'

Brennan hit play then killed the lights in the room.

The first shot stared down the straight from Barrack Hill to Wilts. Jostling for position, the Formula Fords streamed towards the camera with Derek and Alex leading the pack. They were only a few feet apart. Alex had the outside line. Derek had the inside, but he was running a little behind. He needed Alex's cooperation if he was going to make it through the bend cleanly. The two of them bore down on Barrack Hill with everyone else chasing them.

The images propelled me back to that afternoon to relive the experience. My stomach clenched at the knowledge of what was coming next. If Derek had been true to his threat, he would move across to slot his wheels inside Alex's. Unconsciously, I held my breath.

Then it happened, but not as I'd believed.

Something went wrong with Alex's car. The car twitched, the rear end kicking out as if struck by an invisible force. His car jerked right, striking Derek's car. Their wheels tangled and became untangled when Alex's car rode over the top of Derek's. The impact kicked Alex's car onto two wheels for a fraction of a second. When it came down, it slewed hard left and off the track. Instinctively, the cameraman latched onto Alex's car careening off the circuit. He followed Alex's path all the way into the concrete wall. The crunching impact spat Alex's car back across the track. It ground to a halt with Alex slumped forward inside the cockpit, unmoving.

The footage switched to the different camera angle and Brennan hit pause.

'You OK?' he asked.

'I'm fine. Keep going. I want to see the rest.'

Brennan nodded and pressed play.

The rest of the footage was from two other cameras. One followed the action infield at Barrack Hill. The other was an elevated shot taken at Wilts. Just like the first camera shot, they showed the same thing. Alex had crashed into Derek before flying off into the wall, but none of the camera angles captured what had caused Alex's car to twitch in the first place.

Brennan switched the lights back on. 'What do you think now?'

'You're right. Derek didn't kill Alex,' I said.

Lap Twenty-Eight

Monday turned into a dreary, overcast day. I never thought I'd find endless grey sky and drizzle so beautiful, but I did. I was alive. A little beaten up, but alive. The same couldn't be said of everyone who'd entered Hancock's salvage yard last night. I planned on embracing every day as perfect, no matter the weather.

I was sitting in a hotel lobby just off the M42 motorway watching the world outside. Brennan had put Steve, Dylan and me up there for the night. As promised, he arrived just after breakfast to get Steve and Dylan's statements. I hung out in the lobby while he and his team took them up to their rooms.

There'd been quite a reunion when Brennan dropped me off at the hotel. Steve, Dylan and I hugged and cried. I told them I loved them and apologized for almost getting them killed. Neither of them needed my apology. It seemed to have been worth it to them. We'd survived.

Brennan had sprung for separate rooms, which was a good thing. Despite our unfaltering camaraderie, we needed alone time to process everything that had happened. We had adjoining rooms with mine in the middle. Through the walls, I heard Dylan crying while on the phone to his parents and I heard Steve talking to himself. I just sat in the bath ignoring the sting of the hot water on my injuries while I ruminated. I'd been wrong about so many things, but somehow something good had come out of my mistakes. Everything that had happened would prey on my mind for weeks to come, but I shelved all thoughts and recriminations and slept like the dead until Steve knocked on my door the following morning to tell me to wake up.

Brennan's people passed through the hotel lobby on their way out. None of them cast a look my way. I turned to see Brennan walking Steve and Dylan over to me. All three were smiling, which I hoped was a good sign. I crossed the lobby to meet them.

'Are we free to go?' I asked.

'For now,' Brennan said. 'Obviously, you'll be needed in court as witnesses. So you'll be seeing a lot of me over the coming months.'

'Lucky us,' I said.

Brennan patted my cheek. 'It's no treat for me either, son. You're a tenacious little sod, which is to your credit and your detriment. Don't let me catch you at it again.'

'Thanks.'

'There's a compliment in there if you look hard enough.'

'I'm sure.'

'OK, let's get out of here before a sudden bout of affection breaks out.' Steve put a hand in my back and ushered Dylan and me forward.

'Can I buttonhole Aidy for just one sec?' Brennan asked.

I shrugged and Brennan and I waited until Steve and Dylan had pushed their way through the revolving door into the covered courtyard to get the cars.

'I spoke to Derek this morning. He denied attacking your grandfather or the guy from Chicane's or breaking into your home.'

'Well, he would, wouldn't he?'

Brennan frowned. 'Aidy, accept it. Please.'

I should have known better than to expect a straight answer. 'OK.'

'He apologizes for the fight at your grandfather's workshop and the roadside hijacking. He hopes you'll understand why he acted that way. It was for your own safety.'

I wasn't in the mood to argue. There was only so much anyone was going to admit to. There was no point in my pushing the issue. As Brennan had warned me last night, we'd broken enough laws of our own. 'Apology accepted.'

'Good.'

Steve appeared in the lobby doorway with his hands up in a come-on-let's-go gesture. I shook hands with Brennan and pushed my way out through the revolving door.

Steve and Dylan had brought the two remaining cars from our surveillance escapade – the Vauxhall and the Honda. Steve would have a lot of explaining to do about the destroyed Renault when we got back to Windsor. It would have been nice if the three of us could have driven home together, but it wasn't an option. Dylan slipped out from behind his dad's Honda and leaned on the roof.

'You OK driving?'

Dylan examined his broken fingers, now bound to a splint. 'Yeah, I'll live. Hey, I like how that sounds.'

I grinned.

'I've got to get home and check in with my parents, but I'll come by Archway tomorrow to work on the car, yeah?'

I'd been worried that the hell I'd dragged my friend through had damaged our friendship. I'd put him through a lot. But him saying that told me we were OK. 'That'll be good. See you tomorrow.'

Dylan drove off as Steve and I climbed into the Vauxhall. I stared out of the window as Steve drove. I let my thoughts drift, happy not to latch on any particular thought for more than a second. My silence must have triggered something in Steve and he started talking about preparations for the Festival.

'There won't be a Festival,' I said.

'Why not?'

'My sponsor is in police custody.'

'That doesn't change things. Hancock leased the car and engine for the month. Your entry is paid for. All you have to pay for is petrol and expenses. I say race. It's the least these people can do for you. Consider it your compensation.'

It was a nice way of looking at it. Hancock probably needed every penny he could get right now, but there were no refunds in the racing world.

'What do we do about Hancock Salvage's name on the car?'

'Keep it on there. Hancock is still your sponsor. His company is still doing business. You have an obligation and it'll give everyone something to talk about.' Steve smiled at me. 'You're racing in the Festival. I'm going to make sure of it.'

We arrived home in the late afternoon. The house was still in a mess after the break-in, and the wreckage greeted us. As much as I didn't want to bother with the thankless chore, Steve and I returned everything to its rightful place and threw out anything that had been destroyed. Neither of us were particular hungry, but Steve picked up pizza from the local takeaway. We settled in for a night in front of the TV. Dull, yes, but we were sorely in need of some dullness. The news reported a vague account of a gangland shooting in Redditch, but didn't say who was involved. I guessed there was a police gag order in place until they had Rykov's organization nailed down.

'Have you spoken to Alison?' Steve asked.

'No.'

'I think you'd better.'

He was right and I went up to my room and called her. I told her what had happened over the last twenty-four hours.

'So Derek didn't kill Alex?' she said when I finished.

This was my biggest mistake. I'd told Alison that Derek had killed her fiancé. I'd muddied her grieving process with murder accusations. I'd made a mess for so many people. 'No. He didn't. I saw the video from the race. Alex crashed into Derek. There wasn't a thing Derek could have done to prevent it.'

'What made Alex crash into Derek?'

'I don't know. Oil on the track? A lapse in concentration? Any number of things could have caused it. We'll never know.'

'So Derek's threat was just a threat after all.'

'Yes. I'm sorry. I was totally wrong. I shouldn't have made you think otherwise.'

Alison was silent for a long moment. 'It's OK. You didn't convince me. You only echoed what I believed.'

It was kind of her to say so.

'Are you still racing in the Festival?'

'Yes. Steve and I will be working on the car tomorrow. We're testing the car Wednesday and qualifying is Friday.'

'Do you need help?'

'I'd love it.'

'Eric and Laura came over yesterday to see me. We talked and we'd like to make the Festival Alex's official goodbye to motor racing. So, we'd like to help out.'

'That sounds great. If you don't mind getting your hands dirty, come over tomorrow.'

'We will.'

I stayed late at work the following day. It was my attempt to make up for my no-show the day before. I couldn't really explain myself either. Brennan's orders. Relations between my bosses and me had become strained over recent weeks on account of my absenteeism. This wasn't helped by the fact that I'd be out the rest of the week for the Formula Ford Festival. I'd pushed them to the limit and felt my career was on life support.

After a difficult day at the office, I drove myself to Archway.

There was no need for a personal escort anymore. The war with Derek was over. I could return to my normal life, despite the dishevelled mess I'd made of it.

I arrived at Archway to find a packed house and team briefing in progress without me. Steve had Dylan, the Fannings, Alison and her father clustered around the Mygale. He was going over individual duties with them from wheel checks to pre-race inspections. Steve was in his element. A life spent in the pit lane meant he hadn't lost his professionalism or discipline. The Festival was a big deal and there wasn't room for error. It was fun seeing him marshalling his lieutenants, although a tad disappointing that no one had bothered to invite me to my own party. I was the driver after all.

My arrival ruined Steve's disciplined control. The second Alison saw me, she rushed over and crushed me in a hug. After all that had happened, it felt good to be held. I couldn't fall or come to harm if someone held me. Even though the Fannings and Mr Baker were there in front of me, I couldn't help myself and I hugged her back.

'I'm so happy you're safe,' she said.

'Me too,' I said.

She took me in for a second, examining my cuts and bruises. 'You look terrible.'

It wasn't the homecoming I wanted to hear, but it made me smile. 'Thanks. That makes me feel a whole lot better.'

'Shut up. Promise me that you three won't do anything as stupid as that again.'

'We'll try not to.'

She pulled away from me. 'You need to do more than try.'

'OK, we won't. I guarantee it.'

The Fannings came over and Mr Fanning shook my hand. 'I don't know what to say. You three did something very brave.'

It looked as if Steve and Dylan had divulged some details of our activities from two nights ago. It was probably hard not to considering their battered state. It was bound to raise questions.

'And more than a little stupid,' I said.

'Bravery and stupidity go hand in hand,' Mrs Fanning added.

I didn't have an answer for that.

'It's just so hard to believe,' Mr Baker said, slipping an arm around his daughter's shoulders. 'These were people we knew and trusted. Just unbelievable.'

It was, but it wasn't as unbelievable as the dumb ideas I'd built up about Alex's murder. I felt self-conscious in front of Alex's parents and Alison.

'Can we get back to the job at hand?' Steve asked.

I raised my hands in surrender and ushered everyone back to the car.

Steve resumed the team briefing. I stood off to one side while he talked everyone through their tasks and demonstrated how to do anything anyone didn't understand. He stopped when the thump-thump of the music from the Jumping Bean next door became too much for him.

'Let's get some dinner,' Mr Fanning said. 'It's on me.'

We went next door and were seated immediately. There was a nice vibe around our table. A weight had been lifted from everyone's shoulders. Nobody wanted to be serious and we could have kept it going all night, but we all needed an early start. Tomorrow kicked off a series of long days until the end of the Festival.

Mr Fanning settled the bill and we all walked out into the night. The Fannings had driven to Archway, while Alison and her father had taken the train. We walked the Fannings to their car and saw them off. Steve and Dylan went back to Archway to finish up for the night while I walked Alison and her dad to the railway station. I saw them all the way to the ticket barriers. I thanked them and shook hands with Mr Baker. He inserted his ticket and passed through the barrier. Alison hung back.

'I'll be with you in a minute, Dad.'

He looked a little put out at being segregated, but he nodded. 'Don't be too long, OK?'

She smiled. 'I won't.'

She waited until her dad disappeared from sight in the direction of the platforms before speaking, 'I hope you don't mind that I involved Alex's parents in this race.'

'Of course not. This race is important to a lot of people.'

'You've become important to a lot of people,' she corrected, then blushed.

'Have I become important to you?'

Her hesitation was slight, but it was there. 'Yes.'

'But?' I said.

'I'm not ready for someone new. I care for you, Aidy. I didn't think I could so soon after Alex, but there's a big difference between caring for someone and finding someone. Does that make sense?'

'Yes.'

'I suppose what I'm trying to say is that I feel a connection between us, but I'm not ready for more right now and I'm hoping you understand and that you can wait.'

There'd been girls, but they'd all been short term flings. Alison was different. I felt we had something potentially far more serious developing between us. For once, I was willing to be smart about this. 'I'm not going anywhere,' I said.

Her nervous expression turned into a grin. 'Thank you. You're a special guy.'

'It comes easy for some.'

She pulled me to her and kissed me. 'See you tomorrow.'

I waited until she'd slipped through the barriers and disappeared from sight before heading down the slope to Archway.

Steve and Dylan met me with smiles when I let myself back into the workshop. They were pulling out the tools and equipment we'd need for tomorrow and setting them out so they could be loaded straight into the van in the morning. They stopped what they were doing to look me over.

Dylan tapped his watch. 'Someone took their time saying goodbye. Is that the reason for the big smile?

'Leave the lad alone,' Steve said. 'She's a great girl, Aidy. Be good to her. Just keep your hands where we can all see them.'

'I'll try. Thanks.'

They grinned like idiots before Steve tugged on Dylan's sleeve and they went to the bathroom. While they washed up, I admired the Mygale. It looked great sitting on its stands, despite Hancock's name on the side. This was my car. My chance to prove myself. Not to show the racing world that I was as good as my dad, but that I was just good. I wasn't going to be an also-ran at the Festival. I was going to do my best to make an impact.

I eyed my car from the nose and crouched down so I was face to face with it. The wide track of the front suspension with the big black tires, sleek nose and squat radiator pods was a gorgeous sight. I made my sweep of the car, taking in its smooth lines and elegant construction. I trusted Steve and Dylan's expertise with my life – figuratively and literally – but I was only comfortable getting behind the wheel once I'd made sure everything met my standards. I checked the joints, made sure push rods and tracking arms were perfectly centred, looked for leaks, pulled on the wheels to make sure there was no play in the bearings, and ensured every cable connection was tight and tied back. I worked my way around to the rear of the car. This was the perspective a following driver had of my car. I hoped a lot of drivers would have this view at the weekend. I went over the gearbox and rear suspension. Everything looked to be in its place. Then I spotted a chink in the perfection. It was subtle and easily missed. In the excitement of race day, I wouldn't have noticed it.

It was the same problem I'd noticed with Alex's car. I pulled the drop cloth off Alex's car and stood behind it, comparing it to the Mygale.

'What are you doing?' Steve asked.

'Come have a look at this,' I said.

Steve and Dylan crowded around the rear of Alex's car. I pointed at the right rear wishbone mounting with the bolt placed in upside-down.

'You see that? That bolt could have fallen out during the race.'

'I know. We've been over this,' Steve said.

I grabbed the bent tracking arm dangling from the upright. 'We never found the bolt that should have connected the tracking arm to the gearbox mounting.'

'We went over that too. It could have been lost during transport or the crash. I'm still surprised we found as much of the car as we did.'

Dylan was frowning. A look of disappointment had darkened his expression. He saw that something had lit me up and it couldn't be good. 'Aidy, where are you going with this?'

I replayed the tape of Alex's crash in my mind. The twitch that caused the crash still bothered me. It could have been debris on the track that initiated it, but it was just as likely to have been a mechanical failure.

'What if the bolt holding the tracking arm in place had been upside-down too? If it had fallen out during the race, the rear wheel would have steered itself and Alex would have had no control over the car.'

'That's possible,' Steve said. 'So what?'

'If it was done on purpose, that would be murder.'

'Oh, c'mon, Aidy,' Steve said. 'It's over. We know Derek didn't do it. Maybe Jo-Jo or Alex screwed up and put the bolts in wrong. If one fell out, it's negligence at best.'

'There's nothing here, Aidy. Drop it,' Dylan said. 'Derek is innocent.'

'Who said anything about Derek?' I crossed over to the Mygale. I pointed to the right rear suspension. 'Got any idea how that happened?'

Just like the bolts on Alex's car, the bolts connecting the left and right rear tracking arms to the gearbox mountings were inserted bolt head down.

'Either of you two do that?' I asked.

'Jesus, what are you saying?' Steve demanded. 'You know damn well we wouldn't do that. We know how dangerous that is.'

'So did Alex and so does Jo-Jo. They wouldn't make a mistake like that. Who worked on the rear corners tonight?'

'I made everyone go 'round and do a spanner check,' Steve said, 'but no one had the chance to swap out the bolts.'

'Yes, they did,' Dylan conceded. 'There were a couple of occasions before Aidy came home where we weren't all together or watching what everyone else was doing.'

'When?' Steve asked.

'When you were giving the Fannings a tour of the place, Alison and her dad had the car to themselves. When you and I were showing Alison's dad how to use the quick-lift, Mr Fanning was working on the car alone. I'm sure there were other times too.'

'So any one of them could have done it?' I asked.

'Shit,' Steve said and nodded.

'Who are you saying did this?' Dylan demanded. 'The Fannings? Alison's dad? Alison?'

I didn't answer. I was pointing the finger at these people and as much as I didn't want to believe one of them did this, it had to be one of them. Possibly, even Alison.

'You can't be wrong about this,' Steve said. 'Are you sure?'

'I am. Look at the nuts.'

'Christ,' Steve muttered. 'The Nylocs are gone.'

Whoever had flipped the bolts had gone the extra mile of replacing the Nyloc safety nuts with ordinary nuts. A normal nut wouldn't stand up to the car's vibration and would eventually fly off. This was sabotage.

'What do you want to do?' Dylan asked.

'I need to see the tape of the race again.'

I ran up the stairs to the crow's-nest and dug out Brennan's business card. I called his mobile number.

'Do you have the videotape?' I asked.

'Do you know what time it is?' Brennan moaned.

'Just answer the question.'

Brennan sighed. 'Yes.'

'Can you play it?'

'It's at the office.'

'I can wait.'

'You can kiss my arse, son. What the hell is going on?'

'Alex was murdered.' Before Brennan could object, I cut him off. 'I helped you get your man. Now you're going to help me get mine. Alex was killed and someone is trying to kill me. Now get that tape.'

It was half an hour before Brennan called me back. Steve and Dylan waited for the call along with me.

'OK, I've got the tape queued up. Now what?'

I told Brennan what to look for and he played the tape. I heard the soundtrack coming off the tape over the phone while Brennan watched. The drone of engines filled the air. Then they stopped and started again as Brennan rewound and replayed the tape. The sound of the race stopped and Brennan came back on the line.

'I can't see clearly, Aidy, but it backs up what you're saying. I can have the audio-visual tech digitize the tape and clean it up. Then we'll be able to see more definitively.'

I let out a breath. It was true. This was how Alex had been killed. It explained the missing bolt on Alex's car and why Alex's car had bucked before veering into Derek's car. The bolt had fallen out. The moment it fell out, Alex had become a passenger with no control over the car's direction. It was all over as soon as Alex touched wheels with Derek.

I'd lived through one blissful day believing Alex's death had been accident. It hadn't been satisfying, but it had been reassuring that Alex hadn't died at someone else's hand. I should have known the feeling wouldn't last.

'Detective, I'm going to need your help in the morning.'

Lap Twenty-Nine

Steve, Dylan and I arrived at Stowe Park ahead of Alison, her dad and the Fannings the following morning. While Steve and Dylan parked, I checked in with the Hansen brothers. They were in the classroom, setting up for the day's punters. I wondered how much of the truth about Derek had filtered back to the community. Did they know he was a police snitch? I doubted it. The truth about Derek wouldn't come out until Rykov was in jail and by then, Derek would be long gone, living somewhere under a new identity. That didn't help me in the meantime. People saw me as an interfering busybody. There was nothing I could do about it and I didn't much care what people thought of me at this circuit. This was my last time here.

I held out the two hundred in cash. 'When can I go out?'

Tony Hansen counted the money twice, making sure I hadn't short-changed him, then handed it off to his brother. 'Our clients will hit the track at nine forty-five for their first session. There's a lunch break between noon and one. Between those times, the track is yours.'

I walked back to Steve and Dylan. They'd unloaded the Mygale off the trailer. Besides the Hansens, we had the paddock to ourselves, which was perfect for what we needed to do.

The three of us eyed the murder weapons – two cap head bolts and nuts. They were there in plain sight, but perfectly camouflaged. As murder weapons went, they weren't as threatening as a knife or a gun, but they were no less lethal. The fatal blow wouldn't be immediate. The improperly installed bolts were more along the lines of a time bomb. No one could say when they would go off, only that they would and when they did, it was over for me.

Dylan dropped to one knee, spat out sunflower shells and tried the nuts. 'Aidy, they're loose already. You want me to tighten them?'

'No.'

'You can't go on the track with them like that. Even the trip down here has almost shaken them loose.'

'I want to see if our killer has an attack of conscience.'

'You really think that's going to happen?'

I didn't, but I wanted to give the person the opportunity to do the right thing. 'If we switch out the bolts and don't say anything, the killer will know we're on to them and it will force them to do something else. We know about this situation and can control it.'

'This is crazy. Tell him, Steve.'

'It's Aidy's decision. He knows what he's doing.'

'Let's get me ready to go out there.'

I suited up in the van's cab. As I was putting my boots on, Alison and her dad drew up next to the van with the Fannings in the back.

I said hellos, shook hands and received hugs knowing full well that one of these people had killed Alex and booby-trapped my car.

Steve corralled his team and put them to work. Together, they fuelled the car, topped off the coolant system, checked tyre pressures and taped down the bodywork.

Despite there being a killer in our midst, we had a nice little vibe going. We were working well as a team. I took the time to examine these people. I tried to visualize one of them as a killer and I just couldn't make the image come alive. I wanted to be wrong, but knew I wasn't.

When the car was ready to go, Steve fired up the engine. Everybody stood around the car which had become a symbol of triumph over tragedy for all but one of us.

'This reminds me of Alex's last race,' Mr Fanning said. Instead of sadness on his face, there was a smile. 'We were working like this then. I didn't think we could be this happy again. This is a sad, but special moment for me. I just want to say thanks to everyone for being here.'

Mrs Fanning came over, slipped an arm around her husband's waist and kissed him.

'Let's hope Aidy can put up some fast times today to celebrate,' Steve said.

'Let's hope so.'

Alison hugged her dad and he winced from her embrace.

I checked my watch. It was two minutes to nine.

'OK, I've got just forty-five minutes of track time before the students hit the track, so I need everyone to get to their places.'

I climbed into the car and Dylan made the pretence of taping over the latches on one of the radiator pods in order to lean in close.

'The nuts are still loose,' he whispered. 'You'll be lucky to make it around the first bend.'

'Put some silicon over the end of the bolts.'

'That's a temporary fix. I can't say how long that'll hold everything in place.'

'Just do it, please.'

In the confusion of everyone gathering up tools and timing gear, Dylan surreptitiously squeezed silicon bath sealant onto his fingers and daubed it over the end of the bolts.

For the sake of appearances, I broke my ritual and didn't do a final spanner check before getting into the car. Not wanting to break my superstition entirely, I kissed my mum's St Christopher.

'Be careful, mate,' he whispered after he was done.

I wanted to say I would, but my mouth had gone dry and the words wouldn't come. Instead, I nodded and pulled on my helmet.

Steve and Dylan belted me in, cinching me tight into the car. It couldn't escape me and I couldn't escape it. If we were going down, we were going down together.

Steve gave me the thumbs-up to make sure I was good to go. As soon as I mimicked his gesture, he and Dylan climbed into the van.

'Where are you two going?' Mr Fanning asked.

'We're going to take corner times,' Steve said. 'Alison knows how to record lap times.'

Alison hung the stopwatch around her neck and handed her father the pit board and lap chart. She waved at me, then led her dad and the Fannings to the pit lane.

Suddenly, the weight of what I was doing hit me. I was going to catch myself a killer. I took a breath to calm myself. I couldn't catch anyone if I slammed the car into a wall. If I wanted to catch Alex's killer, I just had to drive.

I put the car in gear and trundled over to the assembly area where the race school cars were parked. The pit gate was already open for me and I joined the circuit.

I had the track to myself and I experienced a minor bout of agoraphobia. It felt vast without anyone else out there to race against, but I didn't knock it. If either of the bolts fell out, I didn't want to take anyone else with me.

I accelerated hard up through the gears. The car responded well. It was all holding together, for now. I tried not to think about the nuts vibrating and trying to shake the silicon off. I held my breath going into the first bend and emerged from the corner still in one piece.

The car completed the first lap fine. Every one of my senses was amped up for the slightest flicker that would tell me that one or both of the bolts had let go.

I completed a second lap. Mr Baker held out the lap board with my first time on it. It wasn't bad considering the circumstances.

I piled on the laps, steadily eating away at my times. I was giving it ten tenths, but those bolts were at the back of my mind. I didn't know if it was real or imagined, but I'd swear I felt a looseness from the rear of the car going as I powered through the bends. Either way, I clung to the hope that the silicon was holding fast.

On the last of my twenty laps, Steve and Dylan waved me down the back straight. I stopped the car and they came running onto the track.

'Jesus, Aidy, did you have to push it so hard?' Dylan moaned.

'I'm here to test the car.'

'And catch a killer. Get your priorities straight.'

'Hey, cut the arguing,' Steve said. 'We don't have long.'

Steve and Dylan peeled the silicon off the bolts. This piece of subterfuge went unseen by anyone in the pit lane since the circuit's topography restricted a clear view of the track.

'You're good to go,' Steve said.

'Where's Brennan?'

'He and the cavalry are waiting in the wings,' Dylan said. 'We just have to call him when we have something.'

'OK. Follow me back. I'm going to need you two to back me up.'

I selected first gear and accelerated away. I imagined panic would be building in the pit lane. The stopwatch in Alison's hand would tell the story. I was lapping the circuit in approximately sixty-five seconds. Around the sixty second mark, I should have reappeared in their sights. For every second I didn't reappear, potential calamities presented themselves – a mechanical failure, a spin, or the worst outcome, a crash. I wanted to screw with everyone's emotions. Three of these people would be scared, but for one person, my potential no-show would be a source of excitement. When I pulled into the pit lane, I expected to see disappointment on someone's face instead of relief.

I slowed for the pit lane entrance. I exhaled, glad that the bolts remained in place. It wasn't just for me. I needed those bolts to stay in place for what I planned to do next.

Alison led her dad and the Fannings towards me as I rolled to a stop. I killed the engine and flicked off the master cut-off switch before popping the belt release on the harness. Mr Fanning helped me clamber from the cockpit and I pulled off my helmet.

'You looked good out there,' he said. 'Very consistent times.'

'Except for the last lap,' Alison said. 'You were really slow.'

'I spun out. Nothing serious. Just got a little carried away.'

I examined their faces for a reaction, but didn't get the one I was looking for.

Steve and Dylan drew up in the van behind the Mygale. They jumped out and walked over.

'I think our work here is done for today. Time to pack it up.'

I cast a look in the direction of the clubhouse where the Hansen brothers were schooling their punters. They were safely housed away. 'I feel like having some fun. You want to take a spin around the track, Alison?'

'I can't. I don't know what to do.'

'If I can do it, you can. It's not hard. C'mon, live a little.'

'Go on,' Mr Fanning urged. 'You're the only one of us who's in good enough shape to fit in the car.'

'No, I can't.'

'You know how to change gears and press a clutch, don't you?'

'Yes.'

'Then you're good to go. It's very simple. All you have to remember is to brake before the corners and accelerate through the bends. No one is expecting you to break any lap records. Just have some fun.'

Dylan clapped his hands and chanted, 'Do it. Do it. Do it.'

The peer pressure worked and Alison threw up her hands. 'Alright. I'll do it.'

'Good for you,' Mrs Fanning said.

Steve handed her my helmet. 'Let's get you strapped in, young lady. Your chariot awaits.'

Dylan pulled the belts clear for her to get in.

I held my breath. If Alison was behind the booby-trap, she'd find an excuse not to get in. She climbed in and slid into the seat without a second's hesitation.

'Stop,' Mr Baker said.

'What's wrong, Dad?' Alison asked.

'You don't have the experience for this.'

'She'll be fine,' I said. 'She's more than capable of handling a couple of laps.'

'I don't care. I don't want her going out there.'

'Dad, I'll be fine.'

'See, she's good to go. Steve, fire the engine up.'

Steve reached inside the cockpit, flicked on the ignition and pressed the starter. The engine caught the first time.

Mr Baker lunged for the car and flipped the master cut-off switch, killing the engine. 'I said no.'

'What's the problem' Mr Fanning asked.

'We need to do a spanner check. You had a spin. We should make sure nothing has come loose.'

'Sure. Where would you like to start – the tracking arm bolts on the rear suspension?' I asked.

Mr Baker looked directly at me. Instead of the contempt I'd experienced in the past, I saw only fear in the man's expression. Not fear for himself, but for his daughter. It all made sense in that moment. Up until this point, I knew what had happened, but not the who or why. Now that I knew who, the why answered itself.

'You did it, didn't you?'

Mr Baker recoiled from my accusation. 'Did what? I don't know what you're talking about. I'm just suggesting we take prudent safety measures.'

'It's over. It's time to come clean. We know what you did.'

'I'm sorry. You've lost me.'

'Dad, what's going on?' Alison asked.

'Yeah, what is going on here?' Mr Fanning said. 'Frankly, I'm confused. Has something happened?'

'Yes, it has. Clive doesn't want Alison driving my car because he sabotaged it the same way he sabotaged Alex's car.'

'Is this some kind of joke?' Mr Baker demanded. 'If it is, I don't find it at all funny.'

Mr Fanning left his wife's side and stood directly in front of me. 'You'd better explain yourself, Aidy, and fast.'

'He installed several bolts incorrectly so that they'd fall out and send the cars crashing out of control.'

Steve crouched by the rear of the Mygale and pointed to the tracking arm bolts. 'Eric, look at these bolts. They're in upside-down and the Nyloc safety nuts have been replaced with ordinary nuts. This is a very dangerous situation and Clive knows it.'

'Get me out of this car,' Alison demanded.

I held out my hand to Alison, but she slapped it away. Her father helped her out and she went to him.

'My God, I haven't heard so much bullshit in my life,' Mr Baker said. 'You need help. Really, you do.'

I didn't say anything. Naturally, lines had been drawn in the sand. People needed to be convinced. None of it worried me. I knew I was right and I could prove it. I just let him keep talking and digging his own grave.

'OK, I'll play along. When did I do this tampering?' he asked.

'Last night at Archway. It wouldn't have taken you long,' I said. 'You're good with tools. I saw your garage. You're a real handyman.'

'Is that all you've got? A bolt that I or half a dozen other people could have installed? You could have done it yourself in your endless pursuit for publicity. You have no proof.'

'Don't I?'

I went up to him. Mr Baker backed up a step, but stopped when he saw I wasn't going to attack him. He stood his ground with a smug smile on his face. I wiped it off when I tapped his side. There was no need to put any power behind it. Mr Baker yelled out and fell to the ground like I'd hit him with a large, adjustable spanner. While he writhed, I yanked up his sweater. A bandage wrapped around most of his chest and back failed to hide the ugly bruising covering half his side.

'Steve gave you that when you tried to burn down Archway with him and Alex's car inside. I thought one of Derek's guys had done it, but none of them have broken ribs.'

Alison dropped to her knees at her father's side. 'Dad, tell me he's wrong. Tell me he's lying. Please.'

But Mr Baker shook his head. 'I'm sorry, love. I didn't mean to kill Alex. I just wanted him to crash.'

'No,' she wailed, pounding on her father's chest. 'Why? Why? Why?'

'I wanted him to get hurt to show you the pain this sport brings. If he saw the light and gave it up, you had a shot at happiness. If he didn't, then you would have seen that you had no future together.'

'You son of a bitch,' Mr Fanning yelled and broke away from his wife.

'No, Eric,' Mrs Fanning shrieked.

Steve and Dylan raced to block his path, but he shoved them aside. He cast Alison aside and pounced on Mr Baker.

'You killed my son.'

Rage consumed the normally mild-mannered man. He grabbed Mr Baker by the hair and smashed his head into the tarmac. Mr Baker put up no defence.

'You killed my son.'

Alison dived onto Mr Fanning to tear him off her father, but she was no match for his size or rage. He continued pounding the life out of Mr Baker.

'We welcomed you into our home, you bastard.'

Steve, Dylan and I moved in as a unit. Steve grabbed Alison and pulled her off. She kicked and fought, but Steve just weathered the blows. Dylan and I grabbed Mr Fanning and peeled him off Mr Baker. Mrs Fanning moved in quickly and got in front of her husband.

'Eric, stop it. We've got him. He's not getting away.'

'He killed our son.'

Tears rolled down Mrs Fanning's face. 'I know.'

The fight went out of Mr Fanning and Steve and I released him. Mrs Fanning enveloped her husband in a hug and they sobbed in each other's arms. Dylan guided them away from Mr Baker.

I helped Mr Baker up and sat him down on the pit lane crash barrier.

'Why'd you do it?'

'For my daughter.'

'For me?' Alison screamed. 'I loved Alex.'

'I had to protect you.'

'From whom?' Alison demanded.

'From the world,' I answered. 'This is all about a father's love for his daughter. But this isn't just about you, Alison. It has more to do with Jennifer, doesn't it, Mr Baker? She fell for the wrong man and couldn't see it even when it was hurting her. Eventually, it killed her. You couldn't let that happen again, could you?'

'No,' Mr Baker sobbed, misery distorting the word. 'Nick Jensen killed her. He got her addicted. I tried to help get her off the dope, but she didn't want to know. She cared more for him than her family.'

'But Alex wasn't like Nick,' Alison said.

'He was. He was going to break your heart. He would have ended up hurting you, even killing you. Racing is dangerous and destroys lives. Look at the financial damage it causes. I've walked the paddocks of a dozen tracks. How many of these guys have pissed their financial future away and for what? Pointless bragging rights.'

It was hard to argue this point. For every driver who made it to the top, hundreds crashed on the rocks of financial ruin. 'That's not enough to kill for.'

'No, but I wasn't going to risk my daughter's life. Drivers are selfish adrenaline junkies. Their addiction infects every part of their lives and those around them. How many drivers have died taking others with them? Graham Hill died at the controls of his aeroplane, killing five other people. Mike Hailwood crashed his car, killing himself and his daughter. Colin McRae crashed his helicopter killing three people including his son. If you need any further proof, just look at him.' Mr Baker pointed an accusing finger at me. 'His father's negligence killed his mother.'

A flush of embarrassment coursed through me. I looked over at Steve and saw sorrow in his eyes.

'I didn't want you to know the misery of having your family destroyed by a drug whether it's called heroin or motor racing.'

'You don't know that would have happened,' Alison said.

'I do. Probabilities dictated it. I just didn't know when it would happen. I talked with Alex. He wouldn't have given up racing. He would have carried on until it killed him. It was better this happened before you were married and had kids.'

'You were wrong,' I said. 'He was giving up racing for Alison.'

'You don't know that,' Mr Baker said.

'I do. He told me he was retiring at the end of the season. It was supposed to be a surprise wedding gift.'

Alison sagged in Steve's arms and wept fresh tears.

'You're lying,' Mr Baker said with panic in his voice.

I shook my head. The colour bled from his face.

'Oh, God, no. Tell me you're lying, please,' he said to me. When

I couldn't tell him what he wanted to hear, he turned to Alison. 'I just wanted you to be happy, love. I couldn't lose another daughter.'

'Well, you have,' she said.

Steve pulled out his mobile and punched in a number. 'Detective, we need you.'

Final Lap

'You did well,' Steve said hanging my wreath on the workshop wall. He placed it alongside one of my dad's. It looked good up there.

I'd come third in the Festival thanks to some good driving and a healthy slice of luck. The knockout format of the races led to the usual desperate driving, which sent drivers crashing out. Several of the favourites crashed in the earlier rounds. I kept a cool head and never finished lower than seventh in any of the preliminary rounds then went for it in the final.

But Steve wasn't referring to the Festival. He was talking about catching Alex's killer. Today was an important day. We were crushing Alex's car.

'C'mon, we've got work to do,' he said.

The Festival had been a week ago. I'd reached the post-ball part of my Cinderella moment where everything went back to normal. The Mygale wasn't going to turn into a pumpkin, but the lease was up. The engine had to come out and go back to Armstrong's and the car had to go back to Mygale. There was no chance of this car becoming a permanent addition to my racing future.

I'd met Hancock's challenge and then some by reaching the final of the Festival, so he owed me a season in next year's national championship, but that offer was dead now that he was safely hidden away in Brennan's custody. His lawyers were working out a deal for him, but Hancock Salvage wasn't long for this world. Sale rumours were rife. It looked as if Hancock's competition would benefit and buy up the company, none of which helped me. I still had my existing sponsors but they weren't going to get me to the next level. Luckily, my third place finish at the Festival made for a great advertisement of my abilities. I'd already received calls for driver tryouts in Formula Ford, Formula Renault and the European Saloon Car Championship. I just hoped one of my tryouts turned into something.

Steve and I carefully peeled the decals and racing numbers off the bodywork before getting down to the hard part of removing the engine.

A knock at the door drew our attention. Alison stood in the doorway.

I'd been calling since they'd arrested her dad, but she hadn't returned any of my calls. I'd finally given up after the Festival.

'Could I have a word?' she asked.

'Sure. Come in.'

'I'd prefer to talk outside.'

'Oh. OK.'

Steve patted me on the back. 'I've got this covered, son.'

I followed her outside. It was cold under the arches and I wished she'd come inside.

'How's your dad?' I asked.

'Do you care?'

'Alison, please.'

'Sorry. He's doing as well as can be expected.'

I'd heard from Brennan that they had him on suicide watch. 'I wish things had turned out differently.'

'Everybody does.'

I hadn't felt this awkward around Alison since we'd first met.

'We're leaving soon for the salvage yard to crush Alex's car. I know you wanted to be there. You're welcome to come with us.'

'No, it's not important. I just came by to explain.'

'You don't have to do that.'

'I know, but I want to. My father tried to kill you and Steve. You deserve an explanation.'

I'd gotten my explanation from Brennan after Mr Baker had made a full confession. With Alison and Alex's wedding looming and all previous attempts to break up the engagement failing, Mr Baker latched onto Derek's death threat. He crippled Alex's car in the hopes that Derek would play the part of the scapegoat. When I began nosing around, he had to tie up all the loose ends. He mugged Paul for his camcorder recording, attempted to burn down

Archway to destroy any evidence on Alex's car with the petrol can he'd taken from Alex's garage, and ransacked Steve's house for the phantom videotape I proclaimed to possess. He decided to kill me when he saw history repeating itself as my bond with Alison developed. My burgeoning relationship with Alison explained how he'd been aware of my every move. Every time I shared a development with her, she told her father. But these weren't the details Alison wanted to convey.

'My father was loving and caring. He took Jennifer's rejection of our family hard and her death even harder. He was never the same after that. I don't know if someone's heart can break, but something broke inside him. Since I was his only remaining child, he focused all his attention on me. He became obsessive, checking up on every one of my boyfriends.'

'And giving them a few stern words,' I said without any malice.

She flashed me a glimmer of a smile. 'Yes. You saw what he did. I believed that was as far as he would go. Never in a million years did I think he'd take things any further. I wish I could have done something to stop him.'

'You had no way of knowing. All you can do now is give him your love and support.'

'I'm not sure about that.'

I hoped that wasn't true. Her father wasn't a bad man, just a desperate and sad one. Then, I remembered what she'd said at the banquet. 'I want him to beg me for forgiveness. I'll never give it, not to the person who killed Alex.' Those were easy words to bandy around when a faceless killer was to blame, but a lot harder to stick by when they were about your own father. The mix of emotions had to be tearing her apart. I wanted to help her, but I felt the wall she was putting up in front of me.

'Aidy, you put me in that car knowing full well I could be killed.'

'I had to force your dad to come clean.'

'What if he hadn't? Would you have stopped me?'

'Of course.'

'You should have told me. I trusted you.'

Trusted. The past tense. The implication that she no longer did stung. I could have told her that I didn't know for sure if her dad had killed Alex until he intervened, but there was no point. The damage was done. 'You know I couldn't.'

Steve poked his head out the door. 'I'm making some tea. Can I make you some, Alison?'

She shook her head. 'No, I have to be going.'

'Don't go,' I said.

'I think it's best.'

'Call me.'

'I will.'

I watched her get into her car and drive away. I waved, but she didn't wave back.

Steve came over and dropped an arm over my shoulders. 'She'll come around. She just needs time. You'll see.'

I didn't think so. I'd helped destroy her family. I'd dug into her fiancé's murder only to discover her father was the killer. She'd lost her husband to be and now her dad. My interference was going to send her father to prison for the rest of his life. Someone needed to be blamed and I was the best candidate for the job.

'C'mon, we've got somewhere to be,' Steve said.

We went inside and I pulled the drop cloth off Alex's car for the last time. I stared at the wrecked car.

'You did right by Alex. He deserved justice and he got it thanks to you. His killer will get what he deserves. You should be proud,' he said.

'At what cost?' I asked. 'A lot of lives are a mess now.'

'There'll always be innocent victims.'

I had hoped for a better response from the Fannings, but I didn't get it. Mrs Fanning had called to thank me for finding her son's murderer. The thank you was perfunctory, which was understandable under the circumstances. I hadn't been totally truthful about my interest in their son's death. I called Myles Beecham and told him I'd be stepping down from the administration of the safety fund. I expected sniping, but he was very understanding and told me that was probably a good thing.

'What's the latest from Brennan?' Steve asked.

Brennan called every couple of days to fill me in on the latest developments. I think this was his way of keeping tabs on me. If he kept me up to date there'd be no need for me to run off in search of the answers myself and make a mess of his investigation. Derek and Hancock wouldn't be seen until the day of the trial. Rykov was also under protection. His own people would be eager to erase him before his trial could destroy their organization.

Brennan estimated he wouldn't last a week in prison after his inevitable conviction. Rykov was aware of his endangered status, but he refused all offers of turning against his people. He was loyal to a fault. The man was tough. I counted my lucky stars that I wasn't in his sights anymore. Brennan expected the attempted murder charges to go to trial first seeing as it was the easiest case to prove. It's hard for any lawyer to defend against three people being forced into a car crusher. He told us to keep our calendar free in the New Year.

I heard the familiar sound of Dylan's car pulling up outside before he appeared in the doorway. 'Are you two ready to go? I just got a call. A bunch of the guys are already at the salvage yard. Even Myles and Eva are there.'

'Are we ready?' Steve asked.

There were a lot of things that needed time before being resolved. This was one thing that didn't. 'Yeah,' I said. 'We're ready.'

We loaded Alex's car into Steve's van, drove it to the salvage yard and paid our final respects to a friend.